A Toy Epic

D0806535

Also by Emyr Humphreys in Seren Books

Miscellany Two
The Taliesin Tradition

A Toy Epic

Emyr Humphreys

Edited & Introduced by
M. Wynn Thomas

SEREN BOOKS
*1989

Seren Books is the book imprint of
Poetry Wales Press Ltd
Andmar House, Tondu Road, Bridgend
Mid Glamorgan

©Emyr Humphreys, 1958, 1989
Introduction, Afterword ©M. Wynn Thomas, 1989

ISBN 1-85411-009-8

All rights reserved. No part of this publication may be
reproduced, stored in a retrieval system, or transmitted at any
time or by any means, electronic, mechanical, photocopying,
recording or otherwise, without the prior permission of the
copyright holders.

*The publisher acknowledges the financial support of the
Welsh Arts Council*

Typeset in 10½ point Plantin by Megaron, Cardiff
Printed by Billings & Sons Ltd, Worcester

Contents

Acknowledgements

This edition of *A Toy Epic* would have been impossible without the great encouragement and the material support so generously provided by Emyr and Elinor Humphreys. I am very grateful to them for all their help. Mr Graham Greene very readily allowed me to publish his letter and the Lord David Cecil letter is printed with the kind permission of his family. My uncle, Brinley Rees, has been my literary conscience in this as in so many other projects, and I would like to pay particular tribute to his scrupulous patience. Mae fy niolch, a fy nyled, i yn fawr iddynt i gyd.

Introduction

A Toy Epic made quite an impression when it first appeared in November, 1958. The comparatively sophisticated fictional technique the author had skilfully used was appreciated by the *Times* reviewer, who described it as "a kind of three-part plainsong of the sublimated 'stream of consciousness'." The delicately mixed tone of the book was well characterised in *The Telegraph*. There the reviewer noticed that "the sense of youth, standing fresh and innocent before the opening day already flecked with black cloud is beautifully conveyed. One feels the strange mixture of nostalgia and fear that remembered boyhood rouses — the compassion for what once was and never will be again," A robustly appreciative piece in the *Western Mail* ended on a sensitive note: "his language is pure and strong, with images as sharp and bright as a child's box of paints." The *Church Times* therefore voiced the consensus of critical opinion when it described the book as "a minor masterpiece."

A month after it appeared, *A Toy Epic* was included in the *Times* list of the dozen outstanding novels of 1958. It was in very good company. The sensation of the year was Pasternak's *Dr Zhivago*, but among the British novels mentioned were T.H. White's *The Once and Future King*, Mary Renault's *The King Must Die*, Angus Wilson's *The Middle Age of Mrs Eliot*, and Iris Murdoch's *The Bell*. Public acclamation of *A Toy Epic* was very shortly followed by welcome private confirmation of the novel's quality. At the end of December, Emyr Humphreys received an unexpected and very kind letter from Lord David Cecil:

> I hope you will forgive a stranger for writing to tell you how very much he has enjoyed and admired your book *A Toy Epic*. There are a great many interesting and efficient novels written nowadays but

7

very few which are works of imaginative art. Yours surely is one of the few. Its whole atmosphere is suffused with that mysterious and poetic sense of life which is the mark of such an imaginative work, and yet this is done at no cost to realism. The personalities of all three boys have the vivid immediacy of real people — and also some of the unpredictability. One does not know how they are going to turn out, and certainly I was surprised when Albie failed to fulfil his promise and Michael developed extremist views. Yet both changes convinced me. I was suprised as one is by a real event.

The book is true and beautiful. Thank you very much for it.

The letter augured far more than the recipient could then have guessed. Along with Francis Wyndham, V.S. Pritchett and C. Day Lewis, Cecil was that year responsible for adjudicating the Hawthornden Prize.[1] Instituted after the First World War, this distinguished prize was awarded annually "for an outstanding imaginative work" written by a British subject under forty years of age. Past winners had included Siegfried Sassoon, Graham Greene and David Jones. Early in 1959 Emyr Humphreys heard that the prize had been won by *A Toy Epic*, and in June he went to London to receive the award from his fellow-countryman, Aneurin Bevan.

★ ★ ★ ★

Although it was first published in 1958, *A Toy Epic* had been begun eighteen years earlier, when Emyr Humphreys was a twenty-one year old conscientious objector working on a farm in Pembrokeshire. Having had several poems published in the *Spectator*, he mentioned to the paper's literary editor, Graham Greene, that he had started work on a verse novel. On March 25, 1940 Greene wrote back expressing his readiness to "be of . . . use to you when the book is completed, unless I'm in the army." Encouraged by this response, Humphreys continued to work on the manuscript after moving to Plas Llanfaglan, a large farm near Caernarfon, where he worked from the early summer of 1941 to the summer of 1944. He soon abandoned the idea of a complete novel in verse, but the manuscripts that survive show that most of the opening three chapters of the novel as published in 1958 were completed between early 1940 and late 1942, having been written at night after work on the farm was finished for the day. Some material relating to the boys' time in Llanrhos County School is also extant. But as this is fragmentary it is difficult to know exactly how much of it there originally was.

Graham Greene had meanwhile become an editorial director with Eyre & Spottiswoode, so it was to that firm the completed manuscript was eventually sent. By January, 1943, the publishers had decided to offer Emyr Humphreys a contract that secured first option for them on the novel. But they also pointed out that the text as received was too short for publication and therefore requested him to prepare additional material. An exercise-book from this period records the new plan to which Emyr Humphreys then decided to work: "*Part One*: Fathers of Men. *Part Two*: Michael. *Part Three*: Alfie [who became Albie in the 1958 novel]. *Part Four*: Iorwerth. *Part Five*: ?"

Part One was the first version of the opening chapters of *A Toy Epic* as published in 1958. It therefore dealt with the childhood and early schooldays of the three boys growing up together. Parts Two to Four were the sections dealing with their lives after they left school and went each his separate way. This was the material added on the advice of the editors at Eyre & Spottiswoode, in an attempt to pad the original work out to publishable length. The Michael section (Part Two) was eventually published in Keidrych Rhys's magazine *Wales* in 1947, and is included as an appendix in the present edition.[2] The other two sections have never been published, but are still available in manuscript.

The Alfie section (Part Three) fills two exercise books. It begins with him failing his exams and having to accept a home-town job in Mr Bell's garage. Frustration follows until Alfie meets a girl called Eileen. The description of their sexual encounter is accompanied by quotations from Dante and therefore broadly parallels the relationship between Albie and Frida in the published novel. Iorwerth's story (Part Four) also sprawls over two books, and it begins with the burial of his father. In accordance with his mother's wishes he then goes to college to prepare himself for the ministry. There he surreptitiously reads the unexpurgated edition of *Lady Chatterley's Lover*, and cuts a strange, solitary figure. His oddness draws him to the attention of Beth Rowlands, a fellow-student, and the rest of the narrative follows his growing relationship with her, a relationship complicated by the guilt and confusion he feels as his sexual feelings develop.

Emyr Humphreys sent the new, extended manuscript of the first *Toy Epic* (as it was already called) to Eyre & Spottiswoode some time in early 1943. On July 4, 1943 he received a reply from Graham Greene, who began by apologising for his delay in commenting on the typescript, explaining that he had been busy "working for 62 hours a week" at the Foreign Office. He then proceeded to offer a mercilessly shrewd criticism of the material that had been submitted:

> I read the original part of your novel with a great deal of pleasure, but I'm afraid I felt it was spoilt badly by the expansion. I rather doubt the policy they followed here of suggesting expansion: it might have been better to have kept the original book until you had a volume of several stories ready. Frankly I found the second half badly written, unoriginal, oddly novelettish and pedestrian. This is harsh, and it will be my own fault if you take your future work elsewhere as a consequence, but I have such a strong belief in your talent that I feel one can be frank with you. The completed book in my opinion is unpublishable. I'm not sure whether the expansion was ever possible: when I finished the first part I asked myself how it could be done. I was convinced that the same style of narration had to be kept, and it seemed to me the only thing for you to do was to skip say thirty years and give us the same soliloquies of the same characters middle-aged. That, I felt, would preserve the epic flavour.
>
> But it's no use suggesting ideas to you now. You may find another publisher ready to take the present book: if you don't I hope you'll send me your next. Have you ever gone on with the translations and the journal you were at work on two years ago?

Emyr Humphreys took Graham Greene's hint and sent the returned typescript promptly to another publisher. He chose Faber and Faber, probably on Keidrych Rhys's advice. On September 3, 1943, he received a letter from T.S. Eliot. Faber, he said, had sought two independent opinions on the typescript. The readers felt there was good material in it, and that it showed a great deal of promise. However, the structure was defective and the novel couldn't be successful in its existing form. One reader had reported that he'd found the three voices difficult to distinguish at the beginning. Later the confusion cleared, but then there was a lack of connection between the three narratives as the characters went in different directions. The readers appreciated the detailed nature of the narrative, the accuracy of the record and the poignancy of the scenes. Eliot concluded by saying: "whether the next step for you is to find a new architectural design for this book or to start another one is a question which no one but yourself can decide."

At about the same time, Emyr Humphrey met the great Welsh short-story writer and novelist Kate Roberts at a Plaid Cymru summer-school.[3] Having read his typescript, she drew a simple diagram that made the weakness of the extended novel blindingly obvious to him:

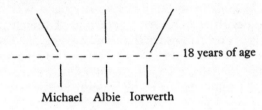

It was then clear that (as Eliot also said) the original framework was not suitable for supporting and inter-relating the later parts of the narrative. Emyr Humphreys decided to put the typescript away, and to start on a new work. This was the novel which was published under the title *The Little Kingdom* in 1946.

★ ★ ★ ★

The Little Kingdom was the first novel by Emyr Humphreys to be published. Others followed in regular succession, including *Hear and Forgive*, which won the Somerset Maugham Prize in 1952, so that by 1955 he was a writer of established reputation. That year he moved out of schoolteaching, which had been his main occupation since the war, into broadcasting when he was appointed Head of Radio Drama for the BBC in Cardiff. Since he was responsible for commissioning and producing radio plays, his conscience would not allow him to broadcast his own work. After he had been two years with the BBC, howewver, he was prevailed upon by Hywel Davies, then Head of Programmes, to write six half-hour scripts in Welsh — the language in which Emyr Humphrey had gradually become fluent after beginning to learn it when he was a student at the University College of Wales, Aberystwyth before the war.

In search of material suitable for broadcasting he turned back to the original *Toy Epic* and began by translating the *Fathers of Men* section which dealt with the boyhood and adolescence of the three characters. A rough translation of part of it into Welsh already existed, prepared by a girlfriend of Emyr Humphreys' during the war. This may have encouraged him to attempt a complete translation of his own, and as he proceeded he slightly modified the forties English text, expanding it and improving it. Then he added substantial new sections in Welsh that were in keeping with the character and tone of the successful forties material. The strong rhythms of the original English version were useful in that they set a pattern of writing he could follow and develop. But his greatest difficulty was ensuring that the assured sophistication of his mature writing style would not destroy the freshness of the young experience he had captured fifteen years earlier. His new title for the completed work was *Y Tri Llais (The Three Voices)* and it was broadcast as a Sunday serial by the BBC in Wales in early 1958.

The programmes were widely admired, not least by Radio Talks producer Aneirin Talfan Davies, who was himself a respected Welsh writer and man of letters. He was also an inspired promoter of literary talent, having been one of the people primarily responsible for commissioning Dylan Thomas to write his play for radio, *Under Milk Wood*. Aneirin Talfan urged Emyr Humphreys to turn the scripts into a novel, with the promise of publication by his family firm of Gwasg y Dryw, Llandybie. *Y Tri Llais* duly appeared in novel form in the summer of 1958.

Y Tri Llais was particularly fortunate in its reviewers, who included several of the most eminent Welsh-language writers of the period. Their knowledgeable discussion of the world portrayed in the book, along with their sophisticated appreciation of the literary techniques employed, are still among the best criticial comments available on the text in either its Welsh or its English form. E. Tegla Davies, for instance, remarked on the way the novel brought all three of the boys, in turn, face to face with the inescapable terrors of living.[4] In a remarkably perceptive extended review, John Gwilym Jones pinpointed several of the novel's particular strengths.[5] He was especially appreciative of the way the author had succeeded in "setting the story in a historical, social, moral, religious and political context without ever making these aspects of the work in any way obtrusive." They "worked like yeast in the text", quietly swelling the story out into a satisfying fullness of shape.

Emyr Humphreys spent the summer of 1958 in London, being trained in television production skills, and it was there, in Cornwall Gardens, that he worked on the English version of his Welsh novel. With him he had *Fathers of Men*, from the early forties, and the complete text of *Y Tri Llais*. He was therefore able to write very rapidly, and in this, its final form, *A Toy Epic* is virtually identical to *Y Tri Llais*. The only major difference between the Welsh and the English texts is the absence from the English of the brief dream sequence with which the Welsh novel opens and closes. Emyr Humphreys's good friend, John Gwilym Jones, had judged this to be the least successful aspect of *Y Tri Llais*, and Humphreys respected his critical judgment. Moreover the dream was an allusion to the great eighteenth century Welsh prose classic by Ellis Wynne, *Gweledigaetheu y Bardd Cwsc (The Visions of the Sleeping Poet)* and Emyr Humphreys realised that the implicit reference would be utterly lost on English readers.

For the novel in its English form he chose the title he had first used fifteen years before. At the time the word "epic" reflected his view of himself as primarily a poet and referred to the origin of the work as a verse novel. In 1958 it still seemed the appropriate word to describe his poetic treatment of the wide vistas of experience that opened before the wondering eyes of three growing boys. "Toy" suggested both a sense of miniaturisation, or reduced scale compared with full adult consciousness, and also the element of play in both childhood and adolescence — with a further musical allusion (via the

13

A TOY EPIC

1

I was brought up in a broad valley in one of the four corners of Wales. On fine days from my bedroom window I saw the sea curve under the mountains in the bottom right-hand corner of the window frame. My sister and I played in the garden. hiding behind the soft forest of asparagus grass, climbing the apple trees. My name is Michael.

I was brought up in the kitchen parlour and bedroom of No 15 Cambrian Avenue. Cambrian Avenue is in Llanelw which is a busy seaside town. Under the kitchen table I first saw motes swimming in a beam of sunlight, and crumbs lying white and edible near me on the floor. At three and a half I played in the cul-de-sac, and numbers 13, 14, 15, 16, 17 and 18 stood on guard about me, watching me with square indifferent eyes. My name is Albie.

I was brought up in the heart of ninety acres, at the end of a broad valley, at the headquarters of Noah, in an anchored ark. My growth was calf-like from the semi-twilight of the darkened kitchen to the sharp light of the empty front garden. I followed my mother, going to riddle cinders, sheltering behind her skirt from the aggressive eloquence of the geese. I followed my father to view the new hunt bull, and my small fist groped along the resistant corduroy breeches he wore. The cart-horse, the duck pond, the cowshed and the hayshed, the stable and the granary constituted my city. My name is Iorwerth.

The Rectory was my home, said Michael. My mother believed the house was far too big. My father's stipend was £300 a year and to this I may add a small private income of £60 a year, the

17

rent of a smallholding far away in Cardiganshire, left to him in the will of his great-uncle Job. I went to the village school and mixed with the village children, being different only in as much as I retired from school or play down a drive sheltered by elms to a large house instead of going home to a terrace house in the village; or in as much as I could watch the parson in his white and distant surplice, with the inward knowledge that I could sit on his knee and even put my finger inside his hard gleaming collar.

My mother was firm and well-bred, the daughter of a vicar, accomplished in playing the piano and embroidery. Because there was little prospect of my going to a Public School my mother strove particularly hard to give me the advantages of a good upbringing, at all times desiring me to be conscious of my good origins.

One rainy afternoon Wil Ifor Jones came to play with me in the Rectory stables. Wil was the daring boy of our class. But his father was a farm labourer, famous for his hard work, for his drinking bouts and for sometimes beating his wife.

"*Nid fel yna mae gwneud*,"[6] said Wil as I failed to spin my top, as my mother came to call us in for tea. "That's not the way to do it, you silly fool."

"Don't you call Michael a fool, Wil Ifor Jones, and don't you use the 'ti' with him either. You should know your place."

I felt vaguely elated that I should be accounted better than Wil, who was a daring boy, and I looked at him curiously. I was more than ever anxious to secure his permanent friendship, but he never came to the Rectory to play again, and at school, for quite a long time, he treated me rather roughly.

In the garden, my mother always wore gloves, and my sister and I, uprooting weeds, moved obedient to her refined remarks. We pulled up weeds in the flower bed around the lawn while my mother clipped the laurel bushes, or, in her absence, we ran about among the laurels and the rhododendrons.

In the house, my mother commanded Mary, the maid, to scrub the large square slabs on the kitchen floor, to wash the dishes, iron our clothes, clean the grate, and sundry other domestic duties, which we watched, my sister and I, with pleasure.

"Mary!" my mother would call in various tones, "Mari-mary!

Mary-mari! Mary-this-house-needs-two-or-three-maids-not-one!"

"Mary!" my father would call in his deep, kind, parsonical voice. "Have you seen my pipe, my hat, my gloves, the red book, the blue book, this, that, or the other?"

Mary, fat and unattractive, would confide in us, and speak to us as equals, and Mary's opinions were ours. She had too much work to do. We agreed. George Jones was a daft fellow. We agreed. Our father-in-the-study had a memory like a sieve. We agreed. Mary was our mentor, our adviser of the business of living. We were credulous clay in her red, scrubbed hands; her rights and her wrongs were ours. We were on her side.

In the evenings she read children's stories to us in hauntingly monotonous English: *What said Dobson are you game for a lark the beak is out we could hide the tuckbox in his study too ris-ky said Peers . . . .*

Mary enjoyed the stories as much as we did and she told us which were best and which ones were no good. Mary was English, she said. Her father was born in Chester, but her father could speak Welsh when he had a mind. Only old Methodies[7] spoke Welsh all the time. We agreed, and answered our father in English which pleased my mother, I think, apart from our accent which we got from Mary. But my father never gave up what must have appeared then a losing battle. That is why my sister and I prefer to speak English. It was Mary's idea. One of her principles.

I run around the cul-de-sac, said Albie, steering my way with a broken stick between my hands, my lips being my engine.

"My father drives a bus!" I shout to anyone who happens to pass.

My father comes through the back door for tea, throwing his stiff peaked cap on the sofa and hanging his leather money bag behind the door.

"Near thing today, by the S bend, between Pantbach and Pydew."

"Oh, yes, Dic. What happened?" my mother's voice is soft and patient.

"Just as I'd got round the first bend, there was a fool of a fellow coming racing towards me. I couldn't see through the hedge, could I?"

"Well, no, Dic, of course you couldn't."

"Good job for him I was going slow or the b . . . " My father looks at me and does not finish what he was going to say.

"He could have had it. Smashed up!"

"Oh, dear." My mother shakes her head and I feel I want to shake mine. "Another cup of tea, Dic?"

"Diawch, Nel![8] I heard a good one down in the yard today. You know little Archie, fellow from Llansannan, conductor on one of our double deckers. You know, little fellow, very small. The one who always says 'A-way John Jones' every time he rings the bell?"

"Well, to tell you the truth, I don't, Dic bach." My mother cuts bread and butter effortlessly, watching also the kettle on the verge of boiling, my father's plate, and me.

"Diawch, you do,[9] Nellie! Terrible temper for such a small man. Like a lucifer.[10] Anyway for you, he got into a quarrel with one of those Royal Yellow chaps. D'you know what he did?"

"I've no idea." My mother holds her head on one side expectantly. My father pauses dramatically now that she has given him all her attention.

"Threw his ticket punch at him!"

My mother looks shocked and startled, but my father is still laughing so I know it is all right.

"He did. Threw his ticket punch at him!"

My father belches. Sitting down all day, gripping the large steering wheel that vibrates constantly between his hands, staring down the winding roads and breathing petrol fumes with every breath of air: he says himself it's no wonder his digestion is bad. "I get shaken to death to earn my living," he says quite often. As a joke. My father loves to make jokes.

"Wish they'd leave me on this circular run for ever more, Nellie," my father says, drinking a cup of tea standing by the open back door. "Nice to pop home for tea. Much better than the country run."

"Well ask them about it, Dic. See if you can get a transfer."

"I will do that, Nel."

"Nel! Nel!"

"Here's your cup of tea, Dic. What's the matter?"

"Thanks. Just a sip. Can't wait. They are saying at the yard that Foster's going to sell out to the Royal Yellow. You can't tell. It's hard to say."

"Jim Morris was saying that the working on the buses is the best place these days. You don't get the sack so easy. You can't tell. It's hard to say."

"Nel! Nel!"

"Here's your cup of tea, Dic."

"Sorry, Nel. Can't stay long. There's talk of a strike at the Royal Yellows. Have you heard?"

"You don't know what to believe, Dic bach. You can't tell."

"It's hard to say. Must be off now. Don't you dance too much attendance on those visitors, Nel. So long, little 'un."

"So long, Dad."

The cap with the glistening peak once more on his head, and his money bag hung over his shoulder, his face turns towards us, smiling between two steps as he passes the kitchen window.

"So long, Dad. Take care, Dad. Ta-ta! ta-ta!"

The first time I am ever allowed to carry out a pint tin of hot tea to the field where my father and Llew are busy hedging, said Iorwerth, it is winter and I am well wrapped up.

"Hedges are cut with the aid of a two-foot rule, aren't they, Llew?" My father is jolly as I run about him. Everything he says seems jollier with the wind blowing it. Indoors he is always more serious. "Look out, my boy. Don't stand too close, my love!" He wields his bill-hook with ardent pleasure, the slim, white-haired man in corduroy trousers and a torn old coat. Half the hedge is bent and neat and half stands untidy and upward, remaining to be tackled.

If you happened to look into my father's diary — Boots' large farmer's diary which he keeps in his desk, — for the year 1926, you would read an account of how, in February, it being cold outside, he allowed me into the barn to watch him chaffing hay for the cattle, breathing heavy and hungry in the warm adjacent byre.

"Ho!" I shouted and danced about.

Clec! Clec! Chuff! Chuff! Chuff! said the oil engine, and the

21

chaff-cutter rattled like mad. My father stuffed hay along the trough into the false teeth of the machine. Those false, false teeth, for when his back was turned I put my hand in thinking I might experience the ecstasy of the shaking machine, and although I cannot remember, the false teeth took my finger, and, I suppose, chaffed it. My right hand now has three fingers and a stump in addition to my thumb. Everyone notices I write with my left hand.

I think it is an advantage to be brought up in the country, spring, summer, autumn and winter. "It is an advantage," said Miss Roberts, our teacher, "to be brought up in the country, and especially on a farm, isn't it Iorwerth?"

"Oh, yes, Miss Roberts," I blush.

"There are little children," continues Miss Roberts, "living in large cities who have never seen a blade of grass."

"Oh, pity. Pity," Our whole class sighs,

Spring, summer, autumn, winter, smartly, slowly, slowly, fast, I walk a mile and a half to school alongside hedges and across fields. Picking the flowers according to the season, a handful of primroses for school, a handful of bluebells home, harebells for Miss Roberts, violets for Mam; or strapped in high gaiters I march as well as I can manage through the more navigable snow.

"Robert Jones! Aren't you ashamed of yourself living almost next door to the school, and ten minutes late! And here's Iorwerth Hughes, who has to walk a mile and a half, never late, never late. Take that impudent grin off your face."

Yes, Robert, please, Robert, take it off. Don't annoy him. Don't scold him. Let's all be friends.

"Iorwerth Hughes has had all his sums correct this morning. He is a very good boy. Come and sit in the front, Iorwerth, here, sit next to Michael."

I slink happily to the front with my pencil and book and I slide my behind along the seat, and Michael, looking at me curiously, slides up.

"Mam," I said, out of breath in the evening when I got home for tea. "Mam, Miss Roberts said I was a good boy today. I got all my sums right. She moved me to the front to sit by Michael Edwards."

"There's a good boy. Tell me, Iorwerth, did Michael get his sums right, too?"

"No, Mam. Only me."

The first day I went to school, said Albie, I was escorted by my mother.

There's Nellie Jones taking her darling to school. She makes too much of him she does. Like a one chick hen. She's sure to ruin him. Mark my words.

"*Good morning, Mrs Jones. Nice day, isn't it? Albie off to school? Hello, Albie! Hello, love!*"

Doesn't he look nice and clean.

"*Ta-ta, Albie.*"

Sulky little chap. Most unloving. Like a little old man. Not natural I call it.

Passing the little gates and little gardens, the housewives bare-armed in doorways, passing the shops and the fish and chip saloon not open yet, I see Mr Pike, the fruiterer, carrying cauliflowers out in round wicker baskets. He speaks to my mother.

"Morning, Mrs Jones. Beautiful morning. Off to school, is he? Big day, eh?"

I see the assistant brushing in the gloom of the shop towards the daylit door sawdust and bits of paper; I see the newsagent and the tobacconist pulling out the placards for the day, which I linger to look at as I believe he wants me to do. But my mother tugs at my arm.

"Come along, Albie, or we'll be late."

My mother hates being late. It is wrong to be late.

"If you don't go to school you'll never learn anything. Come on now, there's a good boy."

What are these tall railings that stand between us and a broad asphalt yard and a dirty red building? What is the wrought-iron gate half open to allow us through? What are these bright and shining faces, these groups, these running figures, this echoing choir of voices? We walk, my mother and I, among talking, shouting girls of all sizes, and very small boys.

My mother has gone. I am alone sitting in a desk among a lot of children of my age. There are blocks on the desk and beads for counting. There is a young lady standing in front of us, and a blackboard. The young lady has a lot of fair hair and a kind face. Like me, please, young lady. We get up, stand in rows between the desks and march out of the room along a corridor, through a glass-topped door, into a large room, a huge room, filled with children, hundreds and thousands of children, and we march to the very front. The young lady makes us stand in rows. I stand trembling with nerves, my nose almost on the gleaming gable of the upright piano. I see a blurred reflection of the endless rows of children that stretch behind me. Bang goes the piano, and I jump with fright.

> *"There's a home for little children*
> *Above the bright blue sky . . . ."*

The September sunlight streams through the high churchlike window across rows of singing faces, rows of wide open mouths. Could there, anywhere, be room for them all? A mighty noise fills the earth, pours through my tender ears. It is not a bad noise; if only it was not so loud; which pause will be the last . . . how long will it go on? Aaaaaamen. It is suddenly quiet.

The man with grey hair and a finger inside a book opens the book. The grown-ups bend their heads and close their eyes. The man with grey hair is speaking with eyes closed. I look along the row of teachers and I am able to see the top of their heads. I look around and the children have bent their heads and closed their eyes also. Now is my chance to understand. They are all silent, their eyes are closed. No one looks at me and I look at everyone. I have begun to explore a new dimension.

Since I was the Rector's son, said Michael, and the village school was a church school my talent received early recognition. At Sunday school also I was expected to give bright answers. Here there were four teachers; Miss Meurig, babies; Mr Jones, boys; and Miss Watkins, girls; my father took the young men and a few grown-ups. Miss Meurig with a cardboard alphabet on her knee taught us the alphabet in Welsh and read Bible stories to us and showed us bright pictures: *Ruth gleaning the field of Boaz, Abraham and Isaac on Mount Moriah.*

24

I gained an early promotion to Mr Jones's class and became its youngest member. Here we memorized the Creed in Welsh. I caused some commotion because I refused to acknowledge that I could read Welsh. Mary, the maid, I suppose, sowed the seed of sedition in my mind. Mr Jones was afraid of my father and hated a fuss. So eventually I had my own way. I would sit in a corner of the pew and eagerly await my turn to read when we read through Psalms together, one verse after another because we read them in English, and I could read English better than the others. If it was a long verse I was delighted and read as fast as I could to emphasize my superiority. For this the others disliked me and kept me out of their games and conversation. I looked back at them, over my shoulder, delighted with my superiority, as I ran alone through the graves to the Rectory gate and they made their way down the broad path to the litch-gate. The advantage of having a path of one's own to come and go by! The advantage! The superiority!

My father had his churchwardens to tea on alternate Sundays, in the seclusion of his study. The one was a farmer with whom he discussed farming and local gossip, and the other the village schoolmaster in whom he endeavoured to awake an interest in archaeology. I was allowed to join them after tea if the conversation was at all fit for young ears. I sat near them, and listened intently until it was time for evensong. Sometimes I had a story book with me, and as I grew older I grew less interested in the conversation and more interested in the book.

But at this time I am a patient audience to Mr Lewis, the schoolmaster, who loved to talk about football more than anything in the world, and my father who wanted to talk archaeology, and to Mr Williams and my father who both talk of the wonders of farming and the genealogies and the strange histories of the families of our parish.

"The *Daily Mail* had a good shot at the Labour Party yesterday. Did you read it, Rector?"

"Llwynhendy is an interesting old farm, you know, Lewis, very interesting. The farm road is definitely the only remaining part of the Roman sarn in this parish. I've established that."

"Rector bach, I never saw such a cow in all my life. She had a bag, well, I've never seen anything more perfect."

25

"Hughes bach's mother and Twm Tan Tŵr's grandmother were two sisters, as you say, but I still don't see how they can be related to Lias Tŷn Gors, Rector, quite honestly."

"I'll show you the book, Williams. I'm quite certain. Michael, pass me that large blue book on the bottom shelf, over there."

"I'll have a look in the old Parish Register, Mr Williams. Get my keys, Michael. I'm sure John Morris is over sixty-five. Quite sure. But I'll be able to tell you for certain."

Mr Lewis speaks slowly. In his anxiety to please, he leaves a sentence unfinished, as though inviting his listener to draw the conclusion he found most agreeable. To myself I say, almost in pain, oh, please yourself, Mr Lewis! Just please yourself, and I devise a conclusion for him that I feel couldn't fail to please anybody, which is what would please Mr Lewis most. But he never knows what I have done for him.

Mr Williams crosses his short fat legs so that I see his underpants above his thick woollen stockings. Oh! I say to myself, almost in agony, adjust your trousers, please, Mr Williams. Mr Lewis taps his finger-tips together and stares through his glasses at something beyond me. Mr Williams smokes like a furnace, I can hardly see his face behind the cloud of smoke that hangs and eddies around him in the windless study. Then perhaps my father will discern the face of the water-clock on the mantelpiece and say:

"Duw, Duw! It's five to six. Come along, Lewis Williams, we must go to Church. They can't get along without us, you know. Michael, go and wash yourself."

"It's Welsh tonight, Dad. Can I stay at home please?

"Go and wash, and don't try and tell me you can't understand Welsh! Go along. It's this maid of ours, you know, Mr Lewis. She can't speak Welsh, she says. If you heard her English! Sheep's English! But then maids are so scarce, so what can we do?"

Mary gets all the blame, but in fact it is my mother who is sending my sister to a boarding school at Llandrindod, for the sake of her accent. Her cousin is the headmistress and therefore my sister gets special terms. There is no talk of a boarding school for me.

My sister, who has spent the time between tea and evensong

with Mary or my mother, now comes to view and races after me across the lawn to climb over the wall into the churchyard. Or, at other times, my mother catches us in time and leads us through the white gate and along the official footpath.

In Church the lamps are lit ready for the darkness that falls during the second lesson. There is a smell of paraffin, and the heating apparatus is boiling over. From a tank in the top corner of the back of the Church comes the sound of mighty rushing boiling waters, and a small cloud of steam. John Elias is ringing the bell, one hand behind his back, his fingers playing about the slit in his jacket. His hair is scanty and parted in the middle, his thin weather-beaten face is creased into a broad toothless smile as he nods at us and raises his eyes at the tank, creasing his forehead neatly, and stretching his smile still further.

The rushing boiling waters roar as we kneel in prayer. My sister and I are afraid. She whispers: "*Dolgarrog*," and I see the front page of the *Christian Herald* that Mary showed us last week — a woman clinging to the branch of a tree with a baby on her other arm, and the water from the broken dam filling up the picture. The sound of mighty rushing waters assails my ears. If the tank of boiling water burst, if the pipes exploded? The tank was at the back of the Church, we sat neatly and quietly in the second pew from the front. Could we get out in time? Through the stained glass window? Or could we climb up the pulpit and stand on the Bible above the rising boiling water?

"*Rhif yr emyn dau gant tri deg a phedwar*,[11] *two hundred and thirty-four*." Thank God for my father's firm voice from the back of the Church. All will be well. Long ago my mother has stopped me from turning round, but the twitch in my neck still remains.

Miss Morris at the organ is behindhand again. Oh, the painful interval. A fat spinster with a straw hat and pince-nez fumbles with her hymn book and peddles away the while, getting wind into the organ's tired lungs.

She's off! We get up. My father in a white starched surplice walks solemnly down the aisle, passing us without as much as a glance. He sinks gracefully to his knees before us. We sing on.

2

As I ran from the shade of the entry into the May sunshine trapped in our small square back garden, said Albie, Mrs Blackwell came hurrying up the entry, her shoes untied, her coat open, and out of breath.

"They're striking," (her husband, too, worked on the buses). "They're striking. Coming out this dinner time, and Foster's got about a dozen volunteer drivers from Rhyl. They're sure to fight, because they're coming in to take over when the boys are leaving. Oh, Mrs Thomas, what'll we do? They're sure to get hurt. The lads are sure to stop 'em. Oh, damn this striking. 'Ow long will it last and what am I going to live on? It's not so bad with you; you've got visitors coming — if they come, too. The trains are stoppin' too they say. Oh, dear mother! What's to become of us?"

My mother does not answer. She pulls her coat on, not troubling to take off her pinafore. I stand watching them both, my mouth open. My mother is breathing fast. Mrs Blackwell has no difficulty in repeating the same words over and over again. "What'll we do? They're sure to get hurt."

Suddenly my mother speaks.

"I don't hold with it. I've told Dic often enough. We're respectable people. I haven't been brought up to this kind of thing. We're respectable people, we pay our way with everybody, we do. I've told him often enough. I'm going there to stop him getting into trouble if I can. Albie, put your coat on."

She grabs me with one hand and takes my coat off the peg behind the door.

"It's nice, Mam. I don't want a coat."

"Keep quiet! I'll have to take him. I can't leave him in the house alone."

28

Bang goes the back door. We go through the front door; determinedly my mother pockets the key. I am dragged along after her, tugged to keep up with their haste. They talk to each other over my head. Mrs Blackwell takes my other hand. Her hand is as sticky as mine. It is hot now; my coat is heavy walking at this pace. There are people in every street walking in our direction. Doors are open, conversations are going on from garden gate to door, from door to door, and shopkeepers stand agitated in the doorways of their empty shops. The crowd thickens as we get into the centre of the town. The railway bridge is black with people. We shall never get through them. Never. I begin to sweat terribly as my mother and Mrs Blackwell thread and push their way forward. I am buffeted about, and my arm aches as my mother draws me on. At the top of the bridge Mrs Blackwell cries:

"Oh! Look at the crowd by the bus station. Oh, look!"

But I am too small to see. The sound of voices flows over me like waves of the sea. The horizon is thick with yells and whistles blowing loudly. New fears grow inside me. If the waves grow bigger, I shall drown in a sea of noise.

"Oh, Mam, let's go home."

She can't hear me. Only the voices about us.

"They're going to stop the blacklegs . . . . They've lined up against them . . . . They won't budge . . . . The police don't know what to do . . . . They're keeping the crowd back . . . . The Super's phoned to Chester. He doesn't know what to do . . . . They'll send for the soldiers. Soldiers . . . soldiers."

Now we are wedged in the crowd. Mrs Blackwell can elbow through no further. She has met a wall of backs.

"Who d'ye think you're poking around . . . . Keep yer bloody elbows to yourself . . . 'ere Missus, don't be familiar . . . . Steady on there . . . 'aven't you no manners . . . ."

We have come to a full stop. My face is pressed against a woman's coat. I can't lift my arm to wipe my face. Mam, I want to go home. The smell of sweat, cheap scent and petrol fumes are making me sick. "Mam, Mam, take me home." I have started to cry without knowing it, like a lost child in a foreign city expecting to be killed.

"Oh, Mam, I'm going to be sick."

If I don't get out I shall be smothered like the two little princes in the tower.[12] Two hairy hands are holding a pillow over my head. I must make a last desperate effort. I scream and scream against the descending pillow, and then darkness falls . . . .

On the sofa at home, in the front room, I awaken as if out of a dream. Rescued from the cruel Tower by kind strong arms, I have been carried like an Arab on a camel, up and down, up and down.

My mother bends over me with a wet towel in her hands. I see my father, too. His nose has been bleeding and he has a cut over his eye which has started to close.

"There, Albie," he says, "you're all right now, aren't you, son? There's a good little soldier. He doesn't cry."

They concentrate their affection and concern upon me and I recover rapidly in its radiance. I thank them with a smile, a signal of contentment and all seems well until they leave my side. Then the circle of warmth is broken and a bitterness steals into my mother's voice.

"Don't you talk to me about bringing him up, Dic. Don't you dare. Why don't you behave like a decent respectable man, if you think anything of him?"

"Listen to me for a second, Nel, will you . . . ."

"Why don't you see that we earn enough to give him a proper upbringing and make something of him, instead of talking big about what he's going to be and about your big strikes?"

"Now wait a minute, Nel . . . ."

"Why don't you see he gets a chance to be something, instead of all this . . . this . . . bloody strike business."

"This is the first time ever I have heard my mother swearing. She is on the verge of tears, and my father is crestfallen and beaten.

"All right, Nel, all right, Nel, I'll see he gets his chance."

"That's empty talk, that is. The same as all that talk about justice for the workers. It's the worker's job to work, and not waste his time with empty talk."

He turns and goes into the back kitchen to bathe his nose.

"Will you listen to the children, Mr Charles?" My father leans forward, said Iorwerth, his prematurely white hair glistening in the lamplight. We, a row of children, stand along the rail of the *Sêt Fawr*,[13] six on either side of the organ facing the congregation.

The young preacher, the stranger in our midst, the unfamiliar interesting face among familiar faces, smiles at us and draws near. He nods his head to each of us in turn:

"Yes, very good. Very good. Now you."

It is my turn and I begin like a veteran.

"A false balance is abomination to the Lord: but a just weight is his delight."

"Yes, very good. Who taught you that?"

"My father." I blush.

"Very good. What is your name?"

"Iorwerth."

"In which book is that verse to be found, Iorwerth?"

"The Bible!" Do I hear laughter? they are smiling.

"Certainly. Quite right. Quite right. But which particular book in the Bible?"

"Oh! Proverbs."

"Yes, very good. Try and learn them all, Iorwerth, will you? They are worth learning, every one of them."

"Yes. I will." I answer at once, anxious to please — and to retreat to the anonymity of our pew. My release is not yet.

"What exactly does '*carreg uniawn*' mean? Do you know, Iorwerth?"

The answer is behind that smiling face, but not in my head. He asks too many questions. Why ask a question to which there is no available answer? My mind grows hot for something to say and my hand flutters about my silent open mouth.

"Rather difficult, is it not? '*Carreg uniawn*' — the correct weight. A 'just weight' in the English."

Light dawns dutifully on twelve young faces. I look across the *Sêt Fawr* at my father, downhearted by my bad performance, but he smiles at me. Relieved, I smile back at him, the kind man who is my shield and my protector, who teaches me new things and reads to me, teaches me rhymes and takes pleasure in me. The thin, kind man who before breakfast, comes in from the stable or cowshed, collarless, washes his hands in the kitchen sink, and reaches into the window recess for the large Bible. The

31

thin, kind man who returning from town in shining leggings, brings me a bar of chocolate, returning with gladness to his own hearth. The thin, kind man who reads so much in the evening while my mother knits on the other side of the fire, like two figures on a Christmas card.

When he was younger, before I was born, he wrote a book about the history of Calvinistic Methodism in the north of the county. He worked on through the night and according to Llew, the farmhand, that was how his hair turned white.

"You know, Ann . . . "

My mother, who is darning, patiently lifts her head,

"You know, Ann, I would rather like to make a start on the second volume."

My mother nods patiently.

"Well, yes, Arthur. It would be interesting I'm sure."

"Two-thirds of a job is the start." My father quotes the proverb, but then he sighs.

"That is certainly true," says my mother.

My father leans forward to press his advantage.

"What about tonight? Couldn't I start tonight, Ann?"

"Well, I don't know, Arthur bach, you are rather tired, aren't you? I'd have a nice rest if I were you."

"Yes, yes. I'm certainly tired." There is disappointment in my father's voice. "Yes, I'm certainly tired."

We walk home from Chapel, my father and mother on either side of me holding my hands. The darkness looms from the hedgerows, but I am unafraid, beautifully safe between my guardian angels. We come to the broad, white gate that leads to the home field. My father lets go my hand to open it. Released I dance through in front, into a familiar darkness, knowing full well that cords of love stretch back to them and that I shall never be lonely, even though I walk to school alone. As we walk through the yard to the kitchen door, the warm smell of animals, dung and hay assails us. We are home.

My father strikes a match so that I can see his face and scarf and bowler hat first, as he lights the hanging lamp, level with his head. My mother has already poked the fire and put the kettle on. She hums a hymn tune to herself as she bustles between the dairy and the kitchen.

"Will you carve the cold meat, then, Arthur?"

"Father," I ask during supper, "Michael Edwards says that Methodists are not as good as Church folk."

My father laughs.

"Well, after all, his father is a parson."

"He says they are better because the Methodists are not official. Is that true?"

"Oh, ho! That's a good one." My father laughs again.

"But is it true."

"No, indeed, my love. It is *not* true." My mother is not laughing.

"Why?"

"You had better explain it, Arthur. It needs to be explained."

"Yes, I suppose I ought to. It will take some time though. Are you willing to listen, Iorwerth? It's a long story."

"Yes," I say. "But I must help mother wash the dishes first."

"That's a good boy."

I see them both smile. I must have pleased them. It is so nice to please them and feel warm inside.

On a delicate April morning, said Michael, when the sun had already gently set the dew on fire, Wil Ifor Jones, Iorwerth Hughes and I stood staring fixedly into the window of Siop Ganol.[14] Wil Ifor, as a matter of fact, was waiting to see the bus, because it was driven, with incomparable skill according to Wil, by his uncle Dic. More than once I heard Wil Ifor ask after his cousin above the clatter of the powerful engine.

"How's Albie, Uncle?"

And his uncle would always answer, "Fine, *boi bach*![15] Champion!"

Then Wil would say, "When is he coming up to stay with us?" And his uncle would answer, often when the bus was already moving, "Oh, he'll come one day. He's sure to come one day."

But as Wil continued to ask the question, his uncle began to make excuses. "He's got to help his mam, you see . . . . She's not so well, you see . . . next summer holidays I'm sure he'll come, eh . . . . So long now, Wil . . . . Be a good boy."

And so the bus would depart leaving only a cloud of evil-smelling black smoke behind, and Wil in a bad temper and

Iorwerth and I like two faithful dogs at his heels.

"You got any money, Iorwerth?"

"Well, no. I'm afraid I haven't, Wil."

"What about you, young squire me lad?" Wil says to me.

I nod eagerly.

"How much have you got then?"

"A shilling."

"Bah-ach!" Wil spits contemptuously.

"I have." My hand of itself dives into my trouser pocket. Ah, that horrid shilling. But I was so anxious to impress Wil Ifor and win his regard. There was no one in school to touch him for daring, fighting and swearing.

"Let's see it then."

A bright new shilling on the palm of my hand. Mother's shilling, a contribution to some Fund or other to be delivered without fail or forgetting to Mr Lewis, the School. Wil and Iorwerth draw near to stare at the shilling in respectful silence.

"Um," says Wil at last. "Enough to buy twenty cigarettes, *myn uffarn i*![16]

"Michael," says Iorwerth, in his goody-goody voice.

"What?"

"That shilling isn't yours, is it?"

Wil laughs scornfully, so that I am compelled to say hotly, "Yes, it is! It is mine!"

"I don't believe it," says Wil, and Iorwerth smiles with self-satisfaction.

"Well, if it *is* yours," Wil says masterfully, "buy six of those. Two each for the three of us, *myn uffarn i*!"

"Six of what?" I say, knowing full well that he is referring to a powerful pyramid of oxo cubes in the shop window.

"Very good chew," Wil says. "Just as good as Amlwch tobacco."

"All right. We'll have six of those." And into the shop I go.

My mother, as always, said Albie, stands over the gas stove, and my father sits down to his plate of egg and chips. "I've had enough of this country run, Nel," he says. "Crawling up all them hills. Fumes are ruining my stomach and that's a fact. Heigh, Albie! I saw your cousin Wil Ifor today again."

34

I glance at my mother where she frowns above the stove. I know very well how much she disapproves of my father's brother, Wil Ifor's father. Drunk and out of work most of the time, and, "his children in a shameful state. And his wife such a sluttish woman."

"Same age as you," my father goes on cheerfully. "Well-grown lad. Not an inch taller than you either. Pity you can't pop up and see him, just for the day . . . ."

"Dic." My mother's voice is loaded with warning. There is an uneasy silence. With a sigh my father decides to drop the subject. My mother's dearest wish is to be respectable and it is also mine.

On our way to school, said Michael, I did not offer Iorwerth any of the oxo cubes I had bought in Siop Ganol. I gave Wil Ifor two. During playtime, I gave him half the last one; and in the lunch hour in order to make sure of his friendship for the rest of the afternoon, I bought six more. I gave his friend Raymond a cube too. While Raymond was opening his mouth to show me its messy contents, Wil Ifor crept up behind me. Suddenly he thrust his hand into my pocket and scattered my jingling pennies across the playground. I opened my mouth to scream with rage but Wil Ifor held up his fist before my face, so instead, I bent down to pick up the pennies. Two were lost.

That night, when my mother came in to say goodnight, she picked up my trousers from the bedroom floor and heard the remaining pennies jingling in my pocket.

"Michael, where did you get these?" The pennies lay like tombstones on her long, white hand.

"Well?" I could think of nothing convenient to say. "Well, Michael? Answer me, or I shall go and get your father."

If only there were an answer I could give. I also knew that my father was not in the house and that my mother disliked scenes.

"Very well, Michael. You shall hear more of this in the morning."

Nevertheless I slept surprisingly well. But next morning as I finished my porridge, my father came down much earlier than was his wont. He was frowning.

"Now then, my boy. Tell me exactly where you got the money found in your trouser pocket last night."

The way he said *exactly* was like an axe cleaving a log in two. There was no hope of escape now. Bit by bit I began to confess.

"In fact, it was your mother's shilling?"

"Yes."

"You didn't give it to Mr Lewis?"

"No."

"How much did you spend?" What could I say? "How much did you spend?" The thunder of his voice seemed to threaten my existence.

"Only a penny, father."

"Only a penny! Your mother found five pennies in your pocket! *Where* is the remainder?"

"I lost some. And some of the children in school stole some."

"What!"

A gap in the universe, my father's mouth hangs open, his body for one moment turned into a pillar of salt. There was no turning back; in order to transform the motionless rock into familiar flesh I had to go on weaving my story.

"I was standing in the yard talking to Iorwerth Maesgwyn. Someone came behind me, put his hand in my pocket and threw the pennies all over the place. I only got five back."

"Who was it that came behind you?"

"I don't know. I couldn't see. He was behind me."

"Did Iorwerth see him?"

"I don't know."

"Where *exactly* in the yard were you standing, you and Iorwerth?"

"About the middle, I think."

"Well, you surely must have turned to see who it was. You did so, didn't you?"

"Yes."

"Well, who was it?"

A piece of toast and marmalade squished between my fingers. I was too scared to lift my arm and push it into my mouth.

"Who was it, Michael?"

An answer could not be avoided. But I couldn't give Wil Ifor away.

"Raymond. Raymond Rawson." The name slipped out.

My parents gazed at each other unhappily across the table. I realized then that although Raymond Rawson's family were new in the village, they were keen church folk.

However, once on my way to school my spirits rose.

It was another beautiful morning. At school I paid close attention to Iorwerth Maesgwyn and avoided Wil Ifor Jones. For the first time, Iorwerth asked me to Maesgwyn for tea. I jumped up and down three times before I said yes. Later I closed my eyes as I stood by myself in the warm sun in the shadows of the school wall. I felt a hand on my shoulder. It was Raymond Rawson.

"I've got a tent," he said. "A big one. Green. In our garden."

"No you haven't," I said.

"Yes, I have. Honest. Come and see it after school."

"Oh, I don't know." It was tempting. Games in the green gloom of the tent would grow as sweet as dreams. How popular I was that afternoon. Everybody wanted me.

"Say you'll come."

"All right. I'll come."

And it was there I went, instead of Maesgwyn and it was there in the green twilight of the tent among Raymond's friends that my father found me.

"Just come out of there, as fast as you can! At once! Your mother is looking everywhere for you."

I crept out into the harsh daylight. I felt my father's heavy hand grasp my shoulder. He led me down the road, saying nothing until we were out of earshot of the house.

"You told me a lie, Michael, didn't you?"

I shook my head in fright. I knew well enough how bad it was to tell lies and be caught at it.

"Barefaced lie! I'm ashamed of you. Raymond didn't take a penny. You spent it all. I'll have the truth out of you, my boy."

A nightmare journey down the narrow lane towards the rear entrance of the Rectory. I was so afraid of anyone seeing us, my father nudging the truth out of me as he pushed me in front of him and I crying unrestrainedly. That night, in the darkness, with a stump of pencil I wrote in English on the wall above my bed, 'I HAVE NO FREND IN THE WIRLD.'

3

Spring is the most mysterious season, they were saying. The trees break into green song. Each leaf opens like a baby's fist and grows towards the sun. Nothing can withstand our growth, today's foot already too big for yesterday's shoe. Observe our steady stretching in the air about us. We grow daily and nightly, and we are plants equipped to draw sustenance from all the elements.

Our heads grow bigger to contain more information. In school our faces among rows of faces each have two ears down which funnels are poured the measured gallons of knowledge. In each face two bright eyes stare at a map of the world. The mouths in the row of faces are shut until the bell rings and then they open and out in the asphalt yard voice the singing music of all the released limbs.

I go to bed at night, said Albie, with a meccano world shifting in my brain like the rails at Chester station, and my head on the pillow can hear a beautiful train steaming out into the night along sweet, shining rails to run through new worlds; or, more often, the street lamp glows in the street and out in the darkness a train that never stops, whistles to announce its swift and terrible passing.

I go to bed, said Iorwerth, to dream of Jesus Christ conducting me through orange groves on the edges of a dusty desert. "Here," he will say, "is your field of work." A cow perhaps will bellow for its calf, or a horse stamp his itching feathery leg on the cobbled floor of the stable.

I go to bed with a loaded mind, said Michael, filled like an omnibus with schoolboy stories. I am attached to the real and possible, dreaming possible dreams of schoolboys in which I may play a prominent part; escapades at the tuck shop and booby traps for unpopular masters: scoring ninety-nine before being run out because of a lazy partner. The rooks in the rectory trees caw as I put on my Eton jacket and slip into the quad of St James's School.

My sister has gone to my aunt at Llandrindod Wells to be brought up there as a young lady. I had hoped that I would have been allowed to go to some kind of a public school, but my father says I must try the scholarship for the County School like everyone else. I resent having to compete, especially since I am aware that Iorwerth Hughes, who is also trying, is better than I, and will therefore appear higher in the lists. Why, when I know in my own mind that I am good, should I be forced to make myself appear dull and stupid? Why can no one else see the injustice of it?

Mam and Dad have wished me luck, said Iorwerth, and I have walked, jumped, and run to the Cross Roads to meet the bus. I have a satchel on my back which contains my lunch, a ruler, pencils, a pen and a bottle of ink. I stand alone and put my hand out proudly to the big-nosed bus. Obediently it stops. I clamber up. It bears me onward on a wave of excitement, until we reach the village, where Michael Edwards with a satchel too gets on board and comes to sit beside me. As the bus moves (but not before, because the driver is his uncle) I catch a glimpse of Wil Ifor inciting his followers to make rude gestures. Michael is very cool at first and says, "Damn this scholarship."

The bus driver changes gear and turns to smile at us.

"You two going to try the Scholarship?"

We nod our heads fairly politely.

"My boy is trying, too. Albie his name is. Very tall for his age. Taller than both of you. Very dark like he is. Doesn't talk much."

We nod again politely. The driver resumes his duties, staring at the road ahead. Michael says to me, "If I happen to fail, you know, I expect I'll be sent away to boarding school. So I don't care really whether I pass or not."

39

But by the time the bus reaches the town he is just as excited as I am. We descend all trembling, at the gates of the County School.

"*Hwyl* boys!"[17] the driver shouts, as the bus moves off. "Tell Albie you saw me now!"

We follow a stream of boys through a door marked *Bechgyn*.[18] We stand uncertain, my confidence and expectation is giving way to fear and despair. I seem to be the only lonely boy, because all the others are talking and laughing and smiling at each other. Michael is smiling and talking to a strange boy. We are rounded up like stray cattle by prefects and made to stand in rows.

The headmaster appears before us, like the hero of a myth, direct from heaven. He is a tall, thin-faced man in spectacles, drawing his long black gown tightly about him as if he were very cold in spite of the bright sunshine. In sharp English he tells us where to go and what to do, and not to cheat. He then wishes us luck. Abruptly he turns away, drawing his gown yet more tightly about him, and like a distant cloud of glory, disappears.

Oh, the minutes of pain and apprehension, pain in the stomach sitting in a large, strange, yellow desk in a strange well-windowed yellow room. The white virgin papers and the question papers are in the arms of a gowned young man who walks authoritatively between the desks.

"Who wanted this paper in Welsh?" He looks around, eyebrows and paper raised.

I, Iorwerth, suddenly remember, it seems the last moment, that I had been told that I did. In the room my arm alone is raised and as I look around I meet all faces turned for a moment towards me, expressing amusement, surprise, curiosity, disdain. And why does the master smile as he hands me the paper? My vest is sticking to my back as I grow hot with embarrassment. It is a relief to pick up my pen and plunge into the work.

The English paper was easy, said Michael, and I wrote a lot about Long John Silver.

The Arithmetic was simple, said Albie. I finished first and walked out of the room between perplexed boys, quietly triumphant. I am able to go home early before the others come out, but I wish to wait for company in order to compare notes and answers. "What did you get for No. 6?" "Five pounds, two shillings and fourpence three farthings?" "That's it! That's it!" "Did you get this for No. 4?" I shall be among the first group going home for dinner along the broad concrete slabbed pavement, and I shall be able to tell my mother over dinner how many sums I have worked out correctly.

The Arithmetic was awful, said Michael. My mind was matted and mazed like the hair of a newly-awakened restless sleeper, like wool on thorns. My new watch thudded on my wrist like a giant pulse. It was a relief to peel the problems off my eyes, and free my limbs from the stocks, and allow my tongue to express or transmute my late discomfort, and make excuses.

We eat our lunch in an empty classroom, Iorwerth and I. The children from town walked off in a superior manner to their various homes. Some even had bicycles and we watched them wistfully as they passed the classroom window. They seemed to us the *élite*.

We were allowed to wander about the school fields and watch senior boys of the school play cricket and the senior girls play hockey. These bigger people completely ignored us, but the boys only a few years older than ourselves chased us and tried to catch us. We saw them spread one small boy on the grass and holding on to his legs and arms, bump him. "I am determined," I say to Iorwerth, "that they shall not do that to me." "So am I," he answers. We link arms and are more friendly now than ever before, standing together watching the big boys play cricket, at last real friends, shedding unworthy thoughts.

I forgive you for being superior and copying my sums from me, thought Iorwerth.

I forgive you for being better than I at school, and for talking Welsh to me, thought Michael.

I forgive you for calling me a Methody quack-quack and a goody-goody, and for choosing Wil Ifor's company before mine.

I forgive you for looking hurt when I make fun of you, for looking pained when I swear in competition with Wil Ifor, and for making me feel uncomfortably guilty.

A party of boys came strolling up towards us, spreading out as

41

they approached, deploying in order to surround us, camou-flaging their intentions by hands-in-pockets and whistling. The leader has reached us and put his hands on my shoulder, said Michael.

"Excuse me," he says laughing, "but we shall have to bump you."

We are surrounded.

"No," I say unsteadily, casting my eye around for an outlet.

"Oh yes!" he says pleasantly, giving me a push on the chest so that I tumble over a boy who has knelt behind me for this purpose without my seeing him. I am deafened by laughter and hands grasp my legs which do not even kick and grasp my arms which are like unresistant rubber.

I lie still on the grass, conscious of an ache of body and spirit and of grinning faces around me. I look around for Iorwerth. Iorwerth has gone, has fled, and, alas, I, only I, am left. I see his back making for the boys' lavatories. I think bitterly "he has deserted me", and get up, brushing my clothes with my hand, walking slowly away with tears in my eyes, towards the far end of the playing fields. I turn about to survey the innumerable children bigger than I, running about the field, each with a definite place in the large red building which stands as a background to them. I am moved to tears at the thought of my own unimportance.

I stood by the side door, said Iorwerth, waiting for it to open, among other early arrivals. I was safe here from any attack, within the shadow of authority, away from the lawless field. The tall well-built boy with jet-black hair who walked out of the examination first this morning was standing next to me, answering questions addressed to Albie with a small confident smile. This no doubt was Wil Ifor's cousin. I, too, entered into conversation with him about the morning's exams. I expect being so much taller made him stand quietly and not hop and skip about as we did. And standing still gave him a knowledge-able air. To be tall is to look over other people's heads and to stand out among crowds, an obvious figure, and the watched do not indulge in antics, but conscious of stares, are still. I liked standing near him. Who is not pleased and flattered when the most outstanding person in a crowd gives him some particular attention; who does not bask in reflected glory?

I intended to say that I had met his father and that I knew his cousin, Wil Ifor. But somehow it did not seem meet. For Albie was a prince among boys, tall, stately and quiet, and so much better than his connections. In any case I am at ease now, no longer among strangers entirely, and not being completely ignored.

Michael has joined the queue a little way down from us. He is within speaking distance, but he makes no attempt to speak or draw near. I should like him to watch me talking to my tall distinguished new friend, Albie Jones, and share my unmitigated pleasure. Look, Michael, this tall boy has taken notice of me. Come here and let me tell him who you are. Come here! Come here! Michael continues to stare straight in front of him; his eyes are red.

When the examination was over, said Albie, I knew that I had done well; the questions were easy to answer, some of them even childish. I walked into town light-hearted, accompanied by two boys from the country, Iorwerth and Michael. Iorwerth has curly hair, a flat half-moon, girlish face and thin legs. Michael is a little taller than he, sturdily built, parting his hair and brushing it back like a grown-up. They both seem to like me, and listen to me with respect. They do not jeer and push and run away; they are not dirty; their noses do not run — they are clean and tidy and talk sensibly with the country accent, not with the town drawl.

"This is where I turn down for home."

"Where do you live then, Albie?" Iorwerth says.

"Down there, Prince Edward Street."

"That's a posh name," says Michael.

"They are council houses." I blush and they look at each other.

"There's a pub in Gorsedd called the Prince Edward Arms," says Michael.

"Let's hope we've all passed, yes?" says Iorwerth.

"Hope so. Well, so long now."

"I haven't passed," says Michael. "And I don't care either. I'll get sent away to boarding school and I'd like that."

I lift my hand in gesture of farewell. "See you in September," Iorwerth calls. And Michael calls, rather louder.

"Won't you come up and stay with Wil Ifor in the village? We could play together then on the Gop."

"P'r'haps. Don't think so though. Mother won't let me."

"So long then."

"So long."

Michael and I go on to the bus station, said Iorwerth.

"Do you think Albie's father will be driving tonight? He's a good driver, isn't he?"

"I suppose so."

Michael stares ill-humouredly at the row of buses in the petrol-and-fish- and-chips-smelling-yard. He is so cold towards me there must be something I have done to offend him. I do not want him to be vexed with me.

"Pity Albie can't come up and stay with Wil, isn't it?" I say.

"Too much of a mammy's baby, I'm afraid," says Michael.

I wish he would put himself in a better humour. I am happy. We climb into the empty bus.

When I arrived home, said Albie, Mam had a nice tea ready for me; a boiled egg, and then two eccles cakes to enjoy. I see how big I am in her eyes, Albert Thomas Jones,[19] known as the cleverest boy at the British School,[20] accustomed now to being top of my class, and very capable too at football and cricket, which earns me respect among other boys. In the warm light of her love, I become beautiful, like a lily that blooms on a stagnant pool. Tall, clean, healthy and intelligent, I stand out among a classroom full of generally unhealthy untidy boys and girls (some suffering from curious diseases and from malnutrition). My mother sees in her vision a divine system of education select me for praise and distinction out of the side streets and the council houses, and save me from becoming an errand boy and cycling down blind alleys. It will mark me out for a career which takes into account the fullest flight of my knowledgeable imagination. Was it my mother who whispered first, "You get on, my boy, I want you to get on." Was it my father who said, "You are better than a pension"? And was it I who dreamt of a wonderful job, superintendent of this or that, manager of a bank, a high official? I am tall and quiet, the object of admiration among grown-ups, the candle of my parents' eyes. My father is quiet and content in his pride, going regularly to work. My mother, unceasingly proud of me, careful of my dress and manners, remembering all she had learnt as a girl when in service about the upbringing of a young gentleman. I am given sixpence ungrudgingly, having described the excitement of the day and my enjoyment of it.

"You deserve to go to the pictures," my father said. "Indeed you do."

I was still vaguely unhappy when I got out of the smelly, clattering bus by the Rectory gate, said Michael, and walked down the drive through the sweet air that blew between the trees. My mother was out to tea, at a big house in the next parish, and my father was in his study when I came in. Mary made my tea and asked me how I had enjoyed myself, what the County School[21] looked like inside, and who was the conductor on the bus coming home. Mary knew all the bus conductors.

After tea I knock at the study door and go in. My father is at his desk, writing letters; as usual to do with the S.P.C.K.[22]

"Well, my boy," he asks me in English, looking at me over his glasses. "How did you get on?"

"Not so bad, Dad," I say as cheerfully as I can, not wishing to appear anything but self-possessed and successful.

"Hum. Have you got your examination papers with you?"

They are all folded inside my pocket, the horrible Arithmetic paper in the centre. I never want to look at it again. The sight of it makes my eyeballs ache.

"Put them on the table, Michael. I'll have a look at them as soon as I finish these S.P.C.K. letters. Was the History paper easy?"

"Oh, yes, Dad. Oh, yes. Oh, yes!" I see again those kind questions provoking my pen which only stopped over the spelling of long words which I can pronounce but cannot spell. I know that my father will go over it in detail later on, and I shall enjoy displaying my knowledge in the light of the Aladdin lamp on the study table.

I spend the evening on the square in the village, relating

between games the trials of the day to Wil Ifor and the boys, very glad for once to hold the stage,

"Do you think you'll go to the County School?" says Wil.

"I don't care. I'd sooner stay here. More fun here."

This was well received, and the boys escorted me to the Rectory gate, much to my pride.

But later, in the dark, after going over the Arithmetic paper with my father, questions and doubts assail me, and load my hot pillow with needles against sleep.

At our farm, said Iorwerth, we milk at five o'clock in the afternoon and when I arrived home, tired but still excited, I ran to the cowshed to relate my story to my father, who smiled at me while he listened, his head pillowed the cow's flank, his hands rhythmically milking. Llew y Gwas[23] poked his large head out between the cows to look and listen every now and then and to laugh as he felt the occasion needed.

I ran in to my mother who was ironing on the kitchen table, who listened to my story as she cleared away a corner of the table to lay out my tea. When I sat down I realized how hungry I was and how thirsty, and I could not talk while I crammed my mouth with home-baked bread and butter and home-made jam, and lifted my large bowl to my face and drank deeply, making a sucking noise like Llew. As usual my mother said, "Don't make that noise"; but today, without reproof in her voice.

After tea, refreshed, I go out into the yard and follow Llew as usual taking the cows to the field for the night. I know now that I cannot hang by their tails nor ride on their backs, therefore my whole endeavour is to imitate the experienced herding of Llew; a sharp cry to a wayward cow, a cut along a broad hide with my stick, or a general hoarse shout to inspire bovine fear and hasten them on their way. Hoi-hoi-hey-hwli-hwp!

My father calls me, whistles for Carlo, and we go to look around the sheep and the fast growing lambs.

"When will you be washing the sheep, Father?"

"In a week or two maybe. We'll see how things go."

Oh, these patient replies, signifying always no need for haste, foolish unwise haste. Will I never learn not to panic, not to be afraid of forgetting, of losing, of being left behind? Will I never learn to take my time, assured of my memory, skill, and, above all, the abundance of time?

The sun is setting behind the clump of fir trees at the far end of the field. Everything is quiet except for sporadic bird-song, the last song of the day, and the bleat of a lamb left behind by its mother. My father stands still, leaning upon his stick, reading the signs of the earth in an alphabet I have not yet mastered. Carlo lies down at his feet, tongue out, eyes turned towards his master's face, watching for any signal. I talk more about the exam and my father listens, without ever taking his eyes off the ever-shifting flock. As we walk back through the sweet-smelling fields my father asks me:

"What do you want to be, Iorwerth, when you grow up?"

And I think what a beautiful question. The choice. I may pick an occupation, a career, like a chocolate out of a handsome box of chocolates at Christmas or a birthday.

"A Preacher, father. A Preacher, I think."

Chosen to please us all, mother, father and me. To stand in a red plush pulpit and finger the gilt-edged paper of the large black Bible, and talk and be listened to reverently by many people; to be one of the servants of Jesus, doing good, succouring the wounded, helping the needy; or a missionary perhaps, in hot lands. To be a man of note and importance among the groups of Welsh Divines hanging on the sitting room wall.[24] This is the prince of occupations, being among the chosen of God and the prophets of Israel, my nation.

That night for the first time, aged eleven and a half, I took my turn at reading a chapter of the Bible, before we went to bed, Candle in hand, I climbed the stone stairs to my bedroom like Dante up the stairs of heaven in the *Children's Encyclopaedia*, and the air of heaven lay about me as I fell asleep and dreamt of my kingdom to come.[25]

On a bright Saturday morning in June, said Michael, I was about to go out after breakfast when my father entered the kitchen, his spectacles in one hand and a paper in the other.

"You've passed, Michael," he announced, "you've passed, but only just."

Whoop! My joy and relief burst like a flare in my mind,

drowning the darkness and the small daily thoughts in my mind in joyful light. The relief was as thrilling, as beautiful and as consoling as a new dawn.

Shall I dance about, shall I run into the garden and race around the lawn? Shall I climb a tree and leap from branch to branch? I execute a figure on the kitchen floor, and grab Mary, who is bending over the kitchen fire, lifting up a heavy cast-iron kettle of boiling water.

"Look out!" she screeches, "you silly foolish boy! Do you want me scalded and burnt?"

I am sobered. My thoughts and temperature return to normal.

"May I see it, Dad? May I see the list? Oh, look, the boy from town we met on scholarship day is top: Albie. Albie Jones. I thought he would be. Iorwerth is ninth. Where am I. Oh, dear, thirtieth!" (What is there to console me!) But my father smiles, more jolly than I have seen him for a very long time. There were two hundred trying! Thirty-two get scholarships. I am among them — only just. Compare the markings. Iorwerth has done well. What brought me down, oh, Arithmetic of course — only 40 out of 200 — and Iorwerth 165. It I had had 165 I would have been . . . let me see . . . eighth!

"If I'd had the same marks in Arithmetic I would have beaten him!"

"But you didn't, my boy, so it's stupid talk."

"Yes, but . . . "

" 'But' is a very big word, Michael."

That horrible paper, my hatred of Arithmetic is intense, and at the same time I long to belittle the science with some new casuistry of my own that would express my special personal hatred.

Oh, but the cloud on my mind has finally arisen, and I may now go out to play unmolested by torturing thoughts of failure. I have invented a new game and I shall call for Raymond and Wil Ifor; we shall play it on the hillside this morning. It is a beautiful day, soon the heat will be crackling in the gorse-bushes; the dew is rising and soon I may roll on the short, dry grass and put my ear to the ground for enemy footsteps and Wil or Raymond will leap suddenly on my shoulders, and we shall roll on the ground laughing in a life-and-death struggle, and the hillside will vibrate under our stamping feet.

Later we shall explore the cave higher up on the hillside where my father did excavations when I was still a baby. It is low, mysterious and lovely, and inside water drips down the slimy walls. Nothing could be more secret and yet from the green rampart that hides the cave's low mouth there is a stirring view of the wide valley, of the roofs of the town on the coastal plain, and a glimpse of the bright sea. It is a good place for smoking. Wil Ifor will demonstrate his special trick, inhaling deeply and then filtering the smoke through a dirty handkerchief which he holds across his mouth so that it leaves a sinister brown stain. It is going to be a beautiful day.

4

The walls of Llanrhos County School, said Michael, are eloquent with its short history. This is Mr Longwind James, first Chairman of the Governors, senior deacon at Moriah, a prominent tradesman, chairman of the Chamber of Commerce, town and county councillor, died 1917 (in bed). May the dust on the picture frame rest in peace. This still and silent group still displays the original pupils of the school, solemn unsmiling boys and girls of another century, in old clothes with young faces. The first headmaster sits in the middle, wearing a mortar-board and gown, a high, stiff collar and a drooping black moustache. This is a photograph taken at the opening ceremony; Lady M — key in hand, half turns to face the cameras, her smile lost in the shade of her immense wide hat. Her skirt brushes the steps leading to the front door. Aldermen, clergymen, unknown officials and their wives are also captured in the same frame. And here in faded sepia are the pupils of the school who were killed during the war of 1914-18, boys in uniform, with sad surprised faces.

In the Assembly Hall there is a Roll of Honour, said Albie, a black wooden image, stretching like a totem pole from the ceiling to the floor. Upon it there are names inscribed in gilt lettering, thus — JOHN ED. JONES, Burton School, U.C.N.W.,[26] 1899. This is the first name, at the top of the list; the last, almost on the floor, is FLORENCE HAYES, Cohen Exhibition, Liver. University, 1927; and after her honourable pupils such as myself must pass without mention.

On either side of the dais at the end of the Assembly Hall are two large portraits; on the left, O.M. Edwards;[27] on the right, Sir Herbert Lewis.[28] The ruling headmaster stands between them, still liable to the law of change. We grow under his feet.

Michael, Albie and I, said Iorwerth, stand in the very front during morning prayers, on the male side of the Hall. Heads ascend behind us from form to form like the marks on the doorpost which my father has made, makes and will make to register my growth. Exceptions break through the ranks like cocksfoot grass in the hayfield, and Albie is the exception in our row. The hall is filled in the morning by one form after another, as a granary floor is covered by emptying sack after sack of corn. Prefects marshal us, authoritative sixth-form boys who make our row straight and prevent us from turning round as the hall fills up behind us. Girl prefects wearing blazers, their strong grown-up legs covered by black stockings, order the small girls across the aisle made by the wide gap between us. When all are assembled, the headmaster emerges from his room at the back of the hall, and as he advances down the aisle he draws complete silence after him as though silence were the wide wake of his gown.

The short service is in English. We sing a familiar tune to unfamiliar English words. The headmaster reads a portion of the Scriptures and then reads a prayer out of a small blue book which he opens on the open Bible. This is the first time for me to see a prayer read; no one in our Chapel reads his prayer. Now it is clear that I am on the threshold of a new world.

My first day at school, said Michael, began with a scramble for seats. I was pushed fiercely by a thick-set boy wearing long trousers. I turned to face him with anger on my lips, but the hot words turned cold on my tongue as I saw his large clenched fist and ugly look, and my face broke out into a false engaging smile.

"All right," I said, "let us sit together. We may as well."

This had a good effect because he, too, smiled and asked my name.

"Michael Edwards," I said. "What's yours?"

"Jac Owen," he answered. And so I came to sit with Jac who proved to be a bit of a bully, but fortunately also easily influenced. I took care to understand him, and this was not difficult. I had only to make fun of teachers and people he disliked, and he was delighted. Also I brought my back numbers of *The Schoolboy's Own* for him to read in prep, and I let him copy my homework. He was impressed by my knowledge of schoolboy literature, and of the science of escapading, the execution of which he always enjoyed no matter how simple or how safe the trick.

At the far end of the playing fields there was a clump of bushes, and behind them we made a hollow where in the dinner time we shared Woodbines[29] together, or called meetings of Jac's gang. Jac had learnt to swallow, and like Wil Ifor he gave exhibitions, drawing tobacco smoke down, it seemed, to the very bottom of his lungs, and then driving out the smoke through his distended nostrils. He claimed to have put a slug in his sister's tea and to have urinated on the parlour fire and I for one believed him. We broke bounds together in the dinner hour too, going down to the railway line to put nails on the rails, and then retrieving them flattened out after the Irish Mail had passed at one o'clock; or we went to the football ground across the road to the school where we explored under the grandstand among empty bottles and cigarette cartons and the excrement of wandering dogs, for pennies and sixpences and even half-crowns. Most daring of all, we cut across the playing fields after dinner, having stuffed our school caps in our pockets, to the promenade.

"Iorwerth," I whisper to him across the desk.

"Yes."

"Jac and me are going to Pleasureland in the dinner hour. Coming?"

"It's out of bounds."

Jac made a growling noise. "Granny's baby," he said.

So instead of Iorwerth, Les came with us. Les's father was managing director of the Steam Laundry and Leslie, the only son, always wore new suits that were grubby with the stains of the sweets he always carried, and creased by the weight of Les's plump bulging body. But Les was a good sport all the same and was always sharing sweets.

In Pleasureland we borrowed many pennies from Les and I don't remember that we paid them back. The machines of chance were lovely and inviting, their noise was enchanting like the all-pervading smell of rock and candy-floss, coconuts, engine oil, and the chemical used by the Indian chief to cloud his

Vision Bowl.

"What time is it, boys?"

"Hell!" said Jac, and started to run at once. A breathless race across the town it was, avoiding people on the pavement, dodging the traffic in the busy streets, and bathed in sweat, being shouted at by a policeman happily chained to point duty, As we passed the church clock, Les looked up and gasping made his famous jerking joke.

"It's ten to two, too."

Jac left school at the end of our second year having sunk to the bottom of IIIB. He became apprenticed to an electrician in town, and we continued to meet. Sometimes we went to the pictures together, Jac, Les and I. Jac told us things about girls we never knew before. He was still the boss, but as time went on we found we grew less eager to make the effort to meet him on a Saturday afternoon, and Jac became less important.

I sit with Albie in the front desk, said Iorwerth, happy under the eye of a teacher, attentive to the lesson, my intelligence aided by my nearness to them. They are real and human; if I put out my hand I can touch them for they are made of the same stuff as I, and belong to my world; they are not enemies observed over a ditch or across a stretch of water. Therefore what they say is real to me and convincing, and since they have entered my world and are real like my father and mother and the animals on our farm and Miss Roberts, and the preachers at Capel Bach on Sunday, the knowledge they impart is real and of my world also. Albie too helps my understanding, by grasping at once the new facts that are to be understood. Between Albie and the teacher I am in the direct line of communication, and all my efforts to understand are pleasurable labour.

When we are doing some written work, out of the corner of my eye I glance at Albie. He does not bend over the paper with his tongue sticking out and following his pen like a dog following his master. He sits upright, eyes only cast downwards, his pen held firmly in his hand moving steadily over the paper.

Equally confident and capable on the football field he is the undisputed captain of the football team. He coolly plans out tactics, commanding his team with quiet authority which has to be obeyed.

"Albie Jones!" Jac Owen shouts.

"Yes?"

Jac advances ominously in the cloakroom.

"My name isn't down to play against IIB."

"I know it isn't." I look nervously at Jac's big fists, but Albie does not flinch.

"Well, it had better be, see?"

Jac looks wild with anger. Albie is pale. Oh, I tremble with concern for my friend.

"Are you trying to say that I'm not good enough, Albie Jones?"

Everyone in the cloakroom is watching. The air between the rows of coats is unbearably still.

"Yes, I am."

There is nothing else for it. Jac must attack him now. After a moment of hesitation that seems an age Jac suddenly swings a blow at Albie's head. But Albie side-steps and Jac lands face forward among the coats. Everyone laughs. Enraged, Jac turns to attack wildly but Albie is cool and his arms are long and he seems able to keep Jac's flailings out of range.

"Smash him up, Jac!"

"Down him, Albie! Knock him for six!"

"Look out, chaps. The slobs are coming."

Slobs is the school word for prefects. The fight comes to an inconclusive end, but Albie keeps his authority over the football team.

And yet he is not popular. His accomplishments are too many; his superiority too definite. The others envy him too much. Among all the school, only I think the world of him. But although he is unfailingly kind to me, careful never to slight me, not pulling a face at the stump of a finger on my right hand, always giving me my fair chance, I know he does not love me, or feel any great attachment towards me. To him I am strange and foreign; he does not understand my excited talk of farm or Chapel. I cannot bring with me to school fresh news to excite him. My father buys a new horse; twin calves are born to the cow 'Seren Wen';[30] the fox is about again; such things do not interest him. I cannot recount to him stories of missionaries I have read

54

in *Y Cenhadwr*[31] or *Y Trysorfa Fach*,[32] nor can I explain to him my ambition to preach, to make long speeches woven from beautiful words, to see the light of heaven descend upon my hearers' upturned faces. Albie's talk is all of wireless and motor cars, the mysteries of engines, also the exploits of famous footballers, and cricketers. His world is a swiftly moving pageant that never leaves the main streets of towns, always hedged between tall buildings, moving through crowds and congested traffic.

During the summer holidays I spent a week at Albie's home, and his mother was very kind to me. This was the first time for me to sleep in a town. The electric light, so easily and neatly switched on or off, the bathroom and the water closet so clean and convenient, impressed me greatly, and these brilliant assets led me to ignore the smallness of the rooms and the inadequate backyards, ranged side by side, the washing of various households almost touching each other, one man's wet shirt rubbing against his neighbour's vest.

I slept with Albie, and this too was a brilliant experience. My head lying on the same bolster as that of my greatest friend, our bare feet sometimes touching as we turned over in bed.

"Albie."

"Um?"

"You sleeping?"

"No."

"What are you thinking about?"

"Nothing. What are you thinking about?"

"About stars. Do you think there are people living on other planets?"

"Shouldn't be surprised."

"I had an awful dream last night. I dreamt I was sitting on the horn of the moon. I didn't mind it at first until I looked down and saw that the moon was on fire. I didn't know what to do. What could I have done, Albie? What would you have done?"

"Die of course."

"But . . . ?"

"Go to sleep now will you, there's a good chap. Good night."

It was indeed happiness to sleep with my friend and to share, first thing in the morning, a drowsy awakening, looking at each other, raised on our elbows, laughing with half-opened eyes.

At breakfast Albie's father talked Welsh to me, and seemed to enjoy it, but Mrs Jones said:

"Don't talk Welsh, Dic. Albie doesn't understand. Iorwerth doesn't mind, do you, Iorwerth?"

But whenever we were alone, Mr Jones and I spoke Welsh. He was a small, lively man with thin, greying hair brushed across his head to cover his baldness. He was always cheerful and kind, but it was difficult to see any resemblance to Albie.

After breakfast we walked through the bright morning air, making for the wide, empty promenade. The sea was sharply blue, and beautifully clean. We played on the smooth sand, until a small company of Seaside Evangelists came to conduct a service on a small platform. I listened attentively. After all, although it was English, they were doing the Lord's work, and everyone who failed to listen was rather at fault. 'Suffer little children to come unto me' they said was their theme. At the end of the service the man on the tiny platform asked those who had been saved to come and stand behind him. I who wanted so much to be saved was anxious to oblige, but Albie said the Pleasure ground was open and that we must hurry away. I saw for a moment the picture in my aunt's parlour — 'The broad and narrow way', and my heart was torn with a painful dissension. In the end I followed Albie. We both changed sixpenny pieces for seven coppers, and tried to win money on several machines. Albie won 1s. 3d. but I lost all mine. Was it punishment for me to lose, I thought? Albie paid for me to go in the bumper-cars. But as soon as we were beginning to enjoy the sport, the machine stopped and we had to get off. We stood watching the cars for a long time and tried to win enough money to be able to ride in them again. But in the end we had left only 2d. each.

We called in a paper shop on our way home. Albie bought a paper on wireless, and I bought *The Boys' Own Paper*, and we read these papers until dinner was ready. Potatoes, mutton and green peas on willow pattern plates, followed by rhubarb and custard. Then we lay back on the sofa and read a little more until it was time for the pictures. There was a serial, and I remember the ending, a motor-car flying over a precipice — 'To be continued next week' — and then a big picture. My eyes burnt when we came out of the darkness into the harsh light of the afternoon.

We had tea in a café. This too was unusual. We sat by the window and watched people passing on the street below. A double-decker bus passed the window, and I thought, if I put my hand out I could touch it. Custard tarts for me, blackberry tarts for Albie. My stomach was full, and my eyes still ached. The fumes of petrol from the streets seemed to invade my senses. I felt sick. I vomited in the lavatory. Albie was kind, and I was hot with shame.

In the evening we went to the Pleasure Lake outside the town and having ridden the Figure Eight, and gone through the Cave of Mystery in a paddle-boat we watched people try things until supper time. For supper we had fish and chips from the saloon at the end of the street.

One hot afternoon, the last afternoon of my holiday, we were returning to No. 15 from the centre of the town. The street was full of traffic and the pavement was crowded with people, mostly trippers, carrying oddments in paper bags and children's sand spades. A boy came cycling in our direction, and tried to take the corner in front of us without slowing, but the bonnet of a car caught him on the turn and knocked him through the air against a stationary car by the opposite pavement. At the precise moment my eyes were intent on a pyramid of glistening bottles of jam in a grocer's window, and only my ears were pierced by the screeching of brakes and horrified female voices. When I turned round I could see only a crowd around the boy who lay crumpled and silent on the street, made visible to me through a wall of backs by my startled, quivering imagination. A policeman blew his whistle several times, an ambulance pulled up and things happened beyond the thick crowd which I could not see nor imagine. Albie had left me, pushed his way into the crowd, but he saw nothing. A woman standing near me said,

"He'll drown in his own blood."

In the twinkling of an eye, I was in the boy's dying place and I saw the blood rising inside me like quick-silver in a thermometer, welling up like spring water, but red and thick, in order to rise over my mouth, my nose, my eyes. I drown, I swirl like seaweed in my own thick red blood.

I lost all taste for my holiday in the town and I was not happy until I opened the gate into the home field. The setting sun was gilding the welcoming map of ivy above the drawing room window. I greeted my parents with loving gladness and after tea I went upstairs, breathing familiar smells with unutterable pleasure, and having unpacked and put on old clothes, I ran out into the freedom of the yard, and went with Llew to turn the cows out after milking.

5

Towards the end of my second year at school, said Albie, my voice began to break and I had to leave the Church choir. I was never more conscious of a difference between myself and the other boys of our form. My skin broke its even, smooth surface and pimples invaded my face like a face in an advertisement for skin cures or laxatives. The black hairs on my upper lip and chin were very obvious, and seemed to me to be exceptionally dirty and unbecoming. When left in the house alone, I took my father's safety razor and tried to shave without soap and water, sometimes cutting pimples and on the whole making a greater mess of my face than ever. My growth was accelerated, my jackets were tight across my shoulders, my short trousers were tight about my thighs.

When seated in my desk at school I look with shame at the large legs that seem to bulge out of my trousers. I become self-conscious, always Albie overgrown, pimply-faced, thick-thighed, therefore I assume the breastplate of good manners and a shield of quietness against the poisoned darts of the boys who wish to attack me. All my wits are employed patrolling these simple defences.

My remarks are unusually relevant and pointed among the irrelevant and pointless chatter of boys. Some I hurt with my sharpness, a few become respectful, others become my enemies, contriving my ill, seeking to bring upon me dishonour, pain and shame. They invent crude weapons to pierce my defence, nick-names are thrown at my back like stones, and stories are set about like smoke to torment me.

Hell, that chap Albie Jones thinks himself! (How often have I overheard their voices.) *Does he think he's better than the rest of us or something? Have you noticed the way he tries to talk? Fancy isn't*

59

the word for it, boy. Did you know he listened to the wireless for hours and hours on end. D'you know why? To improve his English accent. Honest he does. He does you know. Honest he does.

And so, at any moment, a group of quiet boys can suddenly become a nest of vipers flicking their tongues at me, so that as long as I am in their midst I must for ever be on my guard.

During our third year at school, said Michael, we had a new Latin mistress. A tough-looking woman with a masculine stride. Her name was Miss Todd. At first we were all afraid of her. Then I realized, before anyone else I think, that she had a kind heart. I made myself agreeable to her. When I saw that she liked me I was tempted to take advantage of kindness in order to show off in front of the class.

"Michael!"

"Yes, Miss Todd?"

"What have you got there?"

"Nothing, Miss Todd."

"Bring that box out here at once, Michael!"

"But Miss . . . ."

"At once!"

"Yes, Miss Todd." I walk out to the front of the class, my palm tight over the lid of the small red box.

"Well. What is inside of it?"

"Nothing, Miss."

"Don't call me Miss. My name is Miss Todd."

"Yes, Miss . . . Todd."

"Take your hand away from the top of the box."

I hesitate. Delight bubbles inside me.

"Take your hand away!"

Out comes the Jack-in-the box, higher than Miss Todd's head. She jumps back in fright. The whole class roar with laughter. I don't care about any punishment. I know now for certain that I shall be popular with the other boys.

Oh, Albie, said Iorwerth, I wish you would trust me and confide in me. I know you find life in school difficult. So do I. Let me understand you. Come with me to the green pastures of Maesgwyn and walk with me beside the still waters while I tell you why I march through all weathers to the chapel on the hill. Let me take you there, so that you can stay behind after evening service and become a full member of our fellowship. There is room for you in the silence and room for you in our pew and I shall see you there safely by the light of the paraffin lamps. Join me on my journey. Be my companion and let me be your ever faithful friend.

I envy Michael, said Albie, who seems universally popular and without enemies or a nickname. I envy him his ability to get on with everybody, his charming manner, his witty remarks, and the clowning which he performs for the benefit of the form, and the graceful way he accepts the decision of a teacher to send him out of the room, and his flair for being amusing without being cheeky, and the forgiving smile on Mr Hughes's or Miss Parry's face, which his charm and good looks win. He has formed some kind of a Club which meets behind the Sports Pavilion during the dinner hour. I go home to lunch myself, so I don't know what they do. But I wish I belonged to it. I wish he would ask me. And I wish I could trust him, because I want to be like him. But I am imprisoned inside myself, inside my own defences, and there is a great gulf between us that nothing seems to fill.

Oh, Albie, said Iorwerth, the seasons pass and Time is passing, yet nothing seems to bring you closer to me. I sit next to you in class and term after term you excel in your work and we are great friends, but we share no secrets and you know nothing of the things that I most want you to know. If only you were a little more like me, how freely we could communicate with each other.

On a fine afternoon in the summer term, said Albie, Miss Todd took the Latin class (only a dozen of us by now) out of doors to hold the lesson in the shade of a few trees between the bicycle sheds and the playing fields. Beyond these trees new houses were being built and those nearest to where we sat had been completed for some time, although we were still mildly astonished from time to time, in idle unguarded moments, to see them standing in the very space where the grey donkeys from the seashore ate thistles and nettles during our first years at school. These houses only stood because we saw them standing. Our gaze upheld them. We knew how unsubstantial they were and how a layer of air waited between the bricks for us to look away so that the walls could be swallowed up by the waiting earth and the air released to blow again between the tall thistles.

We were reading the eleventh book of Ovid's *Metamorphoses*, each of us with our slim blue school edition. The girls fussed about finding the right place while Miss Todd watched them with ironic patience. We were revising the work before the examinations.

"Well now, if you are all quite ready, we'll start. Line 585, I believe. Do speak up at once if we come to a construction you can't understand. *At dea non ultra profuncto morte rogari Sustinet . . .* "[33]

In the quiet of the warm afternoon, behind Miss Todd's clear voice dissecting the Latin verse, it was possible to hear the traffic moving through the centre of the town, and the voices of teachers and children through the open windows of the school.

How can one fix one's attention on Latin on such a hot afternoon, said Michael, yawning. Take special note of this one she says, but which one it is I don't know. Oh dear, Iorwerth is listening so intently to the woman it makes me quite ill to look at him. Have you any idea, my dear chap, that your mouth is wide open? It's no use my opening my mouth to pull his leg. He just isn't looking. A swot, that's what he is.

"Notice this particularly. It's a part I've advised you before to learn off by heart. The famous description of the Cave of Sleep. If you don't get it to translate, it's pretty certain you'll be asked to appreciate it in one way or another."

Whispers of excitement and apprehension among the girls. Oh, foolish girls, I feel like saying, do you not know that there are more important things in life than children's examinations. Iorwerth of course already knows the passage off by heart. He insisted on reciting it to me on the bus the other morning.

"Iorwerth," Miss Todd was saying, "Iorwerth, how would you translate *crepitantibus* — the sound of water over pebbles. Um?"

I crease my forehead dutifully, said Iorwerth, and think very hard.

"What were you saying, Michael?"

"I said I shouldn't think there would be any noise at all."

"Noise or not, the word has to be translated. Well, Iorwerth? Albie?"

"It's an example of onomatopoeia, isn't it, Miss Todd?" Michael speaks up boldly.

"Yes, I suppose it is." Miss Todd looks at Michael suspiciously.

"Tinkling," I say suddenly. How lovely the way the word flashed into my mind. If she approves it is possible I am a poet. I would love to be a poet.

"We'll take that for the time being then."

I wish she approved more. That was not enough of a reward.

But by this, said Michael, less than a hundred yards away I saw a dark-haired young girl standing in the bedroom window of one of the new houses. She stood quite still, sometimes passing a comb through her hair. I decided to stare at her. She began to sing. Rather a common voice. Miss Todd took no notice of the new noise, except to raise her eyebrows when one of our girls suppressed a giggle. She continued to translate steadily without turning round. I nudged Iorwerth.

"Heigh, Iorwerth! Look! She's going to undress. She is, you know, look!"

The girl began to act for our benefit. She sang as she moved about, *By a waterfall I'm calling you-oo-oo*.

I had noticed the girl, said Iorwerth, before you stuck your elbow in my ribs. In a brief glance, I had a dream about her. She was a figure that moved in the mouth of the Cave of Sleep, and I was about to approach the figure when your elbow broke so rudely into my dream.

She's not worthy of your notice, Michael, said Albie. She's riff-raff. Her father has made a bit of money by collecting old iron. They think they've gone up in the world by buying a new house. You see, I know all about them, so do not demean

63

yourself, my dearest friend, by giving her so much notice. Do not cheapen yourself, Michael, ever, for one moment, because I am anxious to make you a figure I can love and respect. It gives me such pleasure merely to study your lively way of moving, your springy confident walk, the way in which you hitch up your trousers when the turn-ups touch the ground. (He wears long trousers while I who am so much taller have to wear these tight, short trousers which grow tighter every day.) I have watched you now so closely, for such a long time, and yet I never tire of seeing you. I would never dare let you know how much you mean to me.

"*Quo cubat ipsus deus membris languore solutis*. . . .[34] Albie! . . . Albie! Will you read on from there?"

Oh, agony, I am caught. My very silence and stillness reveal what I am thinking. I am lost. I am undone. I burn with shame as the whole class laughs at me.

"I suspect you were paying too literal a visit to the Cave of Sleep, Albie! Now then, it will be your fault if you don't know this work by the examination day!"

"That's what girls do for you, my boy," Michael whispered. "Let this be a lesson to you." And he winked at me.

At fourteen, said Michael, I am in no doubt as to the advantages of making people like me, and by this time too, I have learnt the secret by which the superficial affection of ninety-nine per cent may be won. To begin with, I have the initial advantage of a pleasant face and a winning smile. Added to this I have the knowledge that the subject which most interests each of the ninety-nine per cent is him-or-herself. Turn all conversations therefore towards the island of Self where every individual dwells, and longs for help to harvest the sweet, elusive fruits that grow only on that island. Help in the harvest. The principle is of course simple, but its execution requires skill and technique. To lead a conversation and keep it within the required limitations needs a skilled shepherd of words; to allay the suspicious, to soothe the sensitive, and finally win the allegiance of your patient to the degree you require.

The device works best among people to whom you are new, and, like an unused article in a shop window, bright and attractive. It is not however much good among those who have always known you; the maid who used to bath you even at the age of seven; the sister who saw you cry at the age of eleven at some disappointment, now too trivial and childish to remember; the Father who caught you in an act of which you are bitterly regretful; and most of all the Mother who once bore you within her, a helpless captive in her womb.

Is it not natural therefore that I, who now begin to taste the sharp sweetness of popularity among new friends and faces, should resent the home which has nurtured me, the prison which has reared me? I resent my mother who treats me like a rather stupid and untidy child; my father who has hardened into the caste of Olympian superiority into which he poured himself when he first entered his study. I resent my sister whom we see two or three times a year, home for the holidays, sweeping all before her. I resent Mary who calls me a *hogyn gwirion*,[35] addresses me by the second person singular, and is completely lacking in any respect due to the son of her employer. I resent the children who were with me at the village school, such as Wil Ifor Jones, since they had an unfair advantage, knowing me young and too silly to conceal my weaknesses. Therefore I resent Iorwerth, who is also patently sincere and honest, and who, I fear, does not like me because he suspects me of insincerity and dishonesty. There are times when I cannot bear the way he looks at me.

He is the most difficult of conquests, and yet he must be conquered, for until I am certain that he does really like me I cannot be happy in his presence. I have to see him every day and without his allegiance every new conquest will be a new defeat, and I shall begin to hate the very sight of him, not because of his shortcomings but because of my own. I am not blind to my own failings. How could I be, who am so astute in grasping the failures of others? I am not satisfied with myself at all. I know that I could be happier than this if I were pure of heart, sincere, truly gentle or strong and thoroughly genuine or honestly brave. These are qualities I already understand and long for. But I also know I cannot dare be less happy and I am tyrannized by this thought into maintaining my vicious circle of popularity. If I gaze long enough in the flattering mirror I may yet admire myself. Oh, Iorwerth, you think I am a cheat and happy in my deceits. Oh, Albie, you think I am happy in my popularity. You think my charm charms me too, my smile, which I cannot see, my face which does not conceal from me my own unpleasantness as does the pretty curtain across the scullery cupboard.

When my intention of becoming a preacher became known at our Chapel, said Iorwerth, I was invited to take part in the *Seiat* on Thursday evenings, and here in this small square chapel I prayed aloud so that all could hear me for the first time, my own words echoing around the Chapel, and rising like incense to God. They had been carefully prepared; having finished my homework, I stared into the kitchen fire and scribbled devout sentences in my classwork book. In bed I stared into the darkness, learning my prayer off by heart. My father, Robert Jones Ystrad, Lewis Bloyd Henfryn, and all the preachers I have ever heard and the hymns I have always known have helped me form this prayer. With these old and well-worn phrases I wove a new cage of words in which my youthful love for the God who made me and his heroic Son was able to sing.

"*Our Father which art in Heaven . . . as many as here present . . . Thou to whom all Flesh turns . . . in Spirit and in Truth . . . thankful for the privilege of being here to worship Thee together in prayer . . . may it please Thee to give us of Thy Spirit . . . but Blessed be Thy Name . . . by virtue of Thy only Son forgive our great fault. Amen.*"

I am thrilled to see Robert Jones's grey, close-cropped head turn towards me and say in his dry, cracked voice:

"Iorwerth Hughes, will you now lead the congregation in prayer?"

To walk into the *Sêt Fawr*, choose my favourite hymn, and read a passage, the meaning of which has struck me lately, out of the large authoritative print in the thick Bible. And then to shut my eyes and pray.

> "*No urgent Prayer has ever failed*
> *to reach the Throne of Grace . . . .*"

I am thrilled to walk home with my hymn book under my arm, alongside my father, almost as tall as him now, my voice deepening, talking with him man to man, discussing the meaning of a difficult passage in the fifth chapter of the epistle to the Hebrews.[36]

When I arrive home and take a look around the stock in the sheds to save my father the trouble, I say to myself, I am Iorwerth Hughes, Maesgwyn, a comfortable farm of ninety acres still in good heart, in spite of the evil days which are beginning to fall on farmers. I am Iorwerth Hughes, Form VA, who catches the bus at the cross-roads with books under his arm, I am the traveller between two worlds, learning by experience the slow lessons of tolerance, which every foreigner must learn. At school I am the Israelite in Babylon, resistant to foreign influences, and careful of my household gods, conforming outwardly in every detail to the pattern of a Llanrhos County School boy, but inwardly firm in my own upbringing and persuasion, and faithful to another, higher, Dispensation. I am embarked now upon my career, thoroughly and conscientiously determined to succeed and happy in the certainty of my vocation.

6

On a wet Sunday afternoon in early November, said Albie, my father snoring in front of the fire, a page of the *News of the World* covering his face, I sat at the table doing my homework, Chemistry and French. I heard my mother making her way slowly downstairs. She had begun to suffer from arthritis and her condition often troubled me. I sat staring at my homework book and thinking of a long letter I wanted to write to Michael.

Dear M, dear M, my father is snoring . . . . Dear M, I am rather worried about my mother. She does not complain, but . . . oh, Michael, could you come and stay with us next week, or if not convenient the week after. Oh, sooner or later come and stay for as long as you like or for ever

But, alas, not here. My father is snoring under the newspaper. The council houses of the cul-de-sac seem like rabbit hutches in the rain. I should be somewhere better than this and yet I should not think of it so disloyally.

"Dic! Dic! Get shaved before tea, Dic bach, or we'll be late for church."

"Ah-h-h!" My father yawns and then belches loudly. "Don't feel like going tonight, Nel. Stomach isn't half right." He belches again but not so loudly. "Got wind around the heart!"

"*Twt lol!*"[37] My mother laughs. She often laughs at my father, but laughs a little crossly, I think, as if he were a pet that never behaved as well as it should and had to be continually forgiven.

"You go and get shaved, Dic Jones, and we'll see how bad your stomach is when tea is ready. Harvest Thanksgiving tonight, so hurry up."

"Thanks for what?"

"Thanks for a lot of things, Dic Jones. Now you know that as well as I do. Thanks for being in health, my boy, and for having a job. That's something to be thankful for these days."

As usual, my father does as he's told. In the big, ugly church I sit neatly between them. It is true that there is rather a bad smell from the decaying flowers in the over-heated church, but there is no need for my father to pull such a vulgar face and wrinkle up his nose. My mother lifts a stiff, grey gloved hand to her mouth and coughs over-discreetly to signal my father to behave himself. *Dear M, In fact there isn't really enough room in our house but if convenient I would love to come up to the Rectory for a few days. As you know I haven't had the pleasure yet of meeting your mother* . . . . It is terrible to be ashamed of one's father, especially when he is such a kind and unselfish man. My mother of course does her level best to make him presentable, but in fact she herself, poor thing, is not without fault in this matter. I hate the servile way she has of talking to people better off than us, and even with Griffiths the curate, she is so ingratiating it embarrasses me unbearably. The other day as she was scrubbing the floor of the passage with the front door open to see better, she was literally on her knees in front of the pompous little man with his perpetual catarrh and the dandruff thick on his narrow black shoulders.

"Oh, Mr Griffiths bach . . . ."

"Good morning, Mrs Jones. And how are you to-day?"

"You'll come in for a minute, Mr Griffiths, now won't you . . . . Don't look at all these newspapers on the floor . . . always scrubbing I am, but I never seem to keep it tidy, small as it is . . . now you'll have a cup of tea, won't you, Mr Griffiths, just to please me . . . . Don't mind this chair, if you'll sit in it please . . . . It is so very kind of you to come and see us . . . . I'm sorry about this tablecloth don't look at it please . . . ."

Oh, mother, my mother, don't ever apologize for anything again. In any case, can't you see you're better than he is? I glance at my father again as she coughs discreetly behind her grey glove, but this time it is nothing more than a tickle in her throat.

The special preacher this evening is a young parson from the country, the Reverend J.P.K. Lewis, M.A.,(Oxon.)

"*Duwch!*"[38] my father whispers to me. "I remember this chap. He used to play outside left for the Nomads, Albie! This chap used to play outside left for the Nomads. Good player, too!"

My mother puts her grey, gloved hand to her mouth and clears her throat loudly and frowns. I sit between them, a pillar of correct behaviour, staring straight ahead.

The special preacher is a youthful-looking fair-haired man. A long, intelligent face. It occurs to me quite suddenly that he rather resembles Michael. I wish that my father would restrain himself over the *Amens* at the end of the hymns. The sermon is easy to follow, simple and sincere. A comparison between a grain of wheat and a human soul. The wheat needs deep soil so as to keep its roots alive and moist even in times of great drought. The deeper the roots, the greater the fruit. So in every respect the soul. Improved strains, clean well-tilled soil; the comparison went on. My father nudges me. "Albie! This is a botany lesson, not a sermon!" Then he winks at me which I find intolerable. Christ, said the preacher, Christ was the deep nourishing earth in which the soul can grow. And it is of this that I think as the congregation flows slowly out of the heated church into the damp, foggy night outside. I try to go home ahead of my mother and father. I want to write to Michael at once.

Dear M, dear M, I heard an exciting sermon this evening. You as a parson's son will know this already, but the fact is, the soul of a man is like a grain of wheat . . . .

I read the other day, said Michael, that the world was a stage; and, in my opinion, every good actor needs a bit of peace and quiet to learn his part. A good place to rest is the big leather armchair in my father's study on a Saturday afternoon, especially when everyone is out and I have the house to myself. I am free to brood, a large book open across my knees, and to stare out of the french window from time to time at the silent fields below the house. At home an actor has the right to set aside his part, to be the core of himself, to remain for hours in a sulky silence of self-contemplation, like Narcissus staring at his own image in the motionless pool. I am an eternal actor, characterless until the occasion calls for a character, until a second person calls the cue, requires the suitable answer from a suitable part. I sit motionless until my shoulders are cold and I shiver involuntarily.

70

Between the high bookshelves on the study wall is a door leading to a small room which my father calls his workshop. It is my habit to go in when the house is empty, for it is full of interesting things; a two-speed bike without tyres; an ancient typewriter; a toolbox, old lamps from Church without glasses or wicks, pieces of the old Church organ in the process of being converted into a wardrobe. Officially, I have been told not to enter this room, since the day when I used it as a photographer's dark room. Iorwerth was with me that day too, but that did not save me from punishment. I spilled hydrochloride over a pile of books my father had just bought at a sale. By now, of course, these bundles of books are the most interesting things in the room. They lie here and there in untidy piles, bought by my father at different sales, in the hope of discovering something worthwhile among them. He goes through them at his leisure, moving those of value on to the shelves and throwing the rest out into the stable loft. He rarely burns any, as my mother and Mary the maid would wish. As an historian he says he finds it difficult to burn anything on paper.

This afternoon alone in the house, alone in this small room, I come across a small blue book called *A Ritual for Married Lovers*, translated from the French. I take it back with me to the study and sit reading it before the fire, trembling with anxious curiosity; the saliva dries in my mouth, and then suddenly flows again. When I hear the front door open, I hastily put it in my pocket and take up the other open book I have ready by me. My imagination is troubled, I know that I am on the threshold of a world governed by inscrutable forces and in the deepest forest of this new continent lies a bright fountain, the source of beauty and horror, of a new joy and new sadness, of perpetual unrest.

What can I do to save my friends, said Iorwerth. It is obvious to me that they do not have the joy and certainty of the true faith. I would do much for Albie, if only for the sake of the innocent love I once bore for him, in the days before I turned my back on the funfairs of Llanelw and the vanities of this world. For now I must declare that every hymn I hear has a personal message for me and that my one ambition in life is to follow in the footsteps of Pantycelyn, unworthy though I may be. I know that there is a

7

We enter the sixth form together, and we walk arm in arm like a film version of *The Three Musketeers*, or the frontispiece of a schoolboy story. The camera catches our legs in unison over the invisible threshold of early manhood, for our legs are encased now in long grey-flannel trousers. We walk boldly towards a man's estate, not only to study but also to possess the world. Three brand-new persons, three filled with hope and strength. Three still without fear, three ready for the future. Albie is now six feet tall, proportionately made, the last pimple is retreating from his long masculine face; his smile reveals long white equine teeth, and his black hair is stylized into one restrained and tasteful wave. Michael has changed the least, his growth has been steady and even, only his fair hair has darkened a little. His clothes are worn with a carelessness that could be natural or assumed. Iorwerth is shorter, and thin, his face still girlish and he tidily washed and dressed like a favourite son. His smile is appealing and his eyes are honest.

By keeping my eye on tomorrow, on the future, said Albie, it is easier for me to avoid the blushes that yesterday's follies bring to my face today. To think how infatuated I was with Michael! (Of course, in those days words like Freud and homosexuality and so on meant nothing to me. I find it difficult to remember exactly how long ago it was: there is no telling the time it takes to become ashamed: hours, days, months, years?) I can only say how thankful I am that no one knew of my weakness except myself, and no one saw the emotional storms I suffered alone for such a long time.

It is true that the Reverend J.P.K. Lewis, the preacher who made such an impression on me at the Harvest Festival Service, knew something of my difficulties. When I think now of how determined I was to cycle from Llanelw to Mr Lewis's parish, I sweat with embarrassment. I waited a long time. The winter was in fact over, when I started out one beautiful Saturday morning. I delighted in the journey. Sometimes I rested in the shadow of the hedgerows: sometimes I listened to the sucking noise my tyres made passing over the hot tarmac. The chippings bounced away as my wheels passed over them. I ate the meat sandwiches my mother had kindly prepared on the banks of a quiet river, where I lay so still a water hen came close before knowing I was there. At last I reached the Vicarage, a handsome house almost hidden by a tree and shrub-filled garden. I stood at the door. Overcoming a last hesitation, I rang the bell. Then it seemed as if I waited a long time. Seeing him in the sunlit doorway he was much older than I had thought and his face was worn like the bowl of the pipe he held in his hand.

"Good afternoon."

"Good afternoon, Mr Lewis." At once I began to regret my visit. I no longer wanted an interview so I did not know what to say. The speech I had prepared was no longer relevant, and there was nothing else I wanted to say.

"Well, Mr . . . .er . . . er, what can I do for you?" The vicar frowned politely. "Tell me, am I supposed to know you, Mr . . . .?"

"Oh, no. No. It's . . . I heard you preach at Llanelw."

"Yes?"

"At Harvest Thanksgiving. A sermon about a grain of wheat."

"Oh yes. That one. Yes. That one does go rather well. What can I do for you?"

"I had some questions I wanted to ask you."

"Well, why not come in? We can talk in the study."

"Thank you. But Mr Lewis . . . "

"Yes?"

"I've forgotten now what they were."

Nevertheless once he understood the purpose of my visit he was very patient with me. He gave me some useful advice which I don't clearly remember, and some pamphlets too, on the meaning of Morals, the existence of God, and sex difficulties in the adolescent.

But now at this moment my ambition is to appear mature, adult, responsible, normal, wise, reliable, level-headed, balanced, and altogether a very sound fellow; to this end I cultivate a deliberate manner and a considered yet confident address. If possible I would like to add to this a slightly whimsical air for lighter occasions. Soon, therefore, I shall be ready to turn my back on the past, to take the compass of my soul and indelicately grasp the finger, fixing it for ever in the one direction from which I shall never be distracted.

On my seventeenth birthday, said Michael, I wrote in my journal (not diary) in a manner conscious of the requirements of style: *I am seventeen today, the fifteenth of September, and I must put on record for posterity that on this day shaving became less of a ritual and more of a habit, and from now on each time I study my shaving mirror I shall have one more opinion on one more outstanding question.* At the time I was rather proud of the sentence, but already the smartness has faded and an aftertaste of falseness is all that is left.

Why is it so difficult to be really smart? The truth is that with oneself one must be ruthlessly honest. As I sit in my bedroom before the open window, watching the sad sun lower itself beyond the churchyard trees, I know with overwhelming certainty that only Truth is enough and nothing less than the truth will satisfy me even for a moment, even if it takes my entire lifetime to seek it out: that's what life is for. Therefore, I turn my back for ever on all forms of falseness and insincerity, and I wish to state plainly that I am a Communist and a Pacificist and that Private Property is the basis of the evils of our Acquisitive Society. Politics and Economics are one and indivisible and I read widely in both fields. On Religion I keep an open mind. Roughly, this is my position.

I would be quite prepared to meet my father in open debate on these matters, but to be truthful his ignorance of the contemporary world quite staggers me. He has no idea how sheltered his existence as a country parson has been. And apart from this, a cold gulf lies between us. He is uncertain of me. I do not think he trusts me. It is as if I had, sometime or other in the near or distant past, committed some offence which he has not yet found strength in himself to forgive.

Michael, one year ago, towards the end of September, were you not in the company of Wil Ifor Jones, Reginald Persifal Williams and Irwyn Tan-y-Fynwent shooting rats at the Henblas Threshing?

Yes, father, I was, but . . . .

And when the Threshing was over did you not accompany the same three idle scamps to Coed-y-Gelli, on Henblas land, to shoot rabbits and also pigeons?

Well I may have done for a while, father, but . . . .

And having tired of continually missing your targets did you then not move across Henblas Park and trespass further, penetrating the territory of Goldengrove, and inside that, climbing the high wall around Colonel Bloyd-Waters' summerhouse, knowing full well that the Colonel was abroad at the time and the house empty?

No, father, I never went near . . . .

Did you not fire three times through the bay window, smashing not only the window, but also several valuable objets d'art *of glass and porcelain?*

No, father. No. No . . . .

And then basely flee without confessing, so that to this day the transgressors go unpunished?

How do you know all this, father, without anyone confessing? How do you know?

Ambition, said Iorwerth, is the wind that disturbs the home-field as I walk home in the evening, bending the growing grass and bending me in one disciplined direction. It is, I know, a dangerous wind when caught in awkward corners, when poured like steam into the narrow cylinders of worldly aims. So let my ambition blow like the even wind that crosses this field, impartial, open and honest. It is a bracing heady wind that makes me glory in God, singing, "Lord God, I thank thee that Thou has given unto me the grace by which to learn that Thy service is perfect freedom."

In my bedroom, I have a home-made bookshelf devoted almost entirely, apart from my text-books, to religious works, *Cofiannau* Cynddylan Jones, Lewis Edwards and John Williams Brynsiencyn;[39] a devotional diary containing prayers for every day of the year, and also two or three books in English on aspects of theology. In summer I come up here to my bedroom to study, and in this silence I lay my fountain pen down and sit with my head between my hands pondering which should be my particular field, the home or the foreign mission. I argue for and against each in turn, and imagine myself in either circumstances, trying to estimate to which I am best suited. How deep are my roots in this corner of Wales, my own dear kingdom of fields and woods, and how well could I bear leaving it for a stranger world even than Llanelw filled with Lancashire trippers? My reluctance to leave home, is this not proof of selfishness? So deep are the roots of selfishness, that even if I bend my will to the greater purpose, I achieve a bitter-sweet sensation as I dream of a scene of parting at Liverpool docks, my parents and Dilys Maurice, daughter of the minister of Salem waving and weeping at the quayside; I watch from the taffrail the break of foam and disappearing land; and then after several years I return home sunburnt and almost a stranger welcomed at the kitchen door by an ecstatic cry from my mother and a chaste kiss from Dilys who has waited in another room. I rebuke myself for such an idle dream, but I have not discovered yet the antidote to the weakness of dreaming.

It is also difficult to resist the insidious infiltration of Doubt. Albie, for example, has turned his back completely on religion. This is far more upsetting to me than Michael's attacks. Michael, I know, is only showing-off and trying to be amusing. He shows off even when we are alone, taking a walk to the top of the hill. *You see, old chap, as I keep trying to tell you, since I've become a Communist I've given up taking opium . . . Ior, look, that's the Isle of Man! It is, you know. I always said you could see it from the top here on a clear day. Pretty terrific. We're still under a thousand feet . . . Now listen, Ior, can you prove that God exists? Just one simple proof. Lift your finger now and point him out. There's a wonderful view up here. There's the Isle of Man. Where's God? Come on, old chap, speak up . . . . Nobody can prove that God exists. Nobody* (At last I am goaded. I know the answer to this one.) *Nobody can prove he doesn't exist either.* There is something generous about Michael's laugh. *Good for you! Good old Ior!* He pats my back. He really is my friend.

But with Albie, it's more serious. He moves, like the tortoise in the story, slowly and certainly by careful study to where the winning post might well be. This disturbs me far more.

Oh, Ior, next Saturday will suit me fine — but I must tell you something. In case it embarrasses you. In case you say anything when you come. My father is out of work.

I try to avoid looking at his face which is red with shame or pride.

Of course, there's rather a stigma about it among us. The workers have their own code of honour.

It is amazing how often Albie talks about *the proletariat* and the *workers* as if they were a society to whom he belonged. Not so long ago he used to listen to the radio for hours to acquire a cultivated English accent. And in actual fact, there are no real signs of poverty in his home. Mrs Jones still has her visitors. Mr Jones works hard all day at the washing-up. When I think of poverty, I remember Wil Ifor's home. There, there was a smell I shall never forget, something that seeped out of the walls and the floor even on fine days when the door was left open all day. I can say nothing of that, of course, to Albie.

You know, of course, Ior, that nine-tenths of the population of these islands earn less than three pounds a week? . . . Franco is winning, Ior, because the capitalists want him to win.

But what about God's will, I want to say, what about God?

Hunger is the mainspring of history, Iorwerth . . . the need to eat . . . whoever controls the means of production controls the world.

But, Albie, what about God?

Hitler must be destroyed, Ior. It's as simple as that.

What has God got to say, Albie. Listen, listen.

Clearly, parliamentary democracy is meaningless unless the control of the means of production is also in the hands of the people, the working people. You've got to face these facts, Iorwerth . . . .

I suppose I have to. But can't he understand these books he wants to make me read are nothing to me. What about God, I want to say to him, but he never finds the question relevant. It does not detain him. He stares at the sky and sees nothing: therefore something terrible is wrong with either him, or me.

In school, when they both attack me in the untidy sixth form room and I am foolish enough to get excited about what they are saying, I see from the smile on Albie's face that Michael is making nonsense of what I am trying to say, I cannot compete with Michael's destructive wit or the soundness of Albie's political and economic knowledge.

How can I explain to them that believing in God is for me as fundamental a part of living as sleeping or eating, and that to doubt his existence would be to doubt my own existence, the existence of my home, of my parents, and of the time-enshrined memorials of my life; the gates, the hedges, the grazing cattle, the nettle-covered dung heaps, the broken harrows and the rusty ploughs on our farm. They do not realize that my life moves between two worlds, the temporal and the eternal, and one cannot exist without the other. If I am communicating with nothing, bowing before nothing, travelling towards nothing, then I myself am nothing.

Let's face it, Iorrie bach, we are living in an age that doesn't believe in miracles.

I have no right to hate Michael's laughter which is not unkindly meant, because I am myself a feeble soldier of Christ, an unworthy defender of the faith, an unreliable witness, a reproach and a scandal, too weak to cry out firmly powerful verses such as 'I am the truth, the way and the life'.

More often than not, Michael and Albie notice my silence and then they become uncomfortably kind. This is unbearable and I make a sudden excuse and leave them.

I am absolutely sick and tired, said Michael, of showing off at school, or in front of girls or before my elders, and I will not allow my popularity to turn me into a clown. I have an overwhelming urge to cry out: O World, I am, myself, no more than a small child lost in an endless wood, a prisoner in darkness longing for light, an ill-equipped idealist searching endlessly for the Holy Grail of Truth. I know now that I am of myself little or nothing and only of any importance in so far as I have some of the truth in me which thirsts increasingly for the whole of which it is a part.

And this is my only pleasure. Absolutely. I have known the excitement of an audience, in the school hall, prepared to surrender to my wit and eloquence, and in the very moment of ecstasy my mind has suddenly rebelled against my own insincerity and shallowness. I have lain with a comely girl beside a river, watching the salmon break the glowing surface of the water and listening to the summer evening thriving gently about us, and was happy enough until I felt obliged to put my arm about her waist and to imitate the actions of a lover only to be suddenly nauseated by my own dissimulation and hot female breath. I have entertained my friends and compelled them to listen to me intently long after I myself have become sick of the sound of my own voice. Time and again the desire rises in me to leave my body propped up like a tailor's dummy against the library table, and release my spirit so that it may soar on the wings of impersonal truth and so that I may more speedily be given my vision of the world.

I no longer recall, said Albie, how Iorwerth, Michael and I began to foregather at Les James's house. It is true that Les was always in our form but neither Iorwerth nor I had ever been in his large house until some time after entering the sixth form. Les, to everyone's surprise (and especially to mine, I had been the natural top of the form for so long) had turned out to be quite a brilliant physicist. Michael had always been rather friendly with him — they shared private jokes — and I expect it was Michael with his usual social gifts who led us to Les's house. A splendid rendezvous on a wet Saturday morning, especially since Les was an only son; indeed, about the only thing his parents had in common. Upstairs two or three big rooms were overflowing with the apparatus of every possible kind of game and pastime and the larder was always full of tinned foods for our sudden appetites. Les had also established the right to smoke at home, and it was, in fact, in this cosy den at the top of the house while listening to his gramophone that I smoked a cigar for the first time in my life — even Iorwerth laughed heartily at the sight.

We marvel at the way Les treats his mother.

"Hello, boys! Didn't hear you come in today."

"You couldn't very well if you were fast asleep, old girl, could you?" Les's mouth stretches in a slightly exasperated grin.

"Oh, Les! Isn't he terrible? I don't know what to do with him."

Another day she meets us in the doorway, her hand pressed to her forehead.

"Les. Les."

"What's up?"

"Les, I've got the most terrible headache I've ever had. Do you think I ought to phone Doctor Wynne?"

"Do as you please, old girl."

"Oh, Les, don't talk like that. I can't stand it now. What shall I do?"

"Well, it depends how bad you are, doesn't it, really?"

"Les, come with me to the doctor's."

"Can't you see I've got Albie and Michael with me."

"We can all go. We won't be long."

Les looks at us and sighs patiently.

"Well, is the car ready?"

"I got it back this afternoon. I'm sure there was nothing wrong with it. Your father . . . "

"Well, we'd better go, if we're going."

"I've got a nice idea, boys. Let's all go to the pictures afterwards. I'll treat the three of you. There's a good one on at the Regal."

A luxurious untidy house, the kitchen sink always full of dirty dishes: drink stains on the expensive furniture. It was in this house I met Frida. I was sitting peacefully reading a glossy magazine, waiting for Les, I suppose, when I heard voices raised in another part of the house. The door opened suddenly, a tall girl with long hair glared at me aggressively. She was bare-footed, I remember, her white blouse was unbuttoned, and her hair fell down over her flushed face. Her sudden appearance made a deep and lasting impression on me. I shall never forget seeing her for the first time. She closed the door without having spoken. I wonder if she had already realized in that first moment what an uninteresting fellow I was.

Les came in soon after she had disappeared.

"Did you see Frida? Did she come in here? Did she say anything? Devil of a girl."

I must have begun to blush. Les took out a paper bag of fudge

81

from his pocket (he never seemed to be without sweets.)

"Look out, Albie, my boy. If she gets hold of you, your life won't be worth living. Never seen a girl like her. Have some fudge?"

Even with his mouth full of fudge, he was a prophet. Because Frida was indeed different.

It was easy enough to go walking on a Saturday afternoon with Michael and Doris and Morfydd, and to be appreciatively aware as if for the first time of a young girl's presence, the shapely body and the incredibly smooth skin. And easy, too, on a summer afternoon, to be near Morfydd on the shore after a swim and observe the soft hair of her long legs supporting drops of salt water that gleam like pearls in the sun. But Frida is something more. I cannot describe her.

"Well, if I've got to stay in this appalling house, I may as well make the best of it. Do any of you children know how to dance?"

And of course, Michael jumps to his feet. I feel the pain of being jealous intensely, but I struggle to control myself and to smile sociably as they move about the low-ceilinged room in each other's arms.

"My father was rather extraordinary. Have you got a cigarette, Michael? Switch that damn thing off, Albie. He was, in fact, the only man in the Embassy who could speak eight languages. How many languages can you speak, Brighteyes?"

"English and Welsh. Two." Iorwerth jumped as she spoke and answered her so innocently that we all roared with laughter at his reply as if it were the greatest joke.

Les James' cousin, said Michael, is an impossible girl. Quite impossible. Bit by bit, we managed to piece her history together. Her father had been a diplomat. He was Les's father's brother. So much at any rate was true, although it did seem incredible because Les's father was quite the most rough and ready Steam Laundry managing director ever consecrated. He looked like a self-made man determined to unmake himself by drinking spirits. In any case, Frida's father had been killed some years ago. How it happened we never exactly knew. Frida hinted mysteriously at a crash in the Ambassador's own car. Les said he thought his uncle had been run over when crossing a busy street and that he was drunk at the time. It was never easy to get any clear information about this man. Her mother, too, was dead.

It was perfectly clear to us that Les's mother and Frida couldn't stand the sight of each other; and that Les's father found this rather pleasing. Les didn't seem to mind. Les never seemed to mind anything. We understood that Frida was to stay until the autumn and then go to college: Cambridge, she said; Cardiff, said Les. It was also quite clear to me that poor old Albie had fallen for her from the word go.

"Albie's such a childish name," she says. "Listen. I'm going to christen you anew — Alberto."

"Oh, no." Neither of them notices my groan of protest.

"Why Alberto?" says Albie.

"Sounds so much nicer. Besides, I once knew an absolutely fascinating Italian racing-driver called Alberto."

Albie nods smilingly. I laugh and he blushes.

Frida, Michael, Les and I, said Albie, play tennis at the Municipal Garden Tennis Courts, preferably in the evening when the wind is cool and blows through our thin shirts. Michael calls "Service!" and throwing the first ball high, smashes it grandiloquently into the net. We all laugh and Michael sends the next ball safely at Frida's feet. Frida takes the game seriously. As her partner, I move along the back-line, and my wrist stretches out thick and strong to meet the flying ball and I am fully conscious of applying my strength well as I volley it back over the net well out of Michael's reach. I am good enough to beat Michael and Les alone if that were necessary. I do not mind my grey flannels alongside their whites when I recollect this fact. I know that I am well made and that Frida is pleased to play at my side. We win every time and I enjoy each game to a superlative degree. Moving about with ease and speed, anticipating their strokes, striking the ball hard, makes me smile, showing my strong white teeth.

Later we walk slowly down the path that leads to the Pavilion where we rest and take refreshment. I don't mind Frida talking so much to Michael. We won and because Frida has placed her hand for a moment on my knee, I know that she is pleased and that she finds me acceptable. I believe she has found something

8

The rain runs greasily down the window, while Shelley's west wind with stuffed cheeks blows draughts between the window and the window frame[40] . . . . The sun this morning thrust his crimson trumpet over Moel Fammau[41] rising like a slow crescendo . . . . The birds in the garden trees opposite my bedroom window rattle their morning song like dainty chopsticks on kettle-drums of silver . . . . And I, whatever the morning or whatever the weather, awake, lie still a little while recovering my senses in comfort. I swish my legs through the bedclothes and the bare soles of my feet thud expectantly on the carpet. Each morning is a new beginning and each day is meant to be a further revelation.

I am at heart, said Michael, a student of life. Let me therefore allow myself a certain licence, and like an eavesdropper become intent on knowing my own experience as though it were someone else's and someone else's as though it were my own. At my age, the present has a flavour and keenness elusive and indefinable like the taste of a dinner-knife pressed flat against the tongue, and I have been told it may not always be so. Therefore I am accumulating notes in a scientific manner, which I hope eventually to bring to some kind of order, arrange in some pattern so that at the end of a number of years I can wave my hand at the last page and say, perhaps with a sigh, here is the meaning, here is the answer, and this therefore is my purpose.

I read, of course. Everything in reach. avidly and yet with the same critical severity with which I examine people, such as my mother gossiping on the lawn over the tea-cups with Mrs Vaughan-Owen who burns with ecclesiastical zeal and private malice, or my father losing the thread of his discourse half way through his sermon and screwing up his eyes in desperation, perhaps, to avoid seeing the fog of dumbness closing in about his head. My poor old father was meant to be an historian not a preacher. I begin to realize what agonies he must have suffered in the pulpit all these years. And because of this, and perhaps also because I am a kind of historian myself, I am beginning to feel closer to him now, at long last. We have done some local digging together and I think it has meant a lot to him. In Cae Meta we unearthed a pre-Roman grave and I touched pieces of sticky bone that once stood upright in a wall of flesh and walked across these acres. Because of this wonder we were able to communicate and I know now that it will always please me, to give him pleasure.

The other day I overheard him say to my mother. "You know, Michael has developed into an extremely intelligent boy. It's quite extraordinary. After all the trouble we've had with him. I really think . . . "

"He's inclined to be overfond of criticizing other people," my mother said.

"Well, that is his age, you know. I was rather like that at his age. No, I really think he might surprise us one day by doing something quite remarkable."

I should not have been listening, of course. But my father's last sentence excited me strangely. He was never given to exaggeration as I for example had been given to showing off. I rushed out of the house and down the grass road to the mill, in order to think about my destiny in the quiet countryside. Near the small river, I lay down under a beech tree that I have always loved and I stared up through the myriad leaves at the miraculous sky. What was it I could do? How could I best prepare myself?

Sunday morning is bright, said Iorwerth, for the April sun pierces the opening hedges now only tinged with green: the sunlight strikes the growing grass in the meadow and in the cornfield shows the soft marks of the harrow. On my way to chapel through the empty lane and quiet fields, God's day, this one in seven, seems specially brilliant and even consecrated by the shining sun.

The preacher this morning is well known for his fervour and

eloquence, and since he lives a great distance away and his visits are rare, the chapel is full. Every pew is filled by the representatives of almost every family in the neighbourhood. (Many churchgoers and Baptists have come to hear him.) Spruce families entire or in part fill every polished yellow pew. My seat is next to the aisle, and wearing a light black overcoat and carrying his hat, the small, frail prematurely-aged prophet brushes my elbow as he passes. Once in the pulpit facing us, he seems tall and there is power in his drawn white face. He reads the hymn slowly. His voice is modulated like the voice of an experienced singer, and as he holds the gilded hymn-book unusually close to his face his eyelids seem heavy with spiritual experience. His eyelids are large and tenderly drawn over. His loosened moist lips work out the music of his prayer which soars and descends, appeals, rejoices and despairs. We are caught in his voice; his sorrow is our sorrow, his joy is our joy, he articulates our emotion and we are content to punctuate his expression with our sighs. For we are captured by his voice and the urgency of his message, we are enchanted, transfigured. At the end of his prayer, his eyelids are slowly lifted, and his eyes look out on the usual visible world retaining the stranger's stare, the stare of one who thinks of another kingdom.

His text concerns the Deluge, and the sermon begins like the regular beat of a great drum, pounding out a succession of facts, facts which we must digest, and only when he feels that we have marked them well, does his tempo increase as he slowly draws us on to some great inevitable conclusion. Now his voice is varied and dramatic, it is many voices, many moods, scenes actual and imaginary are blended into a world woven by his voice: with a gesture of his hand — the white, thin hand with narrow supple fingers worked from a thin wrist — clay is spread over a Babylonian world, and a civilization covered in silt. His iron fist striking the pulpit edge with measured beat is the tramp of Roman legions on Welsh roads, and having created the grandeur of Rome in consonantal splendour, she, too, collapses with a shudder of his hand. And what, his voice is thick with warning, what horrible unknown end awaits this corrupt century, this diseased twentieth-century culture, and to what depths of fear and foreboding are we dragged by the dripping syllables of his declining speech. We are lost, our dumb lips almost shout. What hope is there for a world full of war, of famine, of oppression? Where is our salvation? Where now is hope, the looking forward, and faith that makes possible and sufferable today, and charity imprisoned by the powers of this world? Where is now our God?

What Cross shines above our heads where his eyes stare in burning reverence? What cool stream of mercy shall flow over our individual parched tongues. God is in our midst, we shall not be moved. We who are at his feet have a place to lay our heads. Good news indeed has come to us, most excellent news. The voice draws admission from us, draws from the well of every soul homage and gratitude to God, willing or unwilling from lips, which are stubborn or ready to show forth his praise.

When the service was over, I feared the anti-climax of filing out of chapel, the salutations, comments, coughs and chatter, and the polite departures to Sunday dinners. I trembled to think of hearing the great man speak of anything but the good news. And so I fled homewards through the fields.

I have begun to dislike Frida, said Michael. The other day she said to me, "You know, Michael, your mother is really too respectable to be true. I've seen English matrons in the Embassies abroad, but she really has got them all beaten."

She may have meant it as a joke, but it was in appalling taste. Only a completely insensitive person could ever be so tactless. Even if it were true, which I am not unprepared to believe, she had no business to say it.

I am worried, too, about her influence over Albie. She takes him in completely, and that is very bad for him. I have tried to tell him as kindly as I can that Frida is an actress who only comes to life when she can posture in a part. (I used to be like that myself, so I know.) And really (this, of course, I cannot tell him) there is nothing attractive about her. She has bad teeth and her breath smells. She dramatizes herself into some kind of histrionic beauty and that is what puts Albie under her spell. Iorwerth can see this and he agrees with me. (He also disapproves of her; because she swears so freely, I suspect.) So we can never entice Albie out for a walk in the hills on a Saturday now. He waits for her like a faithful watchdog and the sad thing is that there is nothing we can do about it.

As I lay on my towel, sunbathing in the shelter of the east wall of the Llanelw Open Air Swimming Baths, said Albie, through my half-closed eyes I saw Frida yet again climb the iron ladder to the highest diving board, the water dripping from her long thighs. She never tires of trying to improve her diving. Here, perhaps, she feels there is something she will be able to do better than anyone else.

Poised at the board's edge at the right moment, she falls through the air and her narrow body cleaves the water and passes under it in a continuing curve. There is some clapping of hands among the young men who stand dripping wet in the shadow of the diving board. Frida laughs as she pulls herself out of the water, and I laugh and wave so as not to seem jealous of the attention she is getting. She pulls herself up slowly, out of breath as she must be, but to me more radiant than Arethusa arising from the river.[42]

"Just one more, Albie." I nod compliantly. "Only one more then I'll come and sunbathe."

Alongside me I have dark glasses and a pile of books, but I don't seem to be doing much work. Instead I contemplate Frida, and also my own long body as it lies latent in the sun. I would like to take more pleasure in the strength and developing beauty of my body, but Frida says that the mind and the spirit are so much more important than the body, and I must believe her.

"Unless you want to be Mr Universe, of course, I'd take a shade less interest in my body if I were you, Alberto, and a little more in my mind."

How can she guess that I am worrying so much about my work? Is it true, is it true, that my intellect is somehow slowing down? My power to comprehend weakening? As they grow older, Michael and Les, and Iorwerth too, seem to have more confidence about their work, but I know I have less. Is this simply because I come from a poor family and am therefore conditioned to a small horizon, and unable to cope with a wider world? Oh, why must I endure Frida's constant analysis of my character and capacity.

She says, "You know, Alberto, your trouble is that you are

wildly respectable. You are obsessed with being considered respectable."

That's true enough. I am. I am. I always have been. Because my mother, because my father, because the world in spinning cases me into this tiny mould.

She says, "Your Marxism, my dear Albert, has not extinguished more than one-tenth of your *petit-bourgeois* upbringing."

I know that's true. I still labour to acquire a cultured manner. I still labour.

She says, "You see, Albertino, the reason for a strong, silent man is that he's got damn all to say."

I am stung. I am silent. But Frida, if I had the words would you listen? This body could endure the extremes of heat and cold, long journeys across the wastes and deserts of this world, through hot forests and across frozen mountain ranges, This body exists for some heroic purpose, and one day it will bear the vital message through the burning lakes. If I had the words, would you listen? My body was built for some epic form of endurance, but it lies imprisoned by the iron laws of economics and all I need endure is the nagging need to prepare for an exam, for a job, for money, for a decent, respectable place in society, and the nagging love I feel for this girl who does not love me.

If I fail the menacing examination, I shall be chained behind a counter, locked in a local shop. There is nothing else for it in Llanelw. And if I escaped — impossible to contemplate remembering my mother's health — where can I go in a world shrouded in unemployment? I see life as a cage with an open door, imprisoning mice that are too frightened to run wild.

"Albertino, there's nobody at home. Let's go home and get tea. Would you like to have tea with me?"

"Where are the family?"

"Les and the old man have gone to Liverpool and the Prima Donna is paying her monthly visit to Mr Brown in Chester. Spending her immoral earnings."

I am still not used to the way Frida talks.

"Don't you want to have tea with me, Albie?"

She has never talked to me so tenderly before. If I knew for certain that she wanted to be kind to me . . . . O, Frida . . . then the floodgates of my heart would break!

She wears a bright yellow summer frock, and yellow sandals, too. We walk like conquerors along the promenade to Les's home as if the entire spaces of the afternoon, the sea, the sandhills, the houses along the front, the sky itself, were at our command.

"Now, my master; what will you have? Something out of a tin, as usual? No. No. I'm going to make the most spectacular salad you have ever seen!"

Closing the door, is closing the door on the world I belong to for the first time in my life. Inside this house, there is only Frida. It does not matter that this is someone else's untidy house. This is a dream and a dream transcends material objects.

"*Ych afi!*" Frida pulls a face. "Can't think of eating in this disgusting kitchen. Let's go up to my room. The only clean room in the entire house, let me tell you. You haven't seen it, have you? Don't look so shy, Alberto. Follow me."

A room adapted to her personality. It excites me as she excites me. One wall alongside my chair has a lithograph. Frida says it is the original work of Braque. I have never seen pictures hung so low before. She also says Braque is more important than Picasso. I try to conceal that I'd never heard his name before. She must not think I am a complete fool. When she takes down the tea things I look at her books. French, Italian, German. Is it all show or does she really know all these languages, and has she read all the books? I am ashamed of myself for such a mean-spirited thought. I shall ask her to read some when she comes back. I pick up a complete Dante.

"Hello, Albie. Reading all about Hell?"

"Frida."

"Yes?"

"Will you read some to me?"

"Why?"

"Well, I'd like to hear it. They say the music is in the sound, don't they? I've never heard anybody read Dante!"

Frida laughs.

"What is it?"

"Such a big man talking like such a small boy. Don't, don't look so hurt. Listen to this. I'll read this. Paolo and Francesca.

The second circle of Hell. You know the story, of course?"[43]

"Oh, yes." I hasten to lie and then close my eyes to listen more carefully. "It sounds fine." She reads well. I cannot tell whether it's correct or not. "Now will you translate it for me?"

I sit on the floor to watch her finger moving over the text.

One day, for our delight, we read of Launcelot, how love ensnared him. We were alone and we suspected nothing.

That reading, more than once, compelled our eyes to meet, and changed the colour of our cheeks; but it was one moment alone that overcame us.

When we read how her fond smile was kissed by such a lover, he, who shall never be divided from me, kissed my mouth all trembling.

The book played Pander as did he who wrote it. That day we read no further . . . .

At this point, I am bold enough to turn her head towards me and kiss her. I push the book aside and we lie together on the carpet. I know how little Frida is wearing. I am so excited I try to breathe deeply to control my trembling.

Suddenly, we hear the front door opening. In a second, Frida scrambles to her feet, buttoning up her yellow frock with surprisingly steady hands.

"For God's sake, get up, Albie! Come on, hurry! And don't look so guilty. Blast them! What did they want to come back so early for?"

"O, Frida, I love you."

"Do you, sweetie? That's very nice."

"But Frida, you . . . you love me, don't you?"

"Why? Why should I?"

"Well now . . . here . . . loving, I mean . . . ."

"Maybe I do, Albie. But this is no time to discuss problems. Come on. Hurry up. I'm ready now. Let's go down and meet the *hoi polloi.*"

My father is ill, said Iorwerth. He lies in his bed by the window that overlooks the farmyard. Jacob Tŷ Draw has been hired for the summer to help Llew. My mother would have preferred to hire a non-drinking man, but experienced hands are very hard to get. The young men are turning their backs on the land, going off to work in the seaside resorts or the big towns in

England. Jacob takes care not to swear when he's in the house, but I often hear from the barn or the stable poor Llew's high cackle. There never was anyone so willing to laugh at anything as Llew. But I must admit I enjoy listening to Jacob myself. His stories are endless and the language in which he tells them is such rich and racy dialect.

"So I just said to the blacksmith, I may as well tell you, Lazarus, I said, I could not give a damn if your anvil split in two. The place I'm sleeping in stinks five points before the wind, and your missus' cooking is too disgraceful to make a load for a decent mud boat, and moreover, I said . . . "

Llew neighs wildly and I can't help laughing myself, although I know that Jacob is talking away to postpone the moment when they get back to work. Someone ought to make a record of his speech, all the same. I might do it myself, although my parents might not approve. Jacob is an able man, something of a stone mason, knowing how to kill a pig and salt the meat properly; something of a mechanic; able also to thatch a corn stack or catch moles; a good judge of stock, well-versed in the illnesses of animals; but having all these attributes, one suspects, for the purpose of avoiding hard labour. So when he and Llew are working, as befits the son and heir I join them when I can. To turn the top-dress midden in the corner of a field or to drain the ditches at the bottom of the farm, and more or less to set the pace, and to listen to Jacob.

He has stories specially directed to win my mother's interest too, and to stretch the mid-day eating hour until we all become uncomfortable and restless, except Jacob himself, of course. There is a whole chronicle of anecdotes about my great-grandfather, my mother's grandfather, a noted Wesleyan preacher in his day who before that had been a prize-fighter. Jacob claimed that his own father had been saved by my great-grandfather's powerful preaching. At meal-times, Jacob absentmindedly attributes witticisms to this hero that only the day before he had quoted as someone else's. My mother wishes to rise and get on with her work, Llew and I are ready to get on too, but Jacob quite imperturbably continues to unfold his tale. If only my father were sitting in the empty oak chair at the other end of the table, he would bring Jacob's story to an end with a firm burst of appreciative laughter, at the same time pushing his chair back so that he could rise unhurriedly and say, "Well, men, we'd better be getting on with it!" But my father is in bed, thin and pale, and the doctors don't seem really to know what is the matter with him. Only yesterday, I heard Jacob say to Llew: "Poor old creature — the candle is burning down to the socket. I'm afeard for him, I am indeed . . . ."

And so am I. I have a terrible fear of looking into his grey, unhealthy face, and it is a fear that is undermining my Faith. He is so quiet all day as if he were listening for death's first footstep. Is his Religion no comfort to him? What I mean is that it is ceasing to be a comfort to me and that there is no hymn or anthem that can drown the silence of a cold body rotting in the earth, my father's body, my body. That is why a shiver passes down my spine when I think deeply about my father's illness. It is changing him and it is changing me. If only I could still talk to him naturally as Llew does after breakfast, walking to the foot of the stairs and wiping his mouth with the back of his hand before calling, "How are you feeling today, master?"

"I think I'm a little better today, Llew, thank you. How is the weather?"

"The earth is still pretty wet. It will dry I don't doubt with this nice bit of wind, so long as it doesn't rain again, isn't it?"

"Well, carry on with the ditching until it's dry enough to single out the swedes. And ask Jacob to set a few traps by the furthest hedge in the six-acre field before you leave."

In the evening my mother and I sit before the kitchen fire as it burns low.

"You mustn't worry about the farm, Iorwerth. Above all, you mustn't let it interfere with your studies. Your father will get better, you know. It's just that he's got to take special care. The best tonic you could give him would be to win an Open Scholarship — to do well — to do your best. But you mustn't worry about the farm. Your father and I shall manage as we've always done."

I want to ask her to confide in me, to tell me everything, so that we could discuss everything openly. And yet I am relieved when I see her mouth close firmly in a way that has always indicated that she has nothing more to say, because I could not bear to know the full truth about my father's condition. I would also like to comfort my father by sitting at the foot of his bed talking to him, but all I do is to pop my head in in exaggerated haste every morning.

"Good morning, father! Hope you're feeling better today? Is there anything I can get you in town? Good heavens, is that clock right? I've got to run or I'll miss the bus. Take care now, dad. See you tonight . . . ."

How ineffective my love for my father is. How ineffective I am in every way, because I am so afraid of dying, and of Death. I must work harder, harder. There are only three more clear weeks. I must win an Open Scholarship. I must. Must. And put everything else out of my mind, my father's illness, the beautiful face of Dilys Maurice, the farm work, and Death. Yes, even death.

It is quite fantastic, said Michael, to recall how near I came to rejecting my nationality. All summer the name of Wales met me whichever way I turned, and each time it seemed more like a term of abuse. *Cymru* this and *Cymru* that. In the very middle of the examinations, my father had to hold eisteddfod committees in the Rectory, and their noisy deliberations kept me awake just at a time when I should be husbanding my strength and refreshing my brain with a good night's sleep. There were even *penillion* singers in the drawing-room at midnight. And for once I agreed with my mother, it was much too much. All summer I avoided speaking Welsh and I avoided native persons like Iorwerth with their emotional zeal for things Welsh. I considered the possibility of being like Frida (in outlook, not in manner), a cosmopolitan with a special love for the Mediterranean countries or some small island no matter where, so long as it was populated with primitive but happy natives. I considered also the possibility of being English, without any burden of self-conscious patriotism, except in times of national emergency. It seemed to me that *Cymru* was the name of a disease and that the burden of being Welsh was an uncalled-for discomfort and distress.

Early in the holidays, on a visit to Penmon with my sister and an English friend of hers, quite accidentally I met Charles

Phillips and his friend Watkin. (There is nothing very much to Phillips, a shy, young teacher with very little say for himself. He teaches the lower forms and has trouble with discipline.) I found this friend of Phillips a short argumentative lively man from Glamorgan, exceptionally interesting. He was an enthusiastic nationalist. We sat on the sea-shore arguing fiercely, oblivious of the white lighthouse or the sea pushing at the greater rocks, or the passing pleasure steamer, even when it blew its horn as it passed with its load of trippers through the narrow channel between us and the lighthouse. What did I say?

Why nations at all? Yes, why have nations? Surely with the world changing so fast better one language (English) for the whole world and all the world therefore one? Anyway, Wales was too small, too poor, too unimportant, too backward, too old-fashioned and what about the proletariat and what about progress? Our society was too emotional, noisy, inflated, pompous, eisteddfodic; our religion too self-satisfied. Our chapels too ugly, our politics too false, our causes too narrow.

There never was such an argument. My sister and her friend tired of listening. We had tea together in a large hotel. I was in a strangely excited state all the time, as if I were on the verge of making a great discovery.

The following day, merely to continue the argument, I made the journey to Bangor to meet Phillips and Watkin. They were attending some Summer School, and sleeping on straw mattresses in a chapel vestry. I was allowed to stay there too, when I lost the last train. We argued so much, I could not sleep. It seemed a private battle between Watkin and myself. I remember thinking how unsightly he was. Sticky eyes behind thick lens, a habit of sniffing, his lips always wet with excess saliva. But this had nothing to do with the validity or non-validity of his arguments. It was a battle of pure intelligence. Unable to sleep I read in a book someone had left on the floor alongside my bed a twelfth-century poem by Hywel ap Owain Gwynedd,

> *I love her marshlands and her mountains,*
> *Her forts near her woods, her comely domains,*

Her valleys, her meadowlands, and her fountains,
Her white seagulls, and gracious women.

And sometime during that late and restless hour, I obtained
the revelation I have so long been waiting for. By searching the
past I have discovered not only the key to the future but also the
part I myself can expect to play in it.

Albie said, this is a long, troubled and uneasy summer. Frida
has gone away. I write her letters, but they are not long letters.
The fountain of school-eloquence on favourite subjects has
completely dried up, and I have nothing now to ease the pain of
my new inarticulate awareness. A new world lies inside me,
wordless, unexpressed. I can no longer be assured that any
statement I make corresponds to what I mean and therefore my
speech is disfigured with meaningless 'ers' and painful pauses.
There are some who think it is an affectation and they say
impatiently,"Yes, well?" or "Come on, get it off your chest,"
and of course I smile politely, they never know that my halting
speech is a mark of pain. It is not all Frida's fault. If, for example,
in the early morning I observe the dew on the tennis lawn in
front of the school balanced like shattered glass on blades of
grass, I could stand there looking until the armoured rays of the
sun had dried up all the dew, before being able to express
adequately the size and shape of the experience trembling inside
me.
    And then again, if only Frida would write perhaps my pen
would be stimulated to move into action. If only she wrote once;
if only she made, out of kindness, one demonstration of affection
for me.
    *You're quite out of your depth with me, Alberto . . . .*And yet
only a moment ago I felt her hand pass sweetly through my hair.
*Don't think too much about me. I'm not worth it . . . . You see, in
actual fact I dislike myself far more than Les's mother dislikes me.*
    What does she mean? Everything or nothing? I don't know.
    *I can tell you, Alberto, sometimes I dream of finding a really
great man. A man who is going to do something really big. And I
shall be the one to help him. He'll lean on me.*
    Greatness! That excludes me for ever, like a barrier of ice

97

mountains. I haven't enough self-confidence to create a convincing excuse for my present helplessness.

You poor old dear. You mustn't be so immature. You must find an ambition, a dream, a vision, a great aim in life . . . .

But . . . .I want to say, and cannot say it . . . .*But* . . . .How can I put it: loving you, that is my ambition, my dream, my vision, my aim in life.

Just say what you mean, Alberto. Just say what you mean . . . .

Well, that's just it. I attempt a diffident smile. *I don't exactly know what I mean.*

The other evening, restless and bored as I was, and with nothing to do, I went to the Pavilion to watch the dancing. I sat in the gallery and bought half a pint of beer which I had difficulty in drinking. I was lonely and depressed and the melancholy voice of the band made me nostalgic for the easy successes of my childhood, as if I were already an old-established failure. What could I do to keep ahead, keep in front, keep the trust and admiration of my mother and father, keep Frida's interest and win her unattainable love, and win the astonished notice of the entire world. What if, at that moment, I stood on the narrow balustrade above the band and then leapt, with a cinematographic flourish for the chandelier that hung above the centre of the dance floor. Thus having attracted attention, I would alight gracefully on the floor, and then lift up my hand for silence, and then harangue the crowd, deliver a passionate and overwhelming oration . . . but about what? What about?

9

In this life, said Michael, everything depends on purpose. I have a cousin who owns a chain of butcher's shops. He has become very rich because he set out to make money and nothing else. That is exactly how it is. Therefore because of the urge within me towards a perfect purpose (and certainly *not* because of any soft-headed belief in progress or humanity) I have taken as my goal the winning of self-government for Wales. It is such a difficult task, that joy leaps within me every time my mind dwells on the coming battle. Life is a ceaseless conflict, and here at last is the fight worth taking part in. Young as I am, through this certainty of purpose, wisdom has at last been made available to me. If I live to be a hundred, I shall never have a richer purpose, a better vision, and never a wisdom so pure and certain, so free from sadness and regret.

I am very pleased to have won such a good scholarship to Oxford, although I am secretly astonished at having done so well, considering my life-long fear of examinations. And, of course, it is a splendid thing to earn my parents' whole-hearted esteem and a measure of independence at one stroke. And it is splendid to be young even at such an inauspicious time; to be able to enjoy living in spite of the constant threat of another war, to collect pleasure as a bee collects pollen, even among the briar and the thorns. But all this is only an interlude, and I am aware all the time, beneath the gay surface of my life, that somewhere hidden in the future, because of the choice I have already made my destiny waits for me. Time is never wasted.

It is sad to see a wet harvest, said Iorwerth. From the window of my father's bedroom I watch the endless falling of the rain, and the heavy heads of the corn stooks sinking lower and lower in the sodden fields. It is true that I have passed the examinations but I haven't won an Open Scholarship like Michael. It was too much to expect that I ever should. However, my parents were pleased enough, and now my future hangs in the balance more delicately than they suspect. If I am perfectly certain of my vocation to the ministry, I shall go to college. I can go to college, too, if I wish to become a teacher. Otherwise it is their opinion, and also mine, that I were better turned into a fully-fledged modern farmer, and to that end, attend an Agricultural Institute for a year or two. They say it is for me in the next few days to make up my mind. But how can I?

While my faith is disintegrating in the shadow of my all-pervading fear of death, what right have I to stand in any pulpit? Now I am certain of nothing in the world except death: I see the shadow of Death across my father's face, and across the face of the whole world. Death settles, falls from the air not only on animals, the dead sheep maggoting in the sun, the bleeding pig, the diseased cow, but also on my pale patient father in his spotless, white bed, and also on the lovely face of Dilys Maurice, and also upon all things young, beautiful, kind and good. O, my dear friends, fly the Death that smothers all laughter and fills all skulls with crumbling earth and busy worms.

The other evening I was allowed to accompany Dilys Maurice to a *Noson Lawn* organized by the League of Youth in a bare hall in one of the back streets of Llanelw. I was allowed to call for Dilys, I spoke to her father and to her mother, and I was congratulated by both of them on my recent success in the examinations. I should have been happy and I was happy until quite suddenly in the stuffy overcrowded hall I had a nauseating vision of every mouth open in laughter being frozen open for ever.

"What's the matter, Iorwerth? What's the matter?" Dilys had noticed after some time that I was not singing or laughing.

"Nothing." The hall was so hot her whole face glistened with sweat.

"I have said something? Iorwerth, what's the matter? Oh, you are an odd boy sometimes."

How could I describe my discontentment to her, my unbearable restless thoughts, the conflict in my soul that seemed

100

like a childish quarrel with God. My unrespectable thoughts would startle her as they startled me. In the beginning, what right had He to create Death as well as life out of Darkness?

To me who had long been used to succeeding, said Albie, it is very hard to fail. That night, when darkness had at last fallen, I stole out of the house and walked down the deserted streets to the Promenade. But it was no escape. In the sound of the sea and under the stars, failure took on even more overwhelming dimensions. It was bigger than a bad dream and there could be no waking up. I thought the pain would be less severe out of sight of my mother's dumb patience and my father's manufactured jollity. Instead it was much worse. The wind and the stars and the sea spoke only of Failure.

Not Frida's fault. I still say that. During the last twelve months something happened to my will to act. I walked like a somnambulist to this appointment. I had every possible encouragement. Every winter evening my mother made a fire for me in our small front parlour, and every evening my father turned the radio down and sat listening to his favourite programmes with his ear right on the loudspeaker. As for me, I went through all the correct motions. I sat for hours with my head in my hands over open books, I read systematically, I made careful time-tables for work, I trudged steadily through the syllabus like an insurance man working his weekly way down the terrace, but all the time, in my heart of hearts I knew I was walking in this direction. I never had the strength to change my course. I was a prisoner who still lay on his bed of straw even when he knew that the keys of the prison were in his own pocket.

My poor mother and poor father. Now, in the face of the cruel truth it does not cross their minds to find fault with their only son.

"Those old questions must have been terribly hard, Nel."

"Must have been, Dic. Poor Albie. It's such a disappointment for him, the poor lamb."

"We musn't let him get downhearted, Nel."

"No indeed, Dic. It seems so unfair after all the hard studying he's done!"

I cannot bear to imagine the sympathy of my friends, although

I know that there will be others busy passing judgment.

Old Albie Jones got on like a house on fire up to Form Six. And then what happens? Fizzles out like a damp squib! Suppose his mighty brain gave out on him. Not much point in being top of the form as a kid after all, is there?

Michael wrote me an invitation to stay at the Rectory for a week! I shall have to think of a polite way of refusing. Iorwerth called at our house and barely mentioned the results. In his melancholy way he tried to suggest he fared as badly as I had. No word from Frida. Even if she knew, she would not have much to say to a man who had proved himself a failure.

Now, at last, when it is too late, I have an overwhelming desire to escape from Llanelw. If only I could at this moment. Across the sea. Anywhere in the wide world. I must look for a job. I must start earning. That's the aim now. Not to be a burden to my parents a moment longer. I can't bear to think of living another day without earning.

"Hello, Albie!" I did not know there was someone standing behind me. Could I possibly have been thinking aloud? Exposing myself even further to the scrutiny of an indifferent world?

"Hello, Ann. I didn't see you. Taking your dog for a walk?"

Ann is the only daughter of *The Queen's*. She has left school. She lives at the hotel with her father and mother, doing some office work and learning the business.

"Albie, I was terribly sorry to hear about the results!"

Her voice is overloaded with sympathy. I try to smile. I search for the appropriate phrases, something stoic, something strong.

"Don't look so down-hearted, Albie. Come for a little walk with Pero and me. We'll cheer him up, won't we, Pero?"

She talks away about games, as we walk along. Ann is good at games just as I am. Frida used to make fun of her passion for physical training and fitness, but tonight I find solace in her low, busy voice. At the far end of the Prom we stand side by side staring out towards the sea which is hidden in the darkness. I realize she would not mind if I kissed her. She would like it. Why, then, do I not do so? I place my hand on her arm. She turns her face up towards me. It is a chance to find some comfort and I take it.

On such a night as this, said Michael, when the moon swims from behind a cloud like a golden swan advancing across a purple lake, it no doubt seems a romantic gesture to hold a political conference in a castle which stands on a small hill above a meandering river that glitters in the moonlight, and I can understand to some extent why the young people are singing on the lawn and are moved by the sound of their own harmonious voices. But I do not believe that any political movement can hope to succeed on *penillion*[44] singing alone, or even on a *Cymanfa Ganu*[45]. Enthusiasm is more than a noise to be released on the yielding air in a vain attempt to disturb the nearest star.

Therefore I sit apart, to meditate above the castle wall, and to recall the history and the significance of the castle, and to measure what is relevant in the past and what is irrelevant. I re-affirm, in the sound of my musical contemporaries and in the sight of the sentimental moon, that there is no substitute for fortitude and no known solace for defeat. Therefore this is a time for meticulous preparation; a time to sift knowledge and a time to lay foundations. History is only made by those who are ready to make it and the first lesson is to accept the burden of being utterly alone. If I have a destiny and if I carry any message, it is useless to think of being a member of someone else's retinue, or even of marching shoulder to shoulder with a chosen company of intimate friends. He who desires to lead is on his own and the wind that blows from the outer darkness is always cold on his face.

"Michael! Michael! Come and sing with us! Come on! Come on!"

I wave my hand at the eager faces turned for a moment in my direction. In a moment or two I shall join them and sing away as heartily as the best, and my secret will continue to grow silently inside me.

The people across the road were quarrelling again, said Albie, as I came home one evening after being to the pictures with Ann.

"Your kids are like bloody cannibals around the place and that's a fact. If I catch them in my garden again, surely to God I'll skin them alive . . . ."

"Listen, Fred Pierce, you're so weak you couldn't skin a rice pudding, and that's a fact. I've heard people saying that your mother . . . "

I rush to the house, happy to close the door on the ugly scene. It happens regularly every other month between the long periods of armed hostile silence. The two families are quite closely related. Their feud is a source of endless wonder and speculation to my father and mother. For myself, I cannot bear it and I never could. It seems some all-pervading insult to the dignity of the human race. I feel it as a personal affront.

"Mam bach, they're at it again."

My mother stands in the kitchen, in her accustomed pose, an image of uncomplaining patience, watching the gas stove. Strangely enough, this evening she has not wandered, with a fork perhaps still held up in her hand, across the living room to peer through the window and say from time to time "Aren't they awful," her voice a mixture of disapproval and anxious curiosity.

"O, Albie. Listen, Albie. I've got good news. Mr Bell called. He's got a job for you down at the garage; a clean job, clerking. Very good prospects he said, Albie. He was very nice. He said how nice it would be for you to work in the same place as your dad. It will be nice, won't it?"

Two months ago, during the golden age, before the Fall, before half the world became a desert, in Frida's company I passed the garage and I caught a glimpse of my father in a brown overall holding open the door of the Mayor's car for the Mayor's wife with a gesture of unbearable servility. I turned my head away quickly and drew Frida's attention to a particularly fatuous display in a shop window across the road. In my shame, I forgot how pleased my father had been to get his new job, to be able to give up his seat above the smelly, clanking engine of the country bus. I forgot also how much he has aged lately. A map of tiny scarlet veins stretch across his nose from one cheek to the other.

"Mr Bell is a good man, Albie. Nothing mean about him. Two pounds a week for the first year. That's good money for a boy of your age, you know."

For the first year. I heard the clang of the prison's iron door closing behind me. My mother is still smiling at me expectantly. I must, must, say something, say how glad I am and then she will be relieved and happy.

104

I am sitting, said Iorwerth, in a barber's chair. Michael is in the next chair but one. We are having our hair cut at the best barber's shop in Llanelw. Between us the most talkative barber in the place is shaving a baldheaded man with great quantities of soap and eloquence. From time to time, while continuing to talk and shave, the barber stares at the mirror and nods as if he were in complete agreement with himself. Myself I have always disliked barbers' shops, and yet I listen to his chatter as if it were the song the sirens sang.

"Never ought to put Scuddiforth on the wing for a start, He's not a winger. Never was and never will be and that's how they are all the time, won't leave nothing alone. It's try this and try that, and so the boys never get a chance to settle down. Then they complain they don't get enough support. I ask you, what else can they expect? And look at them now, talking about buying a new centre-forward from Darlington — MacSpinney. Well now I ask you, if he's all that good why is Darlington in such a hurry to get rid of him?"

He goes on and on, on from one subject to another, like an evening paper. His mind is the lowest common denominator of the newspapers scattered over the empty waiting chairs behind us. I am ashamed to confess that I am afraid of him. Any moment, it seems to me, he can swell up inside his white overall and cut off my head with a quick snip of his mighty scissors; and swell greater still into the shape of a Monster of Unreason, able to crush whole streets of cities under his blind merciless boot.

"I tell you what I'd do with those bloody Welsh Nationalists, I'd pick out their leaders and pop them in prison and conscript the rest into the army. I'd shoot one or two, just as an example like, and that would be the end of them."

He seems to me the white-overalled emperor of a seething maggoty world in which I want no part. A man like this couldn't exist on our farm. The farm is the place for me; so long as it remains hidden and does not offend this monster.

"I don't think it would!" Michael wipes the hair away from under his collar with a small towel. The eloquent barber looks puzzled.

"I don't think it would be the end of them!" Michael smiles politely and begins feeling in his pocket for change. I am lost in admiration for Michael's calm. "I'm one of them and so is my friend on the other side of you!"

I nod my head, but if there is to be a row, I would prefer Michael not to drag me into it. But the barber is no fighting man. He is blushing and stuttering and squirming under Michael's firm gaze. To me it appears as if he is visibly shrinking and will never stop shrinking until Michael's gaze relents. Perhaps when he is small enough to sleep in a matchbox, Michael will let him go. By the time we leave I have become sorry for the little man.

Parked in the street is the big car Michael has bought for ten pounds. It works very well and there is plenty of room inside, but it drinks petrol and oil. I think Michael has become very fond of it. Today he is quite determined to arrange a trip for next Saturday afternoon, to extend the car a little and to cheer up Albie. We have time to kill until Albie finishes work at five-thirty. It is an unusually fine day towards the end of September, and the few late visitors are congratulating themselves on the wonderful weather. Leaving the car safely parked we move slowly in the direction of the Public Library. On the corner of Water Street near the new traffic lights, we bump into Les in the company of Harry Marks' sister, handsome in a Jewish way no doubt, but to my mind vulgar, talkative and unbearably all-knowing. It never occurred to me that Les had anything to say to her. Les appears so easy-going, always chewing sweets as if nothing in the world could disturb him. He probably puts up with her because he feels it's the thing to do to have some kind of girl friend. Of course, he has always been very friendly with Harry. But she's not nearly as nice as Harry. I shall never really understand Les.

In a very loud voice the girl questions Michael about his car.

"Goes like a watch," says Michael. "Only one thing wrong with it, drinks too much juice. That's why I want a full load next Saturday. Share the costs. Silver collection half way."

"Oh, I wish I could come." The girl quivers with enthusiasm. "You'll have a wonderful time!"

"Why don't you come then?"

"Well, thanks for the invitation but I've got to be at home. We've got relatives from London coming to stay."

"Relations again?" Les lifts his eyebrows.

"Yes. Relations. They're looking out for new business. They might settle here if there's a war."

"Never mind!" Michael slaps Les across the shoulder. "We'll look after the boy!"

"Gosh." Les changes the subject suddenly. "Have you heard what happened to Jac? Jac Owen. You know he joined the Air Force about six months ago? He's been killed!"

"Oh, no." It seems so incredible.

"Who was this then?" The girl is inexhaustibly curious.

"Used to be in school with us!" Les explains patiently. "Before you came here to live."

"What happened?"

"During an exercise over the North Sea. His training aircraft caught fire. Crashed into the sea!"

So Jac Owen became an unlikely Icarus.[46] I was never fond of Jac as Michael was in the old days. He could be so unfeeling, and such a bully. He was a wild one, a great user of bad language, animal in his ways. And yet for some reason he had kept in touch with us after leaving school. I had a Christmas Card from him every year. He used to ask us to meet him on Saturday evenings. Early this summer, before the exams, he came with Michael to Maesgwyn. He was wearing his new uniform. When we went for a walk after tea I remember him gathering bluebells. That is how I see him now, a small blue figure, bending among the trees.

"It's ten to two, too," Michael says quietly.

"Yes!" Les smiles sadly! "He always used to call me '*Ten to Two*'."

"Oh, did he? Why?" the girl asks.

"An old joke." Les does not elaborate.

"Poor old Jac." Michael sighs! "Used to look back on his brief schooldays as the Golden Age. Always used to ask after the teachers and talk about them as if they were mythical figures, odd sort of heroes. There's something so pathetic about dying young, so innocent."

I feel chilled on the street corner in spite of the sun, as if there were a cold wind blowing. One of us, the first perhaps of our generation, has stopped breathing and his broken body floats on the water like a dead fish. Death has taken the first fruits from our midst. After the first shock, the news is, in some strange way a relief, in a way I cannot understand. But when Michael and I continue on our way to the Public Library, I feel less heavy in my spirit than for many a day, as if at last some particle of courage had lodged in my frightened soul.

"Michael." We are standing outside the library. "Michael. It was splendid the way you tackled that awful little barber,"

"Do you think so? You know I was a bit scared of him at first. I had to force myself to speak. I made myself do it."

"A sort of discipline?" My voice is so eager.

"Yes, I suppose so."

"Michael. You know, I think that you are a natural leader."

I blush at the sound of my own enthusiasm. I sound so naïve, but with Michael I don't mind! "I only wish I had a bit of your . . . your . . . attacking spirit." I struggle to sound as objective as I can.

Michael laughs.

"I'm the aggressive type, you see. No modesty. No shame."

We enter the Library as two friends who understand each other very well.

In the Reading Room we come across Mr Phillips, the Welsh master, standing reading *The Times*. He is concentrating, his forehead is creased in a deep frown and he holds the back of his hand against his mouth. Michael is familiar with him. I realize that they are quite friendly. The three of us stare at the newspaper together.

Michael says, "War before the end of the month. That's quite certain." The small print of *The Times* dances in front of my eyes. I tremble at the thought of massed armour attacking thunderously, and the long silence it leaves burning in its wake. In the paper there is a large map of Eastern Europe.

"Don't think it will come myself," says Mr Phillips. "Not yet anyway. Not this time!"

"Why? I should have said myself that under these conditions war is absolutely certain. It's what they want."

"It would be too destructive," says Phillips. I realize suddenly that he fears it just as much as I do. He is not arguing with Michael, but with himself. Trying to convince himself. "You see, international capital has too much respect for its own property, as it were, to destroy it all at one blow. You know, don't you, that the scientists say that it is possible now to build a bomb big enough to completely destroy a single city. A city as big as Cardiff or even bigger. One bomb. Just one bomb would be enough!"

"It's terrible!" My voice sounds feeble.

"I agree, Michael, local skirmishes, yes. But not all-out total war. Nobody can win a World War again."

Mr Phillips' spectacles gleam triumphantly. He has convinced himself.

Michael smiles politely.

"I think they want war. I think it could start as soon as the corn harvest is over in Eastern Europe."

I long to believe Mr Phillips. He is older than Michael. He knows more; he has studied more. I long to reject the note of confidence in Michael's voice, and his belief in his own ability to face unpleasant facts. Why does he always have to be right? Who does he think he is? And is there not an element of dangerous *hubris* in such a bold and outright self-confidence? He speaks more like an Englishman than a Welshman, I think, taking excessive pride in his ability to face unpleasant facts. Nevertheless, I feel that in this matter he is nearer reality than Mr Phillips. We leave the schoolmaster as we found him, poring over *The Times*.

Out in the street, Michael says, "If a war comes, what will you do, Iorwerth?"

I search my heart for an honest answer to a question I have tried to avoid asking myself. From the open window of the hygienic Rock Shop where the sweetmeat is made on the premises, comes a powerful sweet smell and looking inside I see the shining steel arms twist the stiff toffee.

I say, "It's the idea of killing someone else I object to!" It seems an admirable thing to say and yet no sooner is it said than I realize that I object just as much and even more to being killed myself. Why, then, does this make it less admirable? How can we decide?

"What will you do then? Register as a conscientious objector?"

"I suppose so." I sound dejected. "What else can I do?"

"You could stay put," Michael says promptly. "Stay on the

farm. Farm can't do without you. Quite simple."

I blush because the temptation has already occurred to me.

"No. That wouldn't be conscience. You wouldn't do that yourself."

"Well my conscience isn't so sensitive. I'm not a pacifist, Ior. There are plenty of people in this world I would quite enjoy shooting. Of course I could be a C.O. on Welsh political grounds. Could do that. But I don't think I will. I'm terribly keen to learn more about discipline and authority. The army would be just the place for that. I had an uncle in the Indian Army. But he was terribly stupid."

"Well, what will you do?" We arrive on the Promenade, and lean on the railings to stare at the incoming tide.

"I'll join up, I think," Michael seems quite serious, "but on my terms, Ior. I mean that." He looks at me critically and I look back at him much as I want to look away. "I think Wales needs my way and your way." His searching stare melts into a warming smile. I feel warmer towards him than ever before. We are true friends. He respects me and I respect him. Respect is so essential. I believe he is a born leader. He looks at his watch. "Time we went to collect Albie."

10

On a fine afternoon, said Albie, towards the end of September we all went on a trip together in Michael's car. We had the hood down and our voices fluttered like pennants in the wind. For as long as the car was moving at any rate, I enjoyed the illusion of freedom. It was wonderful to escape from the tiny office box that held me beyond the plate glass and chromium front of the garage, from the ominous hum of the grim electric clock, and Mr Bell's regular critical glances.

Everyone believes I am happy in my new work. I say so, for the sake of my mother and my father, and in order to observe some undefined convention. Shortly, however, when I have him to myself, I shall tell Michael exactly how I feel. He has little sympathy with my Marxist point of view and I don't understand his concern for Welsh nationalism, but, because of the strength of his character perhaps, it is in him I wish to confide. I could tell him about the whispers I hear in that tiny office, voices that remind me of Frida's, repeating endlessly, "*You're here for good. You'll never get out, you'll never get out.*"

O, God, to think of the time and energy I spent on the utter fantasy of loving Frida. It must have been perfectly clear, even for me, from the very beginning that she was only whiling away the time with me, to tide over a tediously long stay in an unfriendly house. I am so ashamed and so hurt, I cannot mention it to anyone, except perhaps to her, and she, I know, would not want to hear. Yet she is still in command of my imagination and I still worship her white body. Perhaps, if we could broach the subject calmly and naturally, I could say to Michael, Tell me, have you any idea why Frida wanted to destroy me?

I wish the others were not here. It's Michael I want to talk to. I

111

know it was for my benefit that he organized this outing and my heart is full of gratitude, but I only wish that instead we could have made a short excursion together to some valley where we could enjoy a long conversation on the banks of a quiet river. I need his help to tackle my problems; even if he only sat still and listened it would help. I wish Ann were not here, sitting next to me in the back seat. She's a very nice girl I know, but she imprisons me, just as surely as does the box-like office, inside some image she insists on calling Albie.

Oh, Albie, you played a marvellous game, you really did . . . .I think you're much better in the centre, I really do . . . .I think you're much better than Cyril Boot, I really do, seriously now . . . .Shall we dance, Albie, you're such a good dancer, shall we . . . ? Will you come to supper, Albie, to tea, to supper, to tea, to supper. Your mother knows you're coming . . . .

It's a comfort of course, but a dangerous comfort. It would be so easy to be satisfied with a little and to be permanently linked to a pleasant and healthy girl I don't even enjoy kissing. More dangerous still because my mother likes the idea of my being friendly with the only daughter of *The Queen's. She's such a nice girl*, my mother says, and I know that she is thinking that all my education has not been wasted. *Jolly girl*, my father says, *good sport. Nothing big about her.* They are quite right about her, and I can understand their attitude, but to me she is only a new warder in the prison. I must say to Michael as soon as I can today, *Listen, Michael. I've got to talk to you. It's important and it can't wait.*

I have a premonition, said Iorwerth, that today all of us are together in one company for the last time. This, therefore, is a special occasion, and for this reason I observe my friends closely and I also observe closely the country world through which we are moving. The steep path winds up through the trees to the green sward of the hilltop in the centre of which stands a ruined martello tower. From there we shall have a wonderful view of the coast. I start singing, and the others join in, one after the other. This pleases me, lifts my heart until I am suddenly overwhelmed with a feeling of affection for every one of them. "Oh, look! Look!" Dilys holds my arm, "Just look!" We all stop and look upwards. "Red ones too," Les says very quietly. For a moment the red squirrels linger and then they disappear into the leaves that are changing colour. At the top of the hill we sit down facing the sea. Ann brings out her camera and insists on photographing us as a group. For a while to tease her, Les and Michael refuse to stand still: more than once, Michael stands on his head. Somewhere in Ann's home there will be a picture of us which will lie in a drawer perhaps for many years: Michael stretched on the grass, his fingers locked together under his chin: Albie standing rather self-consciously with one hand in his trouser pocket: Dilys sitting up neatly her head turned a little to face the camera and Les, caught for ever with his tongue out! Youth I suppose is a brief thing like the moment in which a photograph is taken.

For some reason a heated argument arises between Albie and Les. They do not get on at all well these days, they argue about such trivial things.

"That's not the Town Hall at all." Les says, most uncharacteristically impatient and heated. "That's St John's spire."

"It's so far away," says Michael. "Easy to be mistaken from here."

"I'm not mistaken," says Albie, "I know every stone of the old Sodom only too well."

Bit by bit it becomes a political wrangle.

"People have got a perfect right to enjoy themselves if they want to," Les says. "People have got a perfect right to earn a living by entertaining the public."

"To make money from the people who can least afford to part with it!"

"Everybody's got a perfect right to make money." Les calls himself a pragmatic rationalist. He seems to know quite a lot of philosophy and he must read a lot, but I've no idea when. He seems to me to be always enjoying himself. He's going to be a doctor. Michael says he'll make a very good one. I only wish I knew what exactly I was going to be. "Let's face it!" Les uses one of his favourite phrases, "in the cold light of reason!" This seems to me a reaction from being the son of a vague and emotional mother, and a capricious, hasty-tempered father.

"*From fire and brimstone, from the doomed city, fly!*" Michael sings extempore. I join in and an open quarrel is averted. But as soon as we stop, they start arguing again.

"Come on," I say. "Come on. Don't let's row on such a fine afternoon. It may be . . . "

"Blessed are the Peacemakers!" Michael places his hand on my head in a mock episcopal gesture. "Iorwerth is against rowing."

"Well, it is a waste of time on a fine day like this."

"Quite right," says Michael. "Shadows of the evening will soon be falling across our sky! Come on, chaps, on with the motley! What about some tea? Or is it too early?"

"Oh, no!" Dilys laughs happily. "It's never too early for tea."

"Where's this café you were telling us about, Michael?" Les asks.

Beneath the hill, inland, among the trees, we find a small river and near it two mills, one of them now a ruin, and beyond them a small farmhouse converted into a café. We have our tea on the uneven lawn in front of the house. *Bara brith*[47] and flat scones loaded with butter. Harmony reigns and everyone is in a merry mood. "Isn't there a game we can play?" says Les. "What about hide and seek?"

"Bit childish isn't it?" Albie lights a cigarette.

"Who cares? Just the place for a game on a big scale. I like the idea. What about it?"

"Oh, yes. Let's." Dilys and Ann are enthusiastic.

"Town-bred, you see." Michael points at Les with mock solemnity. "Gets excited at the sight of trees. Releases the animal in him."

"Good start for a psycho-analysis." Albie looks knowing. I blame Frida for the enmity that flares up so easily between Albie and Les. Les used to be so outspoken about her although she was his cousin, or is it that Les has turned out to be so successfully clever at examinations? In any case, I wish they could be good friends again, as they used to be in the old days.

Michael now imitates a child counting out. The lot of searcher falls to me. I borrow Les's wrist-watch, and I sit down comfortably to give them all five minutes to disappear. The entire wooded valley is so peaceful and the sounds of peace so soothing to listen to I wait longer than is necessary and get to my feet almost reluctantly.

114

I walk very slowly in the direction of the old mill. The solitude of my surroundings moves me strangely, and at the same time releases me from my preoccupation with myself. I identify myself with the eccentric shape of an old, isolated thorn tree near the bright green ground with its wet indentations that lies between me and the shallow race of the river as it approaches the mill. Inside the ruined shell of the mill the earth floor has been churned up by the feet of sheltering cattle. Of the second floor, there remains only one stout joist. Hundreds of intials and names are scrawled over the patches of whitewashed plaster that remain on the stone walls. Some must have climbed up to the joist to write their names in bold illiterate letters on the highest parts of the wall. Alongside the mill, the rotting moss-covered wooden wheel suffers the endless attack of the white foamed eager mill-race.

I move further into the wood, following a sheep track upwards towards the hilltop. Lost in my delicious reverie I have almost forgotten my companions, when suddenly through the bushes I hear a murmur of voices. I stand quite still, and listen. The glow of happiness begins to drain from me before I am certain that it is Michael and Dilys that I can hear. Two voices that are intimate, that have come to some understanding. They draw me on like a spy who creeps up to see and remain unseen. They disturb me into new forms of shame and disgust. Dilys lies on the grass and Michael lies at her side, his hand lying on her breast. As I watch, Dilys lifts a hand to stroke his hair and Michael leans down to kiss her, his body weighing against hers. I tremble with hatred and disgust. My best friend and the girl whom I respected and adored. For the first time in my life I feel the hatred that can kill.

When I turn away I no longer care whether they become aware of my presence, or whether she sits up suddenly, smoothing her hair with her hands to ask him did he hear someone approach. All I know is that I am unbearably unhappy and wretchedly betrayed by one whom I considered my most admirable friend and a girl whom I believed I loved: the two who stood between me and complete isolation. Now I know as certainly as if I were already dead that I am for ever alone.

In my agony, I lose all count of time, and when at last I return to our rendezvous on the wooden bridge near the café-farm house, everyone has reappeared, and Michael is the first to ask, "Where on earth have you been all this time?" How is it possible for them all not to observe the change that has taken place in me? Is my suffering not visible? I myself, while the others are talking, cannot help looking at Dilys and Michael; looking for some traces of their sin, some evidence of their guilt. How could they ever be the same again? And yet they seem no different. They laugh like everyone else, and for the same reasons.

As I drew her head down to mine, said Michael, my fingers buried in her silky, yellow hair, I knew, as I studied with pleasure her beautiful and desirable face, that she looked at me with a puzzled curiosity, and her eyes seemed to be staring with frank inquiśitiveness even when our lips were pressed together, as though, if she looked long enough, whatever my lips were saying she would find some signal of my secret on my face. Holding her body in my arms, I was swept with the heresy of the five senses as I thought surely in this shapely girl lies ultimate bliss. She drew away from me suddenly as if she had heard someone approaching, beginning to talk rapidly but unsteadily, and she would not allow me to kiss her again. Apart from her, to my great relief, the spell was broken and I was able to regard her dispassionately.

She would never be my Galatea.[48] In spite of her beauty and attractiveness the horizon of her mind was as limited and as rigid as the polished wooden rail that hemmed in the deacon's dais in her father's chapel. As I listened to her trivial chatter, I knew that in a few years time she would marry some chartered accountant, sing the usual hymns in Chapel on Sundays, and on most mornings meet her married friends for morning coffee at Ronnie's or the Kadomah.

As for me, I need the time to lay the foundations of my plans and to mature. In years to come perhaps, I shall find a beautiful eager girl to whom my purposes will become the breath of living. But not yet.

The meantime belongs to discipline, to preparation for my tasks. I shall dedicate myself to the country whose beauties about me I always linger over now, with loyal eyes. And to people like Iorwerth who among us all is its most direct heir. In reality he is a potent symbol, because with all his naïve innocence, he represents the soul of Wales for me. He must be saved from the new Nineveh that skirts the innocent sands. He must not be among the crowd I once saw in a dream, streaming into Llanelw on the eve of its destruction, in pursuit of green money rolling. As they entered the city they were consumed in a green fire. It is for you, my friend, and for your unborn children and their children after them, I shall work, and, if need be, die.

When we paused at the summit of the hill on our way home, said Albie, and I looked back to see our grassy path lose itself among the trees below us, where the river and the mill and the farmhouse lay hidden, all I had left to say to myself was, "For God's sake, will you never learn? Will you never learn?"

After tea, as we separated to find our hiding places, I tried to go in the same direction as Michael, thinking perhaps that at last my chance had come for private talk with him, the long chat alongside a river that I had been hoping for. But his mind was already fixed on Dilys Maurice. She was never a girl I liked and in any case, it's rather unfair on Iorwerth. I don't know whether they had any previous understanding, of course, but she dawdled until we had caught her up and then Michael turned to me and said:

"Look, Albie. Ann's over there, waiting for you. Over there, by the ruined mill. Go on, old chap. Don't keep a lady waiting."

"Yes, but listen, Michael . . . ."

"Dilys!" He had already begun to walk in her direction. "Dilys! There's something I wanted to tell you . . . ."

And she stood, waiting to weclome him. I went back slowly in Ann's direction. Together we walked without talking along the river bank. I had absolutely nothing to say to her, but she kept looking as if I was about to empty the entire contents of my mind at her feet any minute. Her mouth was fixed in a small expectant smile. But I was determined to say nothing. Here in the neutral quiet of the countryside she walked at my side as the representative of my enemies, like a jailer in an open prison. She watched me on behalf of Mr Bell and the office, and the electric clock, on behalf of Cambrian Avenue in particular and Llanelw in general, so that I could not escape, no not even for one afternoon. This valley and hill were, anyway, no escape. From here all roads led back to Llanelw.

"Albie." Ann spoke at last, in an extra-sweet voice, "Albie. Do you still hear from Frida Langan? You used to, didn't you?"

"No." I tried to sound discouraging.

"She was an odd girl, wasn't she?"

"Suppose so, in a way."

"Michael told me once that she had a sort of influence over you." Her effort to sound kind was unbearable. "A spell, he said."

"Did he?" I could hear Michael's patronizing voice at it, expounding my failure, a light topic of conversation for anyone who cared to listen. But what does he or anyone else know of my bitter experience? I could have killed Frida for her indifference and yet I longed for her and I still dream of her.

"Albie," Ann went on talking. "You know if I were you, I wouldn't go telling Michael everything. I'm not trying to say that he's untrustworthy or anything like that. He wouldn't deliberately try to hurt you I know. But really you know, deep down, he's a very cold person. He treats people as if they were all the same, all objects, all . . . oh, I don't know how to put it. I'm not clever. But you understand what I mean."

I nodded and in a moment she had got what she wanted. We were both flowing with talk as fast as the river flowed with water, and I was busy trying to demonstrate how I had most things under control and how well satisfied I was with my world. And eventually, of course, there was nothing for it but to take her in my arms and to start talking about love. I dropped like a witless fly into the web. How shall I ever get out?

From the top of the hill we saw the sun setting in the west behind the unchanging mountains; an unusually beautiful sunset, but it brought no solace to my despondent heart. Michael and Les were discussing the latest crisis.

"The sooner the better," I said savagely.

"What?" They had not been aware that I was listening.

"War," I said. "It's got to come. There's no avoiding it. So, I say, the sooner the better. Liberty and all that, they have to be fought for. That's the only hope for progress."

"Good old Albie!" Michael was laughing. I could have hit

him. He had no right to laugh at me. What I was saying was true.

"None of this freedom for Wales nonsense," I said, "I mean real freedom. For the workers, for all the oppressed classes. For every individual. If you want liberty you've got to fight for it. And you've got to fight to keep it."

"Oh, Albie!" Ann said this in such a reproachful tone that everyone started laughing. But I still tried to be serious.

"For the workers," I said, "the ordinary people of every country . . . ."

But before I could finish the sentence, Les had begun to sing the Red Flag in his funny squeaky voice. I had to hit him or laugh. I laughed. Oh, what an ass I've been today! Will I mever learn?

As the sun set, said Michael, I was alone for a moment on a step of the ruined tower facing westward. Somewhere in the quiet evening air about me, between me and the voices of my friends going homeward, there was a vision. They were calling me and I could not stop them calling. I stood still enough to hear sheep forty yards away cropping the hill turf, and the individual wings of a flock of migrating starlings beating high up in the coloured air. I waited, but perhaps not long enough. They were calling me. I waited no longer, but yet as I ran on to join the others, I knew it would come again.

I saw the bus, said Albie, generating its own light, moving like an electric toy along the narrow undulating road. I remember thinking at the time of the driver, a man like my father, gripping the big wheel tightly with both hands, thinking of his supper and pressing down his hunger by pressing his right foot harder on the accelerator. Just like my father! Anyway the bus went down out of sight into the hollow, and so it passed out of my mind. I was in no mood for singing with the others. Ann kept nudging me to join in and I noticed she kept on nudging Iorwerth, too. At the wheel, Michael sang loudly enough, in spite of the difficulties we had had starting the old car, pushing it up one incline in the road to the other.

The great bus came suddenly into view, a roaring monster with its wicked headlamps pointing straight at us. Michael failed to slow down the car and to avoid the oncoming bus he drove into the wide ditch on our left. The car lurched on for a while on one side, but before the girls had had a chance to scream, it turned over and emptied us all into the hedge.

Mercifully, said Iorwerth, in spite of the wreck in which the car was, none of us was really hurt, except Michael. His left cheek and the backs of his hands were split open by splinters of the windscreen glass. Albie and Les dragged him out of the car. He stood, dazed, in the middle of the road, his hand on his cheek. Dilys was the first to collect her wits and to start thinking of a light and bandages and such things. The bus had gone on, unaware of our fate, but in a few minutes another bus came from our direction and in its dazzling lights we saw all the blood over Michael's face and arms. Dilys was again in full command. She behaved as if her whole life had been a rigorous training for this one occasion. She found material for bandages and attended to Michael's wounds, telling everyone, including the disapproving bus-driver, exactly what to do. She found out the whereabouts of the nearest doctor's surgery. Les of course did his best, but since his spectacles had been smashed he could do but little. When I had recovered from the shock of seeing so much blood, and struggled not to be sick on the bumpy journey down to the village, I was not displeased with my own behaviour. I began to wonder what message the incident had for me. Was it even possible for me to become a doctor? In those few seconds of crises, had I found a new vocation?

Michael lay on the couch in the doctor's surgery, said Albie, I sat by his head and Dilys Maurice sat on the other side. He kept trying to say something, but we told him not to talk. I realized this was Fate. Somewhere all over the world, from one second to another a heart stops beating, somewhere a man is killed. We are like ants. I want to say to Michael, doesn't this prove to you, Michael, that we are like ants with the hob-nailed boot of Fate always hovering just above our heads as we crawl over the ant-heap of History? All we need then is strength to face the guns of chance here at home or, when the war comes, on another continent. But all I say to him is, don't try to talk.

What I tried to say, said Michael, was to tell them to go home. All of them could go home, each his own way. This was the parting of our ways. I am the only one who needs to lie still on the couch under the glaring light, waiting for the doctor to stitch the wound in my cheek. Alone one learns best to wait in uncomplaining patience. Comrades, we no longer have anything at all to do with each other. Or at least you have nothing further to do with me. I prefer to ponder my first encounter with the thing called Fate alone. I want to believe that I belong to the few among men who are chosen to battle with Fate and I can believe this better when I am alone. I want to welcome this accident as the first fall in a long wrestle. What I'm trying to say, said Michael, is, go home now. I'm better alone.

When I get home, said Iorwerth, the first thing I shall do is to run upstairs to my father's bedroom. I shall speak out clearly and I shall say, father, father, I think life is cruel. When you were young, like I am, how was it with you? And now, my father, in your sick bed and the shadow of Death at the door, what is the purpose of living? What does life mean? I want my life to mean something, but have we any freedom at all, except the freedom to pretend to take death as a free choice, or to choose to be resigned to what in any case is outside our power? My father, I am coming home to be with you. I shall never be far away from you again as long as we live. So you must be ready, when I come, to answer my questions.

From a hilltop, I have seen night advance from the east across the face of the earth like the shadow of God, neutralizing contours, making hill and valley, town and country one. When it reaches the western sea its movement quickens and finally blots out the horizon. The earth, bearing continents and seas, shows another hemisphere the sun, and another the outer darkness.

Afterword

"I was brought up in a broad valley in one of the four corners of Wales." From the very beginning, *A Toy Epic* puts itself firmly on the Welsh map. Indeed it fills out that map, by reaffirming the Welshness of a part of Wales that tends to be overlooked whenever the Welsh construct a mental image of their country. The other three corners leap instantly to mind, at least in the form of the outdated stereotypes by which many continue to take their national bearings. The industrialised proletarian South, the rural West, the craggy cultural fastness of the North-West are familiar fixed points of reference. But the North-East of Wales has never captured the public, or the literary imagination. It remains an unknown quantity, an unexplored locality the character of whose Welshness seems to be undecided, even problematic. As such it is a region eminently available for use by a writer who wants to dispense with stereotypes in order to discover and develop more accurate views of the Welsh scene.

And of course it goes without saying that Emyr Humphreys was himself born and raised in this neglected corner. There is indeed a good, close fit between the fictional landscape of *A Toy Epic*, spreading from secluded inland valley down to the brash seaside holiday resort of Llanelw, and the actual geography of the novelist's home patch, which extended from inland, upland Trelawnyd to coastal Rhyl and Prestatyn. There is also no doubt an intimate, if intricate relationship betwen the growing pains suffered by Michael and his friends and Emy Humphreys's own experiences of growing up. But if *A Toy Epic* is therefore partly a sympathetic study of the milieu that originally made him, it is also in part a record of what he subsequently made of that milieu, in the light of the fire lit by Saunders Lewis and his nationalist companions at Penyberth, Llŷn, in 1936.[49]

Emyr Humphreys's imagination was kindled by that fire. He was a non-Welsh-speaking sixth-former in Rhyl County School at the time, and just beginning to be excited by what Saunders Lewis had written in English about eighteenth-century Welsh literature. This discovery of a rich Welsh culture which had hitherto been concealed from him, took on a sharply political significance following the burning by Plaid Cymru members of a training school to teach aerial bombing, which an imperious London government had insisted on establishing in the Llŷn peninsula in spite of virtually unanimous Wales-wide opposition. For Emyr Humphreys the fire highlighted Wales's colonial status. Thereafter he could not fail to see the signs of socio-political subservience wherever he looked, and *A Toy Epic* is a re-reading of his own early background in these revealing terms. In particular it shows how pitifully common was the experience of culture-shame, a state of mind in which the Welsh language came to be regarded as a badge of social inferiority. In their different yet related ways both the maid Mary and Michael's mother contrive to anglicise the boy pretty thoroughly. As for Albie, well his full name, Albert Jones, shows him to be a strange cultural hybrid — his commonplace Welsh surname being preceded and dignified by the name of imperial Victoria's beloved spouse. Morover the 'Cambrian Avenue' in which his council-house is situated is a comically grandiose Victorian street-name redolent of English attempts to add a patronisingly Latinate glamour and a patina of antiquity to the humble Welsh word 'Cymru'. His simple, good-natured father Dick is a closet Welsh speaker, happy to use the familiar language on the sly, as if indulging in a forbidden vice, when Iorwerth comes to stay. But his status-conscious mother, no doubt remembering the time she spent 'in service' as a skivvy, is determined that Albie shan't be, like her, a member of the Welsh-speaking under-class. The pity of it is that the mother's socially induced culture-shame is changed into a disabling condition of cultural deprivation and historical ignorance in the case of her son, who simply doesn't know where on earth he is.

It was Saunders Lewis who, through his written work and his public actions, saved the young Emyr Humphreys from a similar fate. Lewis enabled him to put the Trelawnyd-Rhyl area on the

map by making him see it as one of the "four corners of Wales."
Emyr Humphreys was able to get his bearings by seeing his own
locality in relation to the rest of Wales and by understanding it in
terms of Welsh history. In the process he discovered that his
native Flintshire had already produced two outstanding Welsh
novelists in Daniel Owen[50] and E. Tegla Davies, and that
discovery was very important to his own development as a
writer. As can be inferred from *A Toy Epic*, Emyr Humphreys
was from the beginning very interested in the experimental
fictional techniques of modernist writers like Joyce, Lawrence,
Woolf and Faulkner. But he also identified with what he came to
term the "North Wales school of writers." Prominent among
them was the great fiction writer Kate Roberts, who, although
she was a native of Caernarfonshire in the North-West corner of
Wales, spent the last years of her long life, until her death in
1985, living and writing in Emyr Humphreys's North-East
corner of the country. In the essay on 'The Welsh Novel' that he
published in *Lleufer* a few years after *A Toy Epic* appeared,
Emyr Humphreys emphasised that in North Wales a deeply
traditional peasant culture had modulated by the end of the
nineteenth-century into a conservative middle-class way of life
with the chapels at its centre. This ethos produced novels of high
moral seriousness that, after the fashion of Bunyan's *Pilgrim's
Progress* and William Williams's eighteenth-century poem of
spiritual conversion, *Theomemphus*, examined the frequently
tormented condition of the individual soul.[51] It can easily be seen
that *A Toy Epic* is itself a novel that translates this tradition into
modern, largely secular, terms, as it traces the soul-searching
and soul-making psychological development of three young
men, each of whom undergoes some kind of conversion
experience, and each of whom unconsciously (or consciously in
Iorwerth's case) patterns his life on the religious model, thinking
in terms of a 'vocation', a 'destiny' and so on.

In that same *Lleufer* article Emyr Humphreys also contrasted
the North-Wales novels with the English-language novels
associated with another corner of Wales, namely the South-East.
There the new cosmopolitan society of the industrial valleys
produced, from the thirties onwards, a colourfully picaresque
and panoramic fiction suited to the varied and rapidly changing

world the writers knew. Appreciative though he is of the verve and brio of their work, Emyr Humphreys has always had reservations about their achievement. They seem to him to be dissipating their talents in a form of verbal exhibitionism that is not infrequently calculated to catch the ear of the English. "In this respect," he once laughingly observed, "I thank God that I was born a North-Walian and I don't have the golden endless eloquence of the South Walians, so that being economical comes natural! In my writing I try to use as few words as possible, because this is one way of partially reflecting the great glories of the epigrammatically terse Welsh poetic tradition, as opposed to the oral tradition which lies behind the South Wales style, where the flourishing of many words is considered to be the acme of 'the bard'." The concise yet lyrical style of writing in *A Toy Epic*, upon which many reviewers commented very favourably when the novel first appeared, was partly a style deliberately adopted by the author in conscious opposition to the flamboyant manner of writers from the South-East corner of Wales, which to the ignorant outside world had come to seem quintessentially Welsh. An alternative, corrective, definition of 'Welshness' is therefore implicit in the very style, as well as in the subject-matter of *A Toy Epic*.

One corner of Wales remains to be mentioned, and that is the South-West, This is the region diametrically opposite on the map to the North-East in which *A Toy Epic* is set, and a similarly oblique relationship exists between the novel and that other Welsh classic of boyhood and adolescence, Dylan Thomas's *Portrait of the Artist as a Young Dog*, which for the most part is set in the author's home town of Swansea. The *Portrait* is very much a charmingly provincial work that sets out to capture the somewhat naïve flavour of life in a part of Wales regarded as being a remote and backward corner of a London-orientated Britain. In that respect, the contrast with *A Toy Epic*, which is resolutely Welsh in its terms of reference, could not be more marked. But what the two works have in common is the highly charged atmosphere of the period in which they are both set — the inter-war period of the twenties and thirties. Both works, having been written either during or after the Second World War, are salvage operations mounted by the imagination, attempts to reclaim a lost personal and social world, and this process of historical recovery gives point and lends poignancy to both narratives. But here again they meet only to differ, with the *Portrait* being keyed to the fantasies of private life, while in *A Toy Epic* personal affairs are ultimately inseparable from the social problems, economic difficulties, class tensions, spritual crises and political ideologies of a whole society at a clearly given point in its history.

It is in particular seen, with the benefit of hindsight, to be a society over which the coming war casts an ever darkening shadow. The Grammar School days of the three boys in *A Toy Epic* begin with a mention of the 'faded sepia' photograph on the wall of pupils killed in the '14-'18 war, "boys in uniform, with sad suprised faces"; and they end with the news of the young airman Jac Owen's death and with newspaper reports of troops massing for an armed offensive. The book constantly gives the impression of lives helpless before the might of historical forces, an impression that is ironically confirmed by Michael's innocently confident belief that he will be able to fight the war on his own terms. Fate bears down on the boys as remorselessly as the bus which heedlessly pushes Michael's car into the ditch at the novel's close. There are also eerie symmetries in the narrative that suggest confinement and hint at the inescapable. The car's collision with the bus is, for example, anticipated very early in the novel when Albie's father comes home one day shaken by the near-miss he has had with a car that came racing towards his bus.

The war is not only, however, a catastrophe visited from without upon a peaceful society. It is in part a climactic expression of the tension and violence that is intermittently felt to inhere in that society. It is, for instance, noticeable that soldiers are sent to break up the 1926 strike in which Albie's father is involved and Iorwerth's visit, just before the war, to the bigoted barber who wants to line all nationalists up against the wall and shoot them leads us to a prophetically nightmarish vision of the violently intolerant little man "swollen into the shape of a Monster of Unreason able to crush whole streets of cities under his blind merciless boot." Moreover, Iorwerth's timid life has its own fearful symmetry. As he leaves the barber's shop his apprehensive eye notices the confectionery shop where the "shining steel arms" of the sweet-making machine, "twist the stiff toffee." It reminds us of the gaily rattling, chattering hay-chaffer which tore off and chewed up one of Iorwerth's fingers in the barn when he was a little boy.

II

"I was brought up in a broad valley in one of the four corners of Wales. On fine days from my bedroom window I saw the sea curve under the mountains in the bottom right-hand corner of the window-frame." The short outward journey from secluded inland community to sophisticated seaside resort takes on considerable significance in another Emyr Humphreys novel, *Flesh and Blood*, but it most clearly serves as a *rite de passage* in *A Toy Epic*. Iorwerth and Michael step on board the bus that carries them to the entrance scholarship exam in Llanelw. "I stand alone and put my hand out proudly to the big-nosed bus," says Iorwerth. "Obediently it stops." Up until then the bus has come to the village and gone in its own mysterious time, just as the boys have been usually subject to events rather than directing them. For them to stop the bus is therefore to take a big step forward into a different relationship with the world.

The episode clearly marks a new stage in the development of Michael and Iorwerth, and the novel is itself of course no more than a sequence of such stages in the growth to maturity of the three boys. In a biological sense that process is as simply pre-determined and predictable as Iorwerth's "calf-like" growth "from the semi-twilight of the darkened kitchen to the sharp light of the empty front garden." Indeed the progress of the boys is repeatedly associated with the imagery of light and dark. But as the novel proceeds, this imagery is increasingly used to qualify, rather than endorse, the initial impression that young humans grow as simply as young calves, or as a "leaf opens like a baby's fist and grows towards the sun."

"As I ran from the shade of the entry into the May sunshine trapped in our small square back garden, said Albie, Mrs

Blackwell came hurrying up the entry, her shoes untied, her coat open, and out of breath." The passage reminds us of Iorwerth's movement from kitchen twilight to garden sunlight, and so makes us note the decisive influence that the different social environments, of ninety-acre farm and cramped council-house estate, have on the development of the boys' contrasting personalities. Nevertheless the universal characteristics of the several inescapable phases of physical and mental development, from the first sensuous apprehension of the world in infancy ("crumbs lying white and edible near me on the floor") to the complicated narcissism of adolescence, are sensitively registered in *A Toy Epic*. Also carefully traced is the way in which a sense of selfhood evolves, partly through an inner dynamic and partly through the contribution of external and environmental factors. Initially it is the relationship with parents and neighbourhood that matters, then later the choice of friends and the general influence of one's peer-group proves decisive. But always and throughout the process of becoming a person is fraught with difficulties, and *A Toy Epic* implies that all three boys end up with personalities that are less than complete, owing to stunted emotional growth and arrested development.

Albie is the one who is most clearly seen to suffer, riddled as he is with anxieties that are the product of his basic social insecurity. Rock solid though his parents' genuinely unconditional love for him may be, it is still undermined by Albie's early, permanently unsettling intuition that family life is at the mercy of some remote, capricious power — the "them" his father defers to and grumbles about, to whom his father owes the borrowed authority of his peaked cap, and with whom the bus-driver comes into bloody conflict only to be put in his place even by his own unsympathetic wife. One of the most powerful scenes in the novel is the one where a pitifully bewildered Albie is dragged by the hand into the suffocating middle of a crowd of strikers. Mounting panic causes him to faint. Traumatised by the primitive agony of self-annihilation which is at the heart of such experiences, he constructs a false self as a defence against a threateningly unpredictable environment. He becomes compliant in order not to be exposed and conspicuously conforms to parental and institutional expectations. He cultivates obedience, affects composure, and becomes precociously adult, at the expense of feelings within him which are never allowed to contribute, in the normal way, towards the process of gradual maturation. It is these un-integrated feelings that are brought disastrously into play by his relationship with Frida during what, for Albie, is bound to be an exceptionally confusing adolescence.

It is clear, then, that an environmental deficiency which is specifically social in character, has an intimate effect on Albie's development. Accordingly his opening description of his surroundings eventually takes on an ominous double significance: "At three-and-a-half I played in the cul-de-sac, and mumbers 13,14,15,16,17 and 18 stood on guard about me, watching me with square indifferent eyes." The phrase "stood on guard about me" allows initially for the possibility of the houses being Albie's protective guardians: but his obsessive later use, in adolescence, of prison-imagery, alerts us to the likelihood that these houses are seen as warders who had already imprisoned his tender embryonic ego.

In Albie's young eyes his house is merely a number virtually indistinguishable from other numbers, but Iorwerth Hughes is known from the beginning in his neighbourhood as "Iorwerth Maesgwyn." The family farm is indeed central to his identity, and therein perhaps lies his problem. Iorwerth's naturally timorous character shrinks from any robust, educative contact with the world beyond Maesgwyn where his father and mother are veritable icons of dependability, sitting one each side of the fire in winter "like two figures on a Christmas card." But even on the farm he is not fully protected from the world's malice, and his innocent wish to share the "ecstasy" of the chaffing machine results in a physical maiming which also scars him mentally for life. Iorwerth accordingly develops an imagination for disaster, and a dread, in the Kierkegaardian sense, of violence — that is it both fascinates and appalls him.

On occasions his neurosis endows him with visionary powers. He it is who foresees the carnage to come, when he imagines Jac Owen's body floating "on the water like a dead fish." And it is he who gains a vision of the casual brutality of modern town life, in the form of an imagined glimpse of a boy cyclist caught on the turn by a car and catapulted acrobatically through the air into another car. Prone always to identify with the victims of violence, Iorwerth puts himself in the dying boy's place: "I drown, I swirl like seaweed in my own thick red blood." The sensation of being overwhelmed by a deluge comes to each of the three boys at some point in their young lives and is expressive of a whole period's vague but persistent sense of impending catastrophe. But the threat of drowning is particularly real to Iorwerth, to whom life on the farm is like being brought up "at the headquarters of Noah, in an anchored ark."

His fearful mind takes refuge in reassuringly familiar religious beliefs and in early adolescence he seeks the sanctuary of a parentally approved 'vocation.' Like Albie he develops a false self in order to cope with everything that is threatening both in the external world and in the internal world of his own turbulent feelings. Consequently his genuine capacity for goodness becomes distorted into a nervously censorious priggishness. However, whereas Albie suffers from an instability in his social surroundings, Iorwerth suffers instead from an excessive stability in his over-protective family background. Unfortunately this background does not fail him or frustrate him, as in a sense he actually needs it to, if he is to grow less totally trusting of it and therefore less totally dependent upon it. He is never led on to the perception that a relatively (rather than an absolutely) dependable family circle and a relatively (rather than a totally) undependable wider world are both part of a single indivisible continuum of normal human experience, Consequently he is quite unable to handle those shocks and disappointments that eventually come close to "home", like his father's terminal illness and his girlfriend Dilys's flirtation with his best friend Michael.

As for Michael, he has problems of his own, although it is perhaps his distinctive self-possession that first attracts attention. His privileged social background provides him with an inbuilt confidence, and he is on easy terms with authority because he could, after all, "watch the parson in his white and distant surplice, with the inward knowledge that I would sit on his knee and even put my finger inside his hard gleaming collar." Yet while he relished the advantages that come with social superiority he also successfully rebels against his strict moral background without ever really losing his father's favour. In the village school Wil Ifor, the biggest troublemaker, becomes his friend, and then later he loves to skive off from the county school in the company of the bullying delinquent, Jac Owen. He offends his father repeatedly and quarrels with him outright over matters of faith. But having in these ways emphatically established his independence (as Iorwerth and Albie clearly fail to do) he is reconciled to his father in his late teens on terms that promise to be solid and lasting.

In all these respects Michael's development would seem to be admirably normal and successful, so in what way exactly can his personality, in its final form, be said to be deficient? It is Albie's unappreciated girlfriend Ann who spells it out, in characteristically forthright fashion, at the very end of the novel: "really you know, deep down, he's a very cold person. He treats people as if they were all the same, all objects. Oh! I don't know how to put it. I'm not clever." "Clever" psychologists have in fact coined a term to describe personalities of Michael's sort. They call them 'schizoid' and draw attention to the difficulties such people have in experiencing normal, humanly appropriate emotions. They are essentially detached and isolated individuals, and tend to regard others as their intellectual inferiors, fit only for exploitative manipulation. Indeed, a passion for ideas, accompanied by an arrogant pride in intellect, tends to be a schizoid characteristic and Michael's obsession, towards the end of the novel, with the ideology of nationalism conforms precisely to type. So does his earlier sense of his own hollowness and his conviction that life is nothing but a succession of roles and masks.

A schizoid disorder is generally supposed to originate in a disturbance in a child's relationship with its mother, and it is noticeable that Michael's mother is both a cooler and an appreciably weaker presence in the novel than are the mothers of the other two boys. Here again there are social factors to be considered. Hyper-anxious as she is about observing the manners of the English middle-class, Michael's "well-bred" mother is always respectably reserved, avoids any display of maternal feelings, and employs a maid to look after the children.

"In the garden," Michael suggestively remarks, "my mother always wore gloves": there is similarly no flesh-warmth and no intimate sense of touch in her relationships with her children. Even her anger is cold, as Michael indicates when he recalls what happened on the horrifying occasion in his early boyhood when she discovered that he had mis-spent most of the money she had entrusted to his care: "I knew that my father was not in the house and my mother disliked scenes."

As the three boys grow up together, each chooses one of the others as his model of perfection, believing his friend to be possessed of wonderful strength precisely where he secretly feels himself to be weakest. So they are joined together in a neurotically intimate circle of elective friendship, with Albie admiring Michael's charming self-possession, Michael covertly envious of Iorwerth's warmth and "goodness", and Iorwerth attracted to Albie's worldly sophistication. Moreover each one develops a "crush" on the other, as the awakening sexuality of early adolescence gives an intensely physical aspect to these complex inter-relationships. And since these friendships are the outgrowth and confirmation of established features of the boys' innermost personalities, then they are the template of all their later relationships. So, for instance, Albie's infatuation with the coolly self-confident Frida replicates his earlier fascination with Michael. And following the end of his affair with Frida it is to Michael that Albie returns, wishing that Ann and the others were not there so that he could discuss his problems with the friend who is also, in a sense, his *alter ego*.

A Toy Epic therefore shows us human growth under a complex double aspect. On the one hand it shows us the remarkable distance that is covered in a relatively short space of time, as infants grow up, and as boys move from the restricted world of childhood into the immense world of adult experience — from the valley to Llanelw, and beyond to Chester, to Oxford, and in the direction of an ominously sensed Europe. On the other hand it shows us how the pattern and pace of personal growth is prescribed at a very early stage by one's primary relationship with one's parents and one's immediate environment: "I was brought up in a broad valley. . . . My name is Michael." The whole history of Michael's identity can indeed be read in that single opening statement.

And since the main subject of *A Toy Epic* is the mysterious process of constant change that constitutes the inner dynamic of human personality, it is appropriate that one of the books studied by the boys at County School should be Ovid's *Metamorphoses*. In the form of marvellously baroque myths of fabulous transformations, that book provides insights into the endless fluidity of the passional life that lies at the very heart of human existence. Since it deals primarily with sexual psychology, and with what Ovid calls "the strange mutations of love", his book has a particular applicability to adolescence. Indeed Michael's adolescent imagination inhabits a troubling world that is similar both to Ovid's and to that of the Welsh *Mabinogion*:[52] "I know that I am on the threshold of a world governed by inscrutable forces and in the deepest forest of this new continent lies a bright fountain, the source of beauty and horror, of a new joy and a new sadness, of perpetual unrest." Metamorphosis is not, however, an experience confined to adolescence, and insofar as it implies a perception of both personal and communal life as involving endless change it is perhaps the figure that governs the whole of *A Toy Epic*.

III

"So Jac Owen became an unlikely Icarus", thinks Iorwerth, marvelling at the way the school bully has metamorphosed into an airforce hero. People do, after all, change with changing circumstances, and *A Toy Epic* is very much a novel not only about changing selves but about a changed and changing world. A startled and incredulous Albie notices the stealthy appearance of houses "in the very spaces where the grey donkeys from the sea-shore ate thistles and nettles during our first years at school." But whereas Albie can hardly believe his eyes, Iorwerth can, from an early age, feel change in his very bones, just as the painful joints of a rheumatic can feel every change in the weather. Because, in spite of his unshakeable family background, Iorwerth is clearly the child of a disappearing culture —

the rural, Welsh-speaking, chapel-based way of life that is in rapid decline throughout the time he is growing up. And although he attempts to carry on the Nonconformist tradition, he is doomed to fail, because a great culture-shift has denied him the very resources that are needed to combat social change. In this context, too, his maiming seems to be symbolically appropriate.

The novel provides us with several powerful images of Iorwerth's shortcomings in his capacity as heir to a culture. When he carries food out to his father, who is "wielding his bill-hook with ardent pleasure" as he practises the ancient skilled craft of hedging, the delicate little boy is "well wrapped up" against the cold. Much later, during his father's illness, Iorwerth takes over the running of the farm, only to be over-run by the work. He lacks the authority needed to keep the labourer Jacob Tŷ Draw under control by cutting short the tales he endlessly spins and getting him and Llew back to the fields. Iorwerth just isn't up to the game his father is so accustomed to playing.

Moreover in the recent past a toper like Jacob would never have been allowed near the farm. But now "experienced hands are very hard to get. The young men are turning their backs on the land, going off to work in the seaside resorts or the big towns in England." Nor are they entirely to blame, as the rural under-class live in a state of chronic poverty such as the town proletariat can scarcely even imagine. Iorwerth remembers the air of hopelessness that seemed to seep out of the very walls of Wil Ifor's house. That is why he cannot understand why Albie should complain about the hardship of the urban working-class.

Albie's father, who is also Wil Ifor's uncle Dic, was one of those who left the country in search of better conditions, and so Albie too is the child of social change, a child of the working-class. He is also the means by which his parents hope to bring about a further change in the family's social condition. Education is the ladder of social advancement, and Albie's mother "sees in her vision a divine system of education, select me for praise and distinction out of a welter of side streets and council houses and save me from becoming an errand boy and cycling down blind alleys." It is significant that the terms used here are a secularised version of the old religious language. The

Calvinistic culture from which Albie's family no doubt originally came, had, it will be remembered, traditionally employed a highly sophisticiated theological terminology of personal election and salvation through grace.

But in the secularised Welsh world of the thirties the making of the soul was becoming more the work of the school than of the chapel. No wonder that when he boards the bus bound for County School, Iorwerth is attired like a little latter-day pilgrim. "I have a satchel on my back which contains my lunch, a ruler, pencils, a pen and a bottle of ink." Already the education system has divided the local community and thereby destroyed it. It has promoted and transported Michael and Iorwerth to a distant County School and left a sulky Wil Ifor and other "failures" to rot in the village. It is against this aspect of his schooling that Albie, for so long the anxious conformist, eventually reacts. Under the guidance of Marxism he tries, at least in imagination, to re-establish a sense of common cause, or class solidarity, with the "errand boy" from whom his mother was so anxious to separate him. Sadly he ends up cycling down a "blind alley" himself — the victim of the system which he had confusedly tried to challenge; destroyed by the conflict between conformist and rebel in his own divided personality. Frida is cruelly right when she taunts him with the barbed accusation that he is a working-class conservative and a petit-bourgeois proletarian.

Iorwerth also falls victim to the system, but in a different way. To Iorwerth's bewilderment, the supervisor smirks when the boy asks to be allowed to sit the entrance scholarship paper in his native Welsh. The country lad is as yet too naïve to realise that the state educational system is the instrument deliberately used by the English government since the end of the nineteenth-century to anglicise the whole culture of the country — with the active collaboration of Welsh people who had been made ashamed of their supposed social backwardness. "Bechgyn", says the mocking word over the boys' entrance to Llanrhos County School. It means "boys" but could be better translated by a sentence echoing the insciption over the gates of Dante's hell: "Abandon hope all ye Welsh speakers who enter here." Once he is alerted to his danger, Iorwerth, like Albie, tries to protect himself from the worst influence of the school regime. As an alternative, though, he has only the superannuated culture of the chapel upon which to call, and as the preacher's sermon on the Deluge most clearly shows, it has deteriorated into a culture that appeals to those who feel they have been defeated by History.

"We are enchanted, transfigured", says Iorwerth of the experience of listening to the spiritual histrionics of the preacher famous for his eloquence. They are metamorphosed, and transported to "a world woven by his voice." The sermon is of the type known as a "jeremiad", which prophecies that doom will befall the people because they have left the God of their fathers and gone whoring after strange gods. The preacher likens the condition of Wales and its "diseased twentieth-century culture" to the state of Babylon at the time of Noah, when life in "the cities of the plains" was so decadant and corrupt that God in his wrath sent a Flood to drown the whole earth. But the jeremiad is simultaneously a terrifying and a consoling form of address. Although it threatens, it does so in terms that suggest a remedy is still to be found in a return to the old traditional ways. It allows the deepest fears and anxieties of a bewildered people to surface in apocalyptic visions, yet reassures them that it is the enemy, the powerful oppressor, the rulers of the earth, the unredeemed, who will suffer and that the chosen people will indeed be ultimately saved.

In style, the old preacher's sermon is a throw-back to those of the famous 1904-05 revival, a Wales-wide phenomenon which, as Emyr Humphreys explained in *The Taliesin Tradition*, "can be variously interpreted as the last desperate gesture of a people aware in their subconscious mind that their age-old faith was leaving them, or the first of a series of twentieth-century identity crises". Iorwerth is stirred and comforted by an address which is, in more senses than one, delivered in his own language. After all, hasn't the Bible been to him what tales of schoolboy adventures were to Michael — the book of wonders upon which his starving young imagination eagerly fed? Has he not even consoled himself in school that he was "the Israelite in Babylon"?

Iorwerth is not alone in thinking of Llanelw as a kind of Sodom or Gomorrah — as being one of the latter-day "cities of the plains." The very name of the place is revealing. It may have been based on "Llanelwy", the Welsh name for St Asaph, the cathedral town a few miles from Trelawnyd and Rhyl. But by pointed contrast the word "Llanelw" literally means the "Church of profit", a place-name well suited to the cynically commercialised "Pleasureland" that the coastal resort sets out to be. It offers the boys all the excitements, enticements and entanglements of a restlessly sophisticated, rootless, provinicial town. It packs people together but does not bind them into a community, although it may awaken in some, like Albie, a rudimentary awareness of belonging to a single exploited "class." Iorwerth notices "the washing of various households almost touching each other, one man's wet shirt rubbing against his neighbour's vest." It also easily blinds people to the reality of the world in which they're living: so Iorwerth fails actually to see the accident in which the cyclist is killed because "at the precise moment my eyes were intent on a pyramid of glistening bottles of jam in a grocer's window." Meanwhile the exciting disaster of "a car flying over the precipice" which he had enjoyed as fantasy in the warm darkness of the cinema, is being metamorphosed, behind his back and in "the harsh light of the afternoon", into the real-life disaster of a boy being "knocked . . . through the air against a stationary car by the opposite pavement,"

"From fire and brimstone, from the doomed city, fly!" sings Michael in mock preacherly tones towards the end of the book. But as the final chapter is designed to show, there is no ready escape-route available for any of the boys. When Albie despairingly discovers that for him "all roads led back to Llanelw", he is unwittingly speaking for his friends as well, in spite of Michael's determination to save Iorwerth "from the new Ninevah that skirts the innocent sands. He must not be among the crowd I once saw in a dream, stealing into Llanelw on the eve of its destruction, in pursuit of green money rolling. As they entered the city they were consumed in a green fire." There are echoes here of those sinister places mentioned in Bunyan's *Pilgrim's Progress* — "Vanity Fair" and the "City of Destruction."

Escape by means of retreat into the supposedly idyllic country of the past is what the boys attempt in the last chapter. Their break for freedom is also a search for paradise, but all they find is evidence of the Fall, within them, between them and around them. They attempt to re-enter a supposedly innocent world of childhood — Michael "imitates a child counting out" as the others scatter in the game of hide-and-seek. As he climbs towards the martello tower (a relic of a past war) Iorwerth looks forward to recovering his early valley-perspective on life, believing that "we shall have a wonderful view of the coast." Instead, Les and Albie fall to quarrelling about what features of Llanelw they can see at this distance. "I'm not mistaken, says Albie, I know every stone of the old Sodom only too well." All roads do indeed lead back to Llanelw, and the only hope is to find not a retreat from the town, but a way through it and beyond it.

IV

"I shall dedicate myself to the country whose beauties about me I always linger over most, with loyal eyes. And to people like Iorwerth who, among us all, is its most direct heir. In reality he is a potent symbol, because with all his naïve innocence, he represents the soul of Wales for me." He may do so for Michael, but the author does not encourage us to share that perception. In *A Toy Epic* it is the three boys together who are "a potent symbol of Wales." And they are so by virtue of their different special backgrounds and by virtue of that incompleteness in each of their characters that has already been remarked upon. In their relationships they experience and exemplify the cultural divisions, the language problems and the social tensions that are the sad legacy of recent Welsh history, and which have inhibited the development of a strong and coherent sense of national identity. As the cases of Albie and Iorwerth particularly show, it is only by somehow finding common ground between them that the Welsh language and English-language cultures of Wales can hope to recover from the serious deprivation each suffers through its isolation from the other. Yet as the example of the two boys also shows, communication across a cultural divide is as desperately difficult as it is desperately necessary.

"To him I am strange and foreign," says Iorwerth forlornly of

Albie. Although he is a boy living in a North Wales seaside resort, Albie is clearly a product of the same historical process that brought industrial South Wales into being. His family has moved only the few miles from valley to coast, but in doing so it has undergone the same trauma of passage from one culture to another that countless families from rural West Wales experienced when they journeyed East in search of work, first to the Merthyr district and then to the roaring Rhondda valleys. Like so many of them, Albie has been virtually forced to lose contact with the unique culture sustained for more than fifteen hundred years by the Welsh language. What he has gained in compensation is an embryonic sense of class, as opposed to national, identity. However he has yet to learn that class-consciousness is not the supra-national, trans-cultural phenomenon that his Marxist reading has represented it as being. He needs to communicate with Iorwerth in order to realise exactly what is at issue, at this fateful historical juncture, for a Welshman such as himself. Equally, though, Iorwerth needs to connect with Albie if the culture to which he belongs is to have a place in the modern Wales. Yet to recognise this is also to realise that this was precisely the alliance that failed to form in the thirtes, the period in which the novel is set.

The relationship between Iorwerth and Albie is, therefore, in its modest way, a kind of microcosm of recent Welsh history. It would though, be a mistake to suppose that *A Toy Epic* mirrors only the situation as Emyr Humphreys believed it to be in the thirties. Rather it mirrors in addition the situation in Wales as Emyr Humphreys saw it in the fifties — that is in the period in which the novel was actually completed. This is clear from the *Lleufer* article already referred to. There Humphreys argues there are two cultures in Wales, conservative Welsh-speaking and progressive English-speaking, which he broadly associates with the North and the South of Wales respectively. "The time has come", he goes on, "to call on the Old Wales to save the New Wales and in the process to save itself . . . .Without contact with life in the South, there is a danger that the culture of the North will become a mere fossil. Without roots, and lacking all connection with the traditional North, Glamorgan may well spew all the energy of its valleys into the anonymous mid-

Atlantic . . . .Wales must take advantage of the special relationship existing between the North and the South. Out of this Thesis and Antithesis a Synthesis can be created for the future." It is this "special relationship" that Emyr Humphreys in a way explores via the relationship between Iorwerth and Albie.

It is through Michael, though, that the condition of Wales is most openly addressed in *A Toy Epic* and Emyr Humphreys and Michael evidently have a great deal in common. Both, for instance, experienced a conversion to a nationalist faith at much the same age. They are pretty well agreed too in their analysis of the Welsh problem. Yet it is imperative, when considering Michael, to recall Roland Mathias's perceptive observation that in his work Emyr Humphreys subjects his own convictions to particularly searching critical examination.

Michael's background should be carefully borne in mind. He is raised in an Anglican rectory, and Anglicanism has for several centuries led a kind of double-life in Wales. With the growth of Welsh Nonconformity in the eighteenth and nineteenth centuries, Anglicanism became increasingly regarded as a foreign presence whose privileged status as the state church came under such pressure that eventually the Church in Wales was officially disestablished in 1914. Moreover Anglicanism enthusiastically collaborated with the new, state-controlled education system's programme of anglicisation in Wales. Church schools, such as the one in which Michael and Iorwerth are taught, and for that matter the one in which Emyr Humphreys's own father had been a headmaster, were usually either indifferent or hostile to the native language.

On the other hand, eccentric Anglican clerics had, as Emyr Humphreys emphasises in his interpretation of Welsh history, *The Taliesin Tradition*, been from time to time the unlikely preservers and custodians of Welsh culture, particularly during the "dark ages" of the eighteenth century. And it was precisely the kind of scholarly antiquarian interest in the Welsh past that Michael's father displays that made them such providentially effective benefactors of Welsh culture. So in a sense these two different and conflicting aspects of Welsh Anglicanism could be said to be disputing possession of Michael's young imagination, until the issue is eventually decided by his commitment to nationalism.

Such a "conversion experience" was not uncharacteristic of artists and intellectuals in Wales during the inter-war period — Saunders Lewis himself read English at Liverpool University before the critical state of Wales was brought home to him with the clarifying force of revelation and with the urgency of a call to action. Michael is also typical of the period not only in that his political nationalism derives from a prior cultural concern, but also in that his imagination is fired by a twelfth-century poem by Hywel ap Owain Gwynedd. In other words his passion is not for the Liberal-Nonconformist Wales that Iorwerth represents, nor for the proletarian and proto-socialist Wales to which Albie belongs, but rather for an ancient 'aristocratic' Wales whose golden age was the Middle Ages. The first stirrings of his cultural awakening are felt at Penmon, and this is clearly significant since Penmon was the subject of a famous poem by T. Gwynn Jones, written in the great, intricate *cynghanedd* tradition, that itself stretches back virtually unbroken to the early Middle Ages, and to an even earlier period. The majestic verbal, visual and spiritual culture of the Welsh Middle Ages is itself the subject of this poem, in which T. Gwynn Jones imagines the old Abbey walls resuming their form and former glory — "Rich craft, its portal and door,/ Slender its marble towers;/ Heaven for the weak its hall,/ And holy every chamber."[53]

In addition to being the work of one of the greatest of modern Welsh poets, 'Penmon' is also addressed to one of the greatest of this century's Welsh men-of-letters, W.J. Gruffydd.[54] Therefore in a sense Michael could be said to join the modern fraternity of nationalist artists, scholars and intellectuals when he undergoes his 'Penmon experience.' He participates in their liberating and exhilarating discovery of a Wales whose cultural achievements are far more impressive and historically extensive than most of the Welsh imagine. He thereby realises that it isn't Wales that is 'narrow' but rather his own ignorantly limited conception of his country. But his education isn't complete until he visits the political conference and recalls "the history and significance of the castle." Then his vision grows militant, as he

141

realises that in order to survive not only will Wales have to resist current historical forces, she may also have to mount a counter-attack and take History by storm. This allows him to see how it is at bottom the defeated condition of the Welsh that has made fatalists of Albie and Iorwerth. They cannot believe that they possess the power to influence events. Of course, as has already been noted, by emphasising the inexorable drift towards war the novel has itself to an extent confirmed the two boys' intuition of immediate helplessness. But it clearly repudiates Albie's whimpering, self-pitying cry: "we are like ants with the hob-nailed boot of Fate always hovering just above our heads as we crawl over the ant-heap of History." *A Toy Epic* recognises the long-term relevance of Michael's observation that "History is only made by those who are ready to make it."

"The first lesson to learn," Michael continues, "is to accept the burden of being utterly alone." Emyr Humphreys has himself many times deplored the craven clubability of the Welsh, and has admired the principled and visionary stand of a fearless nonconformist like Saunders Lewis who, as R.S. Thomas has put it, "dared [us] to grow old and bitter as he."[55] Nevertheless in *A Toy Epic* Michael's isolationist stance does give cause for concern, even perhaps for alarm. It is here that the social implications of his "schizoid" character become evident. For one thing, he has no real or realistic sense of solidarity with the very culture he professes to be protecting. His view of Iorwerth as "the soul of Wales" is a sentimental lie, and his contemptuous dismissal of Dilys is the other side of the same false coin: "In spite of her beauty and attractiveness the horizon of her mind was as limited and as rigid as the polished wooden rail that hemmed in the deacon's dais in her father's chapel."

In the second place, Michael's heroic isolationism is presented as being morally suspect. It is tainted by egotism and exhibits megalomaniac tendencies. With his delight in "discipline" and his fantasy of offering strong leadership, Michael is the stuff of which the authoritarian followers of the fascist right were made in the thirties. The cut on the cheek he acquires in the car accident and which he believes is Fate's way of issuing him with a challenge, is curiously reminiscent of the sinister duelling scar that indicated aristocratic young Germans had been 'blooded.'

142

It would be a serious mistake, though, to suppose that by the end of the novel Michael has turned villain. No, he is rather a disturbed and disturbing young man whose impending tragedy is not only a personal but also a national, historical tragedy. He illustrates the fate that can befall the intellectual who tries, in necessarily lonely defiance of his people's historically-induced apathy, to confront them with a challengingly truthful, undeniably accurate image of Wales. And he is surely perceived by the novel as being right in his conviction that only by searching the past can Wales discover the key to its future.

Behind this perception lies a discovery Emyr Humphreys made when the bombing school was burned — the discovery that modern Wales (as represented in *A Toy Epic* by Albie, Iorwerth and Michael) had for too long been prevailed upon to ignore its own history, and was consequently ignorant of its true condition. In *A Toy Epic* the myopic vision of officially sanctioned history is quietly suggested by "the walls of Llanrhos County School" which are "eloquent with its short history." The walls commemorate only Councillors, Aldermen, clergymen, the young men killed in the First World War, and the pupils who have distinguished themselves academically. This is a perfect image of the establishment view of recent Welsh history. By contrast one remembers the stone walls of the old mill visited by the young people at the end of *A Toy Epic*, where "hundreds of initials and names are scrawled over the patches of white-washed plaster." They represent the unrecorded lives and disregarded history of an anonymous people.

The novel does not, however, seek to imply that a single, unchallengable account of the whole of Welsh history remains some day to be written. Instead it allows for the possibility of there being many different, sometimes complementary and occasionally competing, versions of the past as viewed from a Welsh perspective. Michael's father traces the beginnings of modern Wales back (as Emyr Humphreys is himself fond of doing) to late Roman times. On the other hand the charismatic preacher at Iorwerth's chapel can see the time of the Roman occupation only as one of several periods of profane history, as opposed to the sacred centuries of Nonconformist influence in Wales. Iorwerth's father dreams of completing the second volume of his "history of Calvinistic Methodism in the north of the county", a fervent member of his own denomination to the last. These are all rudimentary attempts to fashion a Welsh historiography in the face on the one hand of a vast popular ignorance of the past, and on the other of the temptation to indulge in an anti-historical millenarianism — a favourite recourse of the defeated. So Iorwerth dreams "of my kingdom to come" and even Michael has to beware of a similar temptation.

One of the ways of re-introducing the nation to its own history is through providing it with conscientiously historical but compelling imaginative fictions. Emyr Humphreys has devoted most of his long writing life to doing precisely that. Indeed it can now perhaps be seen that *A Toy Epic* is itself intended to function as at least an aid-memoir for a nation. "The struggle of man against power is the struggle of memory against forgetting" wrote Milan Kundera. In that sense *A Toy Epic* is very much Emyr Humphreys's unforgettable contribution to Wales's continuing struggle for survival.

V

When he reviewed the novel in *The New Statesman* on its first appearance in 1958, Maurice Richardson nervously assured his readers: "There is a little Welsh Nationalism in *A Toy Epic*, but nothing untoward. This is a novel of adolescence." He may have rather missed the point of the work, but he was perceptive when he praised its "contrapuntal form" and appreciated the way it succeeded "in communicating a strong sense of the passage of time and change" during the "nodal period" of adolescence. It would, though, be more true to say that *A Toy Epic* reproduces for us several significantly different experiences of Time. So, for instance, at the end of a frenzied day spent sitting the entrance-scholarship paper in the town County School, Iorwerth returns home at the regular evening milking time on the farm, and has to reacclimatise to his father's slow, deliberate way of doing things: "will I never learn", the boy wonders, "to take time, assured of my memory, skill, and above all, the abundance of time?" Of course he never will learn, because he belongs to a generation which is condemned to live at an altogether different pace. No wonder Michael's new watch thuds on his wrist "like a giant pulse" as he applies his excited mind to the difficult task of answering the Arithmetic paper.

Moreover, a child's sense of time is totally different from an adolescent's. In some of the early sections of *A Toy Epic* several different occasions are unconsciously run together in a small boy's mind to form a single composite scene which is a kind of summation of what "home" means to him. For example in the section in Chapter One when Albie recalls his father coming home for tea, it is clear on reflection that two or more separate occasions have been compressed together to produce the conversation that occurs between his entry and his departure. At the other extreme are those occasions in adolescence when the youngsters begin to contrast their former with their present selves. In the case of Albie this happens at the beginning of Chapter Seven when he blushes at the memory of his earlier infatuation with Michael. Time takes on a completely different aspect therefore for the three as their past grows almost as problematical as their future.

Of course many of the works that deal with childhood employ a narrative form that allows them to explore a complex double-perspective — so that the reader is simultaneously given the child's and the adult's view of events. In *Great Expectations* incidents from the young Pip's childhood are in fact recalled for us by the mature Pip, who is an altogether different, not to say a thoroughly reformed, character. Emyr Humphreys has deliberately denied us this double vision in *A Toy Epic* by making it unclear when exactly, and how, the words in the text are being "spoken". Are they being spoken more or less at the time that the action occurs? They could be, in spite of the frequent use of the past tense. After all, no attempt is ever made in the novel to reproduce the actual thought processes of the characters in a realistic fashion. Instead what is offered is a clearly stylised representation of the states of mind of the different characters, at different ages and on different occasions. Accordingly when the infant Iorwerth "says" that he "followed my mother, going to riddle cinders, sheltering behind her skirt", the words are not meant to be those that actually occurred to his mind. They simply stand for, and speak for, the kind of experience he had, and can therefore be regarded as being continuous with the experience itself. In other words they are the novel's chosen, artificial way of conveying the experiences of a small boy. They are not the thoughts of a later, much older Iorwerth who is recalling his infancy,

One of the most effective features of the novel is the way it skilfully alternates between the past tense and the historic present tense. Once again it needs to be noted that there is no particular psychological significance attached to this technique — it is for reasons of dramatic effect only that the narrative switches from the one tense to the other. Occasionally this can happen in the very middle of a scene, as when Michael describes how the older boys ganged up on him when he first went to the "big" school: "A party of boys came strolling up towards us . . . .The leader has reached us . . . .'Excuse me', he says laughing." Why, though, one might wonder, is the present tense not therefore used throughout, in order to establish a feeling of immediacy? The probable answer is because then the continuous sense of the pastness of the lives being described in *A Toy Epic* would be lost — their pastness, that is, in relation to our, the reader's, present. This aspect of the narrative is perhaps clearer in *Y Tri Llais*, the Welsh version of *A Toy Epic*. That novel opens with a narrator who, as he lies on a hill-top in a state between sleep and waking, hears three disembodied voices rising from the valley below, as if issuing out of the great misty gulf of the past. The whole of *A Toy Epic* is therefore as much about a sense of vanished time, and is as full of a sense of belatedness, as is Dylan Thomas's *Return Journey*, which ends with the tolling park bell reminding the narrator that the children his mind's eye has seen at play are all in reality dead and gone. "Dusk", he realises, "was folding the Park around, like another, darker snow." And *A Toy Epic*, too, ends on a partly elegiac note: "The earth, bearing continents and seas, shows another hemisphere the sun, and another the outer darkness."

The cycle of the seasons is used throughout the novel as a way of indicating that passage of time. But it is the calendar of the school year that is used as the real index to the boys' growth. *A Toy Epic* is divided into ten chapters, eight of which are of

146

almost equal length while the remaining two (Chapters Six and Eight) depart only slightly, yet significantly, from the norm. The first three chapters cover the period from the boys' infancy right through to the end of their days in primary school, and this part of the novel concludes with them sitting their entrance examination to the County School. Their first five years at that school are then described in Chapters Four to Six, and Chapters Seven to Ten deal with their time in the sixth-form, leading up to the fateful university entrance-examination which, in the final chapter, leaves the boys very differently placed as they prepare to move on and out into adult life. Indeed their schooling is throughout shown to play a vitally important part in the formation of the boys' characters, in the development of their social outlook, and in deciding the eventual course of their lives. No wonder that large parts of the novel centre on some aspect or other of the drama of their school careers — the whole of Chapter Three, for example, is devoted to the experience of sitting the scholarship exam.

Other chapters deal not with a single event but with a single phase in the boys' lives. So Chapter Seven is mainly about their attempts to find a goal and purpose in life, and Chapter Eight shows them returning to their separate home backgrounds and exploring them anew, following both a period of absorption in their new life at County School and a period of adolescent self-absorption. Moreover the exceptional length of Chapter Eight marks the fact that it deals with what Albie calls "a long, troubled and uneasy summer." Formal symmetry is sometimes used to bind the different sections of a chapter together by bringing out the thematic correspondences between its different parts. Chapter Two begins with Albie running from the shade of the house entry into the May sunshine, before he is hauled reluctantly through town by his mother and dragged into the nightmare middle of the striking busmen. The same chapter ends with Michael being called out of "the green gloom" of his friend Raymond's tent into the "harsh sunlight", before being led home by his father in public disgrace. Both episodes are moments when a boy's mind is opened to a disturbingly new truth that affects his subsequent psychological development.

Structural correspondence is in fact an extremely important

device in *A Toy Epic*. The opening of the novel, when three voices speak in quick succession, is therefore not only a way of immediately establishing that the work is a triple narrative; it is also a way of establishing the basic principle on which the whole book is organised. The syntactical parallelism here at the very beginning is the first example of a pattern of echo and repetition that acts as the infrastructure of the whole work. So for example the beginning of Chapter Three is a very close approximation in structure to the beginning of Chapter One. To notice the similarity is however also to be brought to reflect on the differences between the two passages. In Chapter One the boys successively describe the world that surrounds each of them in early childhood. In Chapter Three, on the other hand, the emphasis is on the different inner worlds that have in each case been created by them in the very image of their different environments.

The brief sections of which each chapter is composed are also frequently interconnected through the repetition of a word, a phrase, or a situation. Section Five of Chapter One consists of Albie's recollections of his father coming home for tea. Section Six opens with Iorwerth's memory of carrying tea out to his father in the fields. The parallelism stimulates the reader, unawares, to compare and contrast the two passages and so to notice the difference between the two milieus, the two worlds of work, the two families. Sometimes a pointed cross-reference is made from one section to another in order to highlight a social contrast. Iorwerth's mother goes to riddle the cinders in the Third Section of Chapter One, but it is Mary the maid who cleans the grate in Michael's middle-class home in the next section. Dick repeatedly shouts out the name of Nel, the wife around whom the life of Albie's home revolves, whereas the Rector calls for Mary "in his deep, kind, parsonical voice." At other times the links are of a more abstract or general character, as when the opening sections of Chapter Five prove, on examination, to offer variations on the theme of trust and mistrust. A particularly poignant transition occurs in Chapter Eight when Albie's failed attempt to explain to Frida exactly how it is he loves her is followed by Iorwerth's sad realisation of "how ineffective my love for my father is."

As can be seen, the structure of *A Toy Epic* is inseparable from the novel's primary concern, which is to explore the inter-connections and the divisions between three lives and between three social backgrounds. The structure is profoundly functional, just as the 'poetic' features of the novel are a fully integrated part of its particular style of psychological and social exploration. The early reviews were right when they praised the 'lyricism' of the writing, but were wrong when they treated it as if it were an adornment or a lavish accessory. Take Iorwerth's description of his first County School assembly, for instance:

> Heads ascend behind us from form to form like the marks on the doorpost which my father has made, makes and will make to register my growth. Exceptions break through the ranks like cocksfoot grass in the hayfield, and Albie is the exception in our row. The hall is filled in the morning by one form after another, as a granary floor is covered by emptying sack after sack of corn.

Beautiful though they are, these "epic" similes are first and foremost dramatic in character. In other words they are vividly expressive of the character and state of mind of the perceiver of the scene, as well as being highly evocative of the scene itself. Iorwerth brings his country mind with him to the town school, and domesticates his strange new environment by seeing it in familiar terms. And who but poor Albie, in his state of gloomy mental paralysis, would speak of trudging steadily through the exam syllabus like "an insurance-man working his weekly way down the terrace"?

It is, then, through its intrinsic qualities as well as through its extrinsic connections with the history of two periods — the thirties and the fifties — that *A Toy Epic* continues to be of value and of interest. In its Welsh incarnation as *Y Tri Llais*, the novel is still one of the best that is available in the Welsh language. In its English form, entitled *A Toy Epic*, it remains one of the best novels to have been written about Wales, although it is perhaps surpassed by the same author's own magnificent later novel *Outside the House of Baal* (1965). Moreover while it remains, as Emyr Humphreys once put it, "anchored in historical reality by its landscape", *A Toy Epic* also manages to make daily life in one

149

Bibliography

First published by Eyre and Spottiswoode in the autumn of 1958, *A Toy Epic* was reprinted in paperback by Arrow Books in 1961 and in hardback by Severn Books in 1981.

Emyr Humphreys has also published, to date, sixteen other novels in English. *The Little Kingdom* (London: Eyre and Spottiswoode, 1946) and *Outside the House of Baal* (London: Eyre and Spottiswoode, 1963. Reprinted as an Everyman Fiction paperback, 1988) deal with a Welsh background not dissimilar to that portrayed in *A Toy Epic*. However Humphreys's most ambitious treatment of Welsh material comes in the sequence of novels *Bonds of Attachment*. The chronology of events can be followed by reading them in this order: *Flesh and Blood* (London: Hodder and Stoughton, 1974); *The Best of Friends* (London: Hodder and Stoughton, 1978); *Salt of the Earth* (London: Dent, 1985); *An Absolute Hero* (London: Dent, 1986); *Open Secrets* (London: Dent, 1988); *National Winner* (London: MacDonald, 1971). The first four are currently available in a Sphere Books paperback edition. Emyr Humphreys's distinctive interpretation of Welsh history can be found in *The Taliesin Tradition* (London: Black Raven Press, 1983. Reprinted in paperback, Bridgend: Seren Books, 1989).

Reviews of *A Toy Epic* appeared in the following newspapers and periodicals: *Anglo-Welsh Review* 10, no.26, 1959 (Roland Mathias); *Church Times*, 16 January, 1959; *Sunday Times*. 23 November, 1958 (J.D. Scott); *Telegraph*, 21 November, 1958 (Kenneth Young): *Times*, November, 1958; *T.L.S.*, 28 November, 1958; *Western Mail*, 22 November, 1958 (Douglas Phillips). The Severn Books reprint of *A Toy Epic* was reviewed in *Anglo-Welsh Review* 72, 1982 (Andre Morgan). Initial reaction to *Y Tri Llais* included the following: *Yr Arloeswr Newydd* I, 1959 (John Gwilym Jones); *Y Cymro*, 20 Tachwedd, 1958 (Harri Gwyn); *Y Faner*, Tachwedd, 1958 (E. Tegla Davies).

The best introduction to Emyr Humphreys's work is Ioan Williams, *Emyr Humphreys*, published in the *Writers of Wales* series (Cardiff: University of Wales Press for the Welsh Arts Council, 1980). A useful brief summary of his life and work can be found in Glyn Jones and John Rowlands, *Profiles* (Llandysul: Gwasg Gomer, 1980); and in Meic Stephens (ed.), *The Oxford Companion to the Literature of Wales* (Oxford University Press, 1986). Emyr Humphreys's earlier novels are discussed in

BIBLIOGRAPHY

Roland Mathias's collection of essays on Anglo-Welsh literature, *A Ride Through the Wood* (Bridgend: Poetry Wales Press, 1985). There is a sensible comparison of *A Toy Epic* with *Y Tri Llais* by Andre Morgan in *Planet* 39 (1977).

A list of Emyr Humphreys's English publications up to 1965 can be found in Brynmor Jones, *A Bibliography of Anglo-Welsh Literature* (Llandysul: Gwasg Gomer, 1970). A full description of works by and about Emyr Humphreys will be included in the forthcoming *Anglo-Welsh Bibliography and Database* that is being prepared at the College of Librarianship Wales, Aberystwyth by John Harris and John Davies.

Notes

Introduction

1. A distinguished literary biographer and critic, Cecil was at the time Goldsmiths' Professor of English Literature at Oxford.

2. Keidrych Rhys had started his colourful and highly influential literary periodical *Wales* before the war, and the young Emyr Humphreys had been one of the early contributors. Others included Dylan Thomas, Glyn Jones and Vernon Watkins.

3. Kate Roberts (1891-1985) was one of the most impressive and imposing figures among the whole galaxy of talents responsible for the twentieth-century renaissance of Welsh-language literature. Emyr Humphreys scripted a series of programmes in English about her life and work that was televised on Channel Four UK in 1988. The script was simultaneously published in bookform under the title: *The Triple Net: A Portrait of the writer Kate Roberts* (Channel Four publications, 1988).

4. E. Tegla Davies (1880-1967) was a Wesleyan Methodist minister and prolific popular author, whose best novel *Gŵr Pen y Bryn (The Master of Pen y Bryn*, 1923) has been translated into English.

5. John Gwilym Jones (1904-1988) was a fine Welsh-language dramatist, short-story writer, novelist and literary critic. His friendship with Emyr Humphreys was already of long standing in 1958. He had even been responsible for seeing Humphreys's first novel, *The Little Kingdom*, through the press in 1946 when the author was engaged in post-war relief work in Italy.

The Text

6. "That's not the way to do it."

7. The reference is primarily to the Calvinistic Methodists. This church was affectionately known as "Yr Hen Gorff" ("The Old Body") because in

the northern counties of Wales it was, by the end of the last century, the most enduringly powerful of the Nonconformist sects.

8. "By heavens, Nel."

9. "Of course, you do."

10. Inflammable, like a match.

11. "Hymn number two hundred and thirty-four."

12. The two boys supposedly murdered in the Tower of London on the orders of their wicked uncle who became Richard III.

13. The Big Seat, where the deacons sit in Nonconformist chapels.

14. Middle shop.

15. "My lad."

16. "By God."

17. "Goodbye, boys!"

18. "Boys."

19. The first two names bring together the spirit of British loyalism and the cautious sentiments of mainstream Welsh radicalism that are typical of Albie's respectable working-class background. He is named after Queen Victoria's lavishly lamented spouse, Prince Albert, and after Thomas Jones, Rhymney-born Secretary to the British Cabinet, from the premiership of Lloyd George to that of Baldwin. Jones was the orchestrator of the labour movement that established a workingman's college at Harlech.

20. The "British Schools" were the nondenominational elementary schools of the first half of the nineteenth-century. After 1870 a state system of such schools was established, but until then Nonconformist Wales had had to tolerate the Church of England's widespread control of elementary education. The gradual integration of Church Schools into the state system, after the Balfour Act of 1902, was at first fiercely resented and systematically opposed by Welsh Nonconformity. But by the time Michael and Iorwerth were attending their Church School in the late twenties, serious opposition had long since died away.

21. The Welsh Intermediate Education Act of 1889 ensured that Wales was

covered by a network of "Intermediate" (later "County") secondary schools. Entrance to such a school was by extremely competitive examination, and no educational provision was made by the state for those who failed.

22. "The Society for the Promotion of Christian Knowledge."

23. Llew the farm-hand.

24. In the last century no devout Welsh home was complete without pictures of "yr hoelion wyth" (literally "the big nails") on its walls. These were the outstanding preachers of the particular denomination to which the family belonged.

25. In the third part of his *Divine Comedy*, Dante meets Beatrice who is his guide through Paradise. Volume Seven of the *Children's Encyclopaedia* includes a photograph of a piece of sculpture showing Beatrice taking Dante by the hand and leading him upwards.

26. The University College of North Wales, Bangor.

27. O.M. Edwards (1858-1920) helped create an idealised picture of "y werin" (the cultivated Welsh "volk") and became in turn the hero of Welsh-speaking Wales. He was the author/editor of several immensely popular periodicals and books that helped form a national consciousness in Wales by popularising Welsh history and literature. Following a period as tutor in History and Fellow of Lincoln College, Oxford, he was appointed Chief Inspector of Schools in Wales in 1907 and became a renowned educationalist. He is also remembered for his efforts to secure a modest place for Welsh and the study of Welsh history in the thoroughly anglocentric education system of his day.

28. Sir John Herbert Lewis (1858-1933) was born in Mostyn Quay, Flintshire and became the first chairman of Flintshire County Council. He was one of the founders of the Intermediate School system in Wales.

29. A brand of cheap, strong cigarettes, particularly popular with working people.

30. "White Star."

31. *The Missionary* (1922-74) was the Calvinistic Methodist monthly that reported on the work of Welsh Methodist missionaries all over the world.

32. *The Little Treasury* (1862-1966) was the Calvinistic Methodist monthly for children and young people.

33. "The Goddess doesn't tolerate any further questions on behalf of the dead." (Ovid, *Metamorphoses*, Book XI, line 583)

34. "Where the god himself lies, his limbs loosened by lassitude." (Ovid, *Metamophoses*, Book XI, line 612) The goddess Juno sends her messenger Iris to the cave of the god of Sleep to persuade him to reveal the death at sea of Ceyx to his unwitting wife, Alcyone. Iris enters the dark, sound-proof lair: "The god of sleep, stretched on the coverlet,/ Lies there, his figure languorous and long." Lethe's waters flow beneath the cave — and the words of this part of the poem flow through Michael's unconscious mind as he listens to the girl singing.

35. "silly boy."

36. In this chapter of the epistle, Paul compares the ministry of Christ to that of the high priests of the Jewish religion. He emphasises that Christ was indeed the chosen of God, as the priests had claimed to be. "And no man taketh this honour unto himself, but he that is called of God, as was Aaron." It seems likely that Iorwerth's mind is full of the wish to please his father by entering the ministry.

37. "Utter nonsense!"

38. "Gracious!"

39. These were biographies of dominant figures in the life of Nonconformist Wales during the late nineteenth-century. J. Cynddylan Jones (1840-1930) was a Calvinistic Methodist minister and prolific theological writer, who worked indefatigably on behalf of the Bible Society.
Lewis Edwards (1809-87) was a literary essayist and theologian, who established the influential periodical *Y Traethodydd* and founded the Calvinistic Methodist college in Bala.
   John Williams (1854-1921) was a renowned Calvinistic Methodist preacher, whose name is associated with Brynsiencyn, Anglesey, where he spent most of his life. He took an active part in promoting the formation of the Welsh military division during the war of 1914-18 and was its honorary chaplain.

40. The reference is primarily to the opening of "Ode to the West Wind": "O wild West Wind. thou breath of Autumn's being."

41. A mountain well to the south of the speaker, between Ruthin and Mold.

42. Arethusa had been a nymph of the woods and meadows until the river god Alpheus pursued her. Fleeing his advances, she prayed to Artemis for refuge: "The freezing sweat poured down my thighs and knees/ A

darkening moisture fell from all my body/ And where I stopped a stream ran down; from hair/ To foot it flowed, faster than words can tell,/ I had been changed into a pool, a river." (Ovid, *Metamorphoses*, Book V)

43. In Dante's *Divine Comedy*, the second circle of hell is reserved for carnal sinners, "in whom reason by lust is sway'd." There he meets Francesca of Rimini and her lover Paolo, the brother of her deformed husband. Dante is overcome by compassion for the lovers. It's worth noting that their affair began with the reading of Launcelot's story. His adulterous love for Queen Guinevere resulted in the destruction of the brotherhood of the Knights of the Round Table, and Albie's infatuation with Frida is similarly the cause of an estrangement between him and his two friends.

44. This is a form of singing unique to Wales. One melody is played on the harp, while a counter-melody is sung, off the beat, by the singer(s).

45. This "Singing Festival" has been a popular feature of Nonconformist worship in Wales since the first half of the last century.

46. Daedalus, the great craftsman who built the Cretan labyrinth, constructed an ingenious flying machine out of feathers and wax. Exhilarated by the experience of flight, his son Icarus flew too near the sun, and the melting of the wax sent him plunging to his death in the sea.

47. Literally "speckled bread." A kind of fruit loaf.

48. Galatea was a Nereid, loved by Acis. When Acis's rival, Polyphemus, crushed him under a rock, she transformed her lover into a river. (Ovid, *Metamorphoses*, Book XII)

Afterword

49. The burning at Penyberth was one of the most significant events in the history of the modern Welsh nationalist movement, and it had a great effect on artists and intellectuals. In spite of practically unanimous Welsh opposition, the government had insisted on demolishing an old farmhouse in Llŷn whose history dated back to medieval times. In its place they proposed to put an aerial-bombing range. Three leading members of *Plaid Cymru* — Saunders Lewis, Lewis Valentine and D.J. Williams — set fire to the building-site on September 9, 1936 and immediately reported their action to the police. When they were tried in Caernarfon the jury could not agree on a verdict. In order to secure a conviction the unusual step was taken of transferring the case to England. At the Old Bailey each of the three (two of whom were among the finest Welsh writers of their generation) was sentenced to nine months imprisonment. Thousands assembled in Caernarfon to welcome them after their release from prison.

50. Daniel Owen (1836-95), the most gifted of Welsh novelists, was born in Mold, Flintshire. His four outstanding novels are all strongly influenced by his deep attachment to the Calvinistic Methodist faith.

51. William Williams Pantycelyn (1717-91), as he is generally known, was a hymn-writer of incomparable genius. After his religious conversion, he devoted his life to Methodist activities. His long poem *Bywyd a Marwolaeth Theomemphus* (*The Life and Death of Theomemphus*, 1764) is a work of great physical force and subtlety that deals with an individual soul's progress from damnation to salvation.

52. *The Mabinogion* is the modern title of twelve great Welsh tales from the medieval period.

53. T. Gwynn Jones (1871-1949) was a remarkably versatile writer, who excelled as a poet, both in *cynghanedd* (the strict classical metres) and in modern experimental forms. The English lines quoted here come from the translation by Joseph Clancy, which attempts to convey something of the richly archaic quality of the original Welsh. Penmon in Anglesey was the site first of an early Celtic church and then of a medieval monastery. The poet recalls a visit he paid to the place in the company of his friend W.J. Gruffydd, when they were briefly transported in imagination by the beauties of the scene to the distant period of the monastery's hey-day.

54. W.J. Gruffydd (1881-1954) was a literary critic and accomplished poet. In his prime he was one of the principal arbiters of taste and fashioners of literary opinion in Wales.

55. Saunders Lewis (1893-1985) was one of the greatest Welsh-language writers of the modern, or any other, period. As well as being an exceptional dramatist and poet, he was a fine scholar, an incisively authoritative literary critic and an inspired political journalist. A founder member and longtime President of *Plaid Cymru*, he worked to restore a free Wales to its proper place in European culture.

lecturer said that morning: "10,000 horsemen rode across that plain, and for two years laid siege to this castle. And when at last the thin emaciated Welsh commander handed over his sword to the well-fed victor, he did so saying that now English, the castle was henceforward fit only for sanitary purposes." Michael turned this story over in his mind with much pleasure. Such fore-fathers knew the meaning of glory. In spite of the centuried fight against a powerful opulent relentless enemy, in spite of famine, pestilence, disorders, sieges, invasions, pillage and awful slaughter, in spite of the death of friends, of lovers, of fathers and of children, still to retain courage and wit, still to cherish the lightening of language.

"Michael Edwards" shouted someone. "Come and sing with us."

Although he would have liked to have joined them earlier, his ignorance of Welsh folk-song and the principles of harmony had restrained him. Now the action of rising and walking across the wall embarrassed him. He would have preferred to remain seated alone, listening to their voices from a distance, and made anonymous by the entrancing proportions of the surrounding country. Anonymity appealed to him now as it had hardly ever done before. The whole proceedings of this summer school thrilled and interested him, and conscious of his own lack of knowledge and inadequacy he was content to be the most obscure of observers. For now rediscovering, as he thought, a lost nation, a new nation, he felt like an explorer whose discovery overwhelms and absorbs him in its magnitude. Never before had he realised so clearly how much there was to learn and discover not only about his own country, but about — searching for the right words, he could only use 'life' and 'the world.'

He joined the singers, who were some of the young people, university students most of them. Standing in their midst and singing as quietly as he could, Michael observed his companions. Two fat girls stood opposite him, their hands thrust into their blazer pockets, as though caught there, and they gesticulated with two halves of cloth. The four other girls were assorted in shape and size with featureless faces and aimless figures. The men, Michael continued to observe critically, seemed gauche and unrobust. One had a pronounced stoop; he

160

curved inwards from his neck to his waist, and another standing next to Michael, was small and rotund and losing his hair. His breath, as he sang lustily, smelt stale. Another fidgeted, and his hands were raised, fluttered, lowered like a wounded bird as he thought of placing an arm round a companion's shoulders and then thought the better of it. They spoke to each other quickly, and their laughter and accent and an ignorance of their subject-matter made their rapid conversation difficult for Michael to understand. He felt distant from them, indifferent and almost hostile.

"Anfarwol!" said Idris, still fidgeting, and his eyes glowing with excitement. He broke out into rapid comment on the singing, praising Morris, twitting Mary and Maud, and rebuking his brother Glyn. All his remarks were breathless and punctuated with high pitched laughter.

"You don't know harmony?" he said turning to Michael and when Michael shamefacedly shook his head, he exclaimed "Duw! Duw!" with such genuine amazement that everyone laughed.

They started to sing again and Michael studied Idris with a prejudiced dislike. "False teeth, greasy hair, cabbage ears" he said to himself with childish satisfaction.

Soon he left the singers and climbed down the bare battered stone stairway to the square lawn in the centre of the castle. Somewhat selfconsciously he passed through the various groups who stood there talking (as though at a garden fête at night — without tents and stalls). This was only the second day of the summer school and he still felt a stranger.

"Michael!" he turned, and saw Mr Philips beckoning him. "Come here a minute."

Mr Philips stood talking to a small man wearing a white open-necked shirt with an unusually wide collar. His head was small and dark and the brown colour of his skin, contrasted with the sharp whiteness of his shirt, gave him an unreal air in the moonlight. His eyes were keen and penetrating, the skin about them humorously wrinkled, but his mouth was small and sardonic.

"This is the young man I was telling you about," said Mr Philips. "Michael this is Mr Gerallt Gruffydd" (Michael looked at the poet with awe and reverence) "I told him you intended going to Aber next session. He has promised to keep an eye on you for me!"

The poet sucked his cigarette holder and smiled "I have made such a promise Mr Edwards; but I have no intention of keeping it, so don't worry."

"Michael was reading your last book on our way down in the car Mr Gruffydd. He seemed to be enjoying it, too. He's only recently begun to read Welsh, but he's getting along nicely."

Michael saw again the red bonnet of the car through the windscreen and the green hedges and fields and full-blown trees giving way to the open moorland and the carpet-like coarse grass that swept up to the mountain sides to give way to the darker green of ferns which in turn gave way to the purple heather. It was to this he raised his eyes from the printed page, and in looking, savoured the poetry. Mr Philips had interrupted his reverie by saying that the moor was scheduled for afforestation soon. "Afforestation madness," he said bitterly. And here before him was the author of that printed page which he had so much enjoyed while passing over the green moor. In this dark head those lines of beauty were originally shaped, worked, moulded, built into the printed pattern of significance. Where had the final act of writing been performed, in what study or bedroom or on what summer lawn, and how many hours had been spent to attain the effect of effortless perfection?

"What course do you intend to pursue at Aber?" Gerallt Gruffydd asked politely, holding his cigarette-holder in suspense awaiting Michael's answer.

"History," said Michael, and then elaborated briefly. He felt his presence a brake on their conversation; narrowing it he thought, to subjects that must be boring for them.

As he walked down the empty moonlit street towards the chapel-vestry which served as a camp for some members of the school, he felt an unusual pang of loneliness. Surely this was the emptiest street in the world; blind, deaf and dumb these rows of shops and houses. A man stood under a lamp post, hand in pocket like a poster against unemployment, and he did not even turn as Michael passed. Clocks alone spoke in the dumb darkened houses, and struck, as he paused to listen, twelve o'clock, one after the other as though carrying the burden of a monotonous round.

He had no friends here; nor had he, for that matter, friends anywhere. He began to count them on the fingers of his hand. There was Mr Philips, he did feel that he could call him a friend, and yet of course not friend in the intimate sense of the word. Mr Philips was his mentor, who deliberately stimulated his intellect, and, should Michael ask advice, would no doubt be a sympathetic adviser.

Then he thought of Alfie, and of Iorwerth. He liked them both, enjoyed their company and yet, he thought, he could never bring himself to any great degree of intimacy with them. They confided in him far oftener than he confided in them.

He could bury his head in Doris's yellow hair and lose himself for a short while in her undoubted beauty, but talking with her for any length of time, like reading her letter that morning, created in him the desire to hide the commonplace mind she displayed in soft contralto or in crabby schoolgirl hand.

Bending his fingers down one by one he extracted the flavour of ironic satisfaction by saying to himself "not enough to make a hand," and the very utterance brought him some relief, for he entered the vestry through the Chapel side-door with a lighter heart.

The vestry had been cleared of its normal furniture and palliasses had been arranged on the dusty floor-boards along three sides of the long rectangular room. Isolated in the centre of the room stood a trestle-table on which were one or two suitcases and a large haversack. Michael had made his bed earlier, and all he had to do was to change into pyjamas and roll out his blankets. He looked about him as he took off his shoes. There were three people in the vestry apart from himself, and obviously strangers to each other. The groups and parties and friends were still out, frolicking and singing on the beach or in the castle. Looking across the room, under the trestle-table, Michael saw a bald-headed middle-aged man sitting on his palliasse. He was drawing his pyjamas over his legs already covered to the ankle with woolly flannel. Afterwards he took off his long-tailed shirt. When Michael caught his eye, he smiled weakly, half opened his mouth, closed it, and accelerated his preparations for bed. When his bald head finally settled on the pillow, Michael stared at the clothes neatly wrapped up on the chair beside him; on the back of the chair was a black coat and a waistcoat over which was hung a gleaming white wing-collar; a pair of pin-striped trousers lay across the seat, and on it a large watch and chain, a penknife and a small pile of coins. Side by side on the floor stood the bald-headed man's concession to summer — a pair of grey canvas shoes.

Near the middle of the wall on Michael's left a tall muscular man stood naked putting on a pyjama coat. There was a hard beauty in his body and he moved about with ease and grace. His face was handsomely boyish but truculent. He brushed his brown springing hair, before turning on his side to sleep.

The person who most interested Michael was his neighbour, who lay on his blanket, wearing his jacket trousers and shoes, having taken off only the crimson shirt which lay in a heap at the foot of his bed. He had no stockings.

His head was covered with iron grey hair, cut, it seemed, evenly into a one inch stubble from neck to forehead. He was reading, and smoking a stocky pipe with an immense bowl, which when he drew in his breath glowed like a brazier. He seemed to take no notice of anyone. His attention was directed entirely to his book; apart from an occasional loving glance at his pipe.

When Michael finally lay in bed he turned his head on the pillow to steal a glance at his companion. He was surprised and shocked to find that the grey-haired young man had laid aside his book, and was staring at him, as he lay turned towards him and balanced on his elbow. His face, apart from an unruly grey moustache, was uncommonly proportionate; the features of a film star or a tailor's dummy, Michael thought with surprise. His eyes were mellow, and when seen clearly out of the clouds of smoke, seemed to swim in a sea of benevolence.

Eventually he took is pipe out of his mouth and asked "Where do you come from?" and when Michael told him he said, "Oh yes. I've been there. It's being rapidly spoilt. I know the vicar there too; he dabbles in archaeology."

"He is also my father," Michael replied coldly.

His companion merely smiled and continued to stare at

Michael, until his amusement appeared to fade. He picked up his book and continued reading.

"An artist or a poet," Michael thought with interest, but he failed to screw up enough courage to resume their curious conversation. He was tired and he soon fell asleep.

Sleeping, he dreamt that the grey-haired young man was still staring at him with amusement . . . .

"Who are you?" Michael asked with unrestrained curiosity.

"My name is Goronwy Owen; some of the literary friends with whom I correspond call me Goronwy Ddu o Fôn. So you see I am a bard, a would-be-epic-poet now unhappily employed as assistant-master and general scivvy at a second-rate school at Donnington, an execrable village in Shropshire. A more detestable, unprofitable, incongenial occupation for a poet you could scarcely imagine. A good line may come to my head, then the unholy clatter and din of those English colts and dunderheaded tadpoles I have the misfortune to teach drive all away, and leave me with nought but a headache and a violent desire to get drunk."

He said all this without moving and without altering the conversational tone of his pleasant baritone.

"Of course," he continued, "I complain. I seek help — a living or even a curacy in Wales. I have written many letters. Very good letters, too. But there it is, I've grown accustomed to disappointment now. You might say I'm inoculated against most varieties of despair. I take a great joy in the pipe and the pot, and a few quiet moments in the garden, walking about smelling flowers and musing (pardon the pun) the intricacies and harmony of verse. Do you know 'Cynghanedd' young man? Every intelligent young man should be versed in the art. It is discipline for the soul, as well as a pleasure."

"Who is the fine-bodied young man across there?" Michael asked.

"The Prince Hywel ap Owain Gwynedd, the warrior-poet, who when his wars were over and his freedom secured, walked on the sea-shores of Gwynedd, or between the meadow land and the mountains, and sang the praises of his domain. In summer, perhaps, he would lie by the river, head pillowed on the bare white arm of his lover, plucking the white clover flower and counting the arts of peace."

"And who is the bald-headed man who sleeps opposite us?"

"He is Ceiriog, a nineteenth century side-whiskered songster. The Railway Company have given him a week's holiday. Would you believe that he writes lyrics? He writes them well too, although myself I have no taste for that sort of thing."

"Why have you come here?"

"I was invited, so was Prince Hywel, and so was Ceiriog who travelled free being an employee of the company. Taliesin and Aneurin are here staying at the Druid's Head. The three Llewelyns have come, so have several Princes of the Blood, Dafydd ap Gwilym and many famous bards. All the hotels are full. Prince Hywel daren't reveal his identity, so he's staying here. I'm too poor to pay an hotel bill, and Ceiriog is too thrifty.

"Who invited you?"

"He who invited you."

Goronwy pointed to the dais at the far end of the room. There in the semi-darkness sat a small pale-faced man at a desk writing. His white face was outlined clearly; large forehead, long nose, and thin determined mouth.

"Who is he?"

"He has been called Arthur, Hywel, Gruffydd, Llewelyn, Owen Glyndŵr, he has lived many centuries and has seen bitter defeats, and yet he lives. You may call him flame-bearer, leader, undying patriot. As he grows older he increases in skill, in wisdom and in learning, and he becomes more stubborn and harder to kill."

"Where is his sword?"

"You see it in his hand."

"Where is his armour?"

"In his head."

"Where is his shield?"

"In his heart."

"When is his hour come
From what tower or tomb?
Shall there be song and beaten drum
Or will the choristers be dumb?
Shall I see it, shall I hear it,
Should I greet it, should I fear it,

Shall I be far or shall I be near it?"
"You shall see it, you shall hear it,
You should greet it; you shall be near it."

Michael awoke. Behind the cascades of dust ascending the sun-beams he saw the silent row of sleepers against the opposite wall. Beside him the grey-haired young man lay sleeping; he had drawn one blanket over him and Michael smiled as he regarded the feet, stockingless, shoes still on, that stuck out at the bottom of the palliasse. He smiled, remembering his dream.

Chapter II

The map of Wales is endearing; whether old, with quaking coasts and quivering rivers and covered with copper-plate place names by Humphrey Llwyd; whether seen as a face or a figure by our patient embroidering grandmothers; whether in the school atlas, where the sea skirted plains and the valleys are two shades of green, and the mountain slopes two shades of brown, and the peaks an ominous black, or whether the intimate clay relief map, where you may squeeze yourself into a valley and say "Here I am!" . . . . It is durable and endearing, and the key to so many pictures and images. The old exile covering a river with his finger says: "Although I am lodged now by an Italian lake and all about me is dazzlingly fair to look upon, yet this Italian spring with all its splendour cannot warm my heart as did the river banks of Dyffryn Clwyd once, when I heard the first cuckoo calling from the enchanted wood. How that single song lifted my heart. If all the birds of the south assembled near me now, plumed in so various colours, and sang the music of their most harmonious and paradisical song my heart would not rejoice as much as it did then in a quiet valley in Wales" . . . .

The map we follow is accurate and modern, covered with self-important railway lines that link up the unimportant hinterlands with the centre of civilisation and commerce. It carries away surplus goods and surplus population to where they are needed. It is indispensable to the wheel of industry, it is the slender vein that carries the life-blood of the modern world; such parts of the map that are untouched, untapped, are desert, desolate, dead flesh, waste land . . . . . .

At 10 o'clock the train departs from the station. The passengers are in their places, the luggage van is closed; love-letters, business letters, congratulations, condolments, good news, bad news, lie quiet in the mailbag in the corner. The commercial traveller opens his morning paper and relaxes, forgetting for half an hour, the cares of business; the railway employee sits forward eager to be gone, sensitive to a slight delay, as he swallows the smoke drawn from the stump held in his permanently blackened hand; the housewife, off for a shopping expedition, breaks off a piece of chocolate and with narrowed eyes plans the expenditure of time and money. While in the far corner, Michael sits holding a book, unable to concentrate, thinking of the new life awaiting him at the end of this journey.

On the station platform Mrs Edwards stood for a moment gazing after the departed train. Goodbye Michael, new amiable likeable young man, she thought; how you have changed in the last few months, grown older, more sociable, when you leaned out of the carriage door smiling and waving your hand, you remind me of your Uncle John, turning round in the gig that left the rectory to take him to the train in the late summer in 1913. It seemed for a moment that your raised arms and smiling faces were interchangeable.

Only John went to Oxford and Michael goes to Aber. She regrets that Michael was not going to Oxford too. She knew the value of a college crest hung on the study wall, in rectory, vicarage, deanery or palace.

John and Michael so alike. Sociable, popular and good looking, the same fair hair, sharp blue eyes and slightly protruding teeth, enhancing their smiles. Likeable, yet in some way distant and reserved. John killed, now nearly twenty years ago, living again, young and starting out again. John who first brought David Edwards to stay at Llanorwig.

She jerked herself out of this unaccustomed day-dreaming, and closed her hand over her shopping list in her pocket.

"Groceries from Evans'

168

Call at the Vaults for Communion Wine.
Order 'God in the Universe' at Smiths for D.
Order cards for Whist Drive.
Call at the Dressmakers . . . ."

"Come along Alfie," she said, turning to the very tall youth standing at her side. "I must be getting on with my shopping or I'll never be back at the rectory in time for tea."

The train crept steadily along the map, through towns whose names began four miles out at sea, parallel to the dirty sands, the sooty seawalls, the mud-laked sea marshes, small docks and grassless dykes, and came within the hour to the city of Chester. Here Michael changed trains, removed himself and personal luggage from platform X, trotting over the bridge, to platform Y, then finding he had ten minutes to wait, took in the scenes and sounds and odours that stood and swam under the station roof.

Away over the ends of platforms in a deserted bay, a black and shining engine stood polished by the pale bars of the sun which fell through the glazed station roof glass. A solitary greaser in grimy blue overalls stood by one of the huge unspun wheels. He may possibly have been working but from where Michael stood there was no sound or movement in the portrait. It merely hung at the far end of the station, realistic and yet unreal.

Women passed near him, sometimes jolting him with swinging, gleaming, glamorous, round black cases; scent and powder assailed his nostrils intimately for a moment, an apology made a broken tinkle in his ear. Or men passed more soberly dressed, taking long steps, smelling assertively of different tobaccos. From the Restaurant and Buffet behind him issued the blended odour of foods and beers; a porter passed, pushing a trolley load of grease-tins, some open looked like appetising half-solidified cream-toffee; it had a smooth and almost soothing smell. But as the private conversation merged into the public uproar, so every separate smell was dominated by the bitter pungent smell of burnt coke and coal, and gaseous smoke.

A child jumped with joy and excitement, a porter hurried down the platform calling the names of stations, a woman with large breasts shook with uncontrollable laughter, then suddenly smacked her small boy over the ear, a dirty stunted adolescent with carefully oiled hair walked along with a pile of newspapers under his arm, whistling as though his belly was full of steam. Young men and young women, old men and old maids, walked, dashed, trotted, talked, shouted, waved, banged carriage doors, threw bags on racks, leaned out of carriage windows, breathless but still talking or laughing. Energy moved in the station like a piston, driving animate, and inanimate, steel and flesh, entire, complete, cause, accident and effect co-ordinated in a second that dominated time and space.

Vaguely, as he waited, Michael felt hostile to the life in the station, unwilling to drown his voice in a sea of voices, face in a sea of faces, the energy of his body in the communal unreasoned energy of the mass; unwilling to be ruled, and willed by an extra-human force, this dark, ominous, cavern of power.

The train escaped out of the cavernous station. It fled precipitately by innumerable backyards, which shot past the carriage window like bullets from a machine gun, identical, and aimed in the same direction. Then passed the torn faces of film stars, enormous tins of salts and jams for a giant belly, yard-wide smiles, capital letters, tall exclamation marks. With a shrill whistle of relief, the train entered the quiet country, cows and horses on the left in England and on the right in Wales, stood about or grazed in fields like pictures. Michael sighed, and leaned back in his seat.

"Cigarette?"

A pale spectacled young man wrapped in a thick blue tweed, out of which rose a thin frail neck, held out a packet of cigarettes in Michael's direction.

"You going up to Aber? I saw the label on your case," he looked up at the rack.

"You're new, aren't you? I thought I hadn't seen you before. Fine place, Aber. You'll like Col. life. If you haven't been there you can't imagine how great it is. I'm looking forward to seeing the old place again after the long vac. It will be a bit different I suppose. Old faces gone, new people about. But we'll soon settle down to the same old routine. Plenty of work, but plenty of play.

"Are you religious? I mean do you believe in God? I know it's a queer question to ask, especially someone you've never met before; my name's Coke by the way, Joss Coke. But then it's such an important question isn't it? One enjoys one's life so much more believing in God. We have a service every morning at 8.40, before 'niners' begin (that's nine o'clock lectures). I'm a member of the Student Fellowship of Worship. Try and come, Edwards. It's worth it you know. Where are you digging — staying?"

"16, Heol Fach."

"16, Heol Fach! Well! I'm in 15. Next door! Lucky we've met. I can show you around and introduce you to some of the fellows."

Coke told Michael how the constitution of the general body of students worked; he gave short sketches of the best-known people at College among undergraduates and staff. He told Michael that the women students lived in two large hostels, but the men could, within limits, lodge wherever they liked in the town. He said 'kicking the bar' meant taking a stroll along the promenade as far as the extreme north end, where the promenade railing marked the end of the road. The main women's hostel he said was opposite. In winter, the rough high tide would sometimes slap against the steps, and splash the tall green double-doors. 'Res.' was Resolution Hill, the great rock which brought the promenade to an end. 'Refec.' was the Refectory, an eating-place underneath the Men's Club-room, owned by the student body, 'Corpo.' was Corporal Thomas, caretaker of the main building, who rang the bell between lectures. 'Pres.' was the Student President; S.R.C. was the Students' Representative Council. They would arrange a welcome, Michael was told, for the freshers. Coke said Michael would have to sit a mock-examination, and he warned him not to give frivolous answers, for that would mean he would be classed 'Special Case' and be compelled to perform at the Freshers' Concert and Rag. The Students Christian Union gave a tea for Freshers, and secretaries of the different societies spoke.

Coke then began to recite some of the College songs, until noticing the country he jumped up and put his head through the window. The wind grasped his hair and lifted it from his head, and kept its grasp when he turned his head to say that they were near the Main Junction where some of the students from South Wales joined the train. Coke's excitement grew as the train advanced and as soon as the junction came in sight he began to

171

wave, and before the train stopped he had begun several conversations. There were about thirty students, men and women, crowding towards the train, waiting impatiently for the passengers who were changing trains to get out. Snatches of song, laughter, shouts, feminine screeches of amusement, filled the air. Coke tried to make himself understood to a friend furthest away from the train, and beckoned him to share his carriage.

But instead, into the carriage bounded half-a-dozen husky young men, whose noise and presence, it seemed to Michael, awoke at once images of winter, long college scarves wound around necks, and men in coloured vests and shorts hurling themselves about, slithering through the mud or clutching the ball, darting with heroic vigour towards the touch-line. Their robustness seemed to have smothered Coke, who sank into his corner with a silent fixed smile on his face. Coke! or Cokey! each one had shouted as he entered, and then resumed his contribution to their party's revelry. Their Welsh was not easy for Michael to follow; they used words and phrases strange to him. Were they talking about a match . . . or pulling Sam's leg about the red-haired girl from Abercwmboi . . . .or telling a funny story, or running down a lecturer, or cursing the National Government. All these things were connected for them, part of a mutual understanding which they enjoyed. They sang often, boisterous roaring songs, and when Michael glanced at Coke he saw his mouth, too, was moving. Sometimes a brawny red-haired freckled Paul Robeson sang verses and they all joined in the refrain.

"You a fresher?" said one turning to Michael. For a moment Michael felt they were all examining him, eyes of all colours from half a dozen heads examining his face, body, clothes, everything about him. When they had taken their impressions, he was ignored for the rest of the journey.

At five minutes to five, the train came within sight of the sea, the afternoon sun lit up the river along whose banks the train now moved. Then the passengers of the train began to reach down their luggage and wind up their conversations; some who had quietly resented the students' domination of compartments, some who had glared from their corners, some who had joined in the chorus and the laughter, some who had sighed for their vanished youth.

On the platform everyone appeared to be meeting friends, shaking hands, slapping backs; young men poking each other in the ribs, young women half-embraced each other. Cliques of women students walked off arm-in-arm, heads inclined towards the centre of the row, which closed when they paused, and opened out as they proceeded, shaking with laughter.

Trunks of all colours, old and new, strong and weak, all shapes and sizes, roped or strapped, came tumbling out of the luggage van to follow their owners. Porters moved about busily, unmoved by the general excitement.

Coke left Michael as soon as the train stopped; he leapt out to wring hands and have his hand wrung.

Alone, Michael walked slowly out of the station, observing the many students who passed him.

He was to share the room with Watkins. Watkins was arriving on the 6.30, said Mrs Green, as she cleared away the remains of Michael's tea. She was a small, bird-like, talkative woman. Her husband worked nights, she said, so Mr Edwards wouldn't see much of him. She hoped Mr Edwards would like the room: cupboard and shelves for his books on the left of the fireplace; cupboard and shelves on the right of the fireplace for Mr Watkins. Lots of books had been kept in them. She had students staying in the house since she was married, fifteen years ago. Mr Roberts and Mr Jones, in the back room, had been with her since they came to Col. two years ago. They were studying science, she thought Chemistry — she wasn't sure.

She hoped Mr Edwards and Mr Watkins would get on well together. It was so nice to be friendly with your co-digger. She understood Watkins was very clever; a State scholar. He was going to do Law. He came from London. His cousin used to stay here when in col. seven years ago. Seven years! It was only like yesterday. He was very clever. Took first class honours in Law; a barrister now in London.

She grasped the tray and lifted it level with her waist, and stood facing the door. Over her shoulder she said she hoped Michael would like Aber. He would be sure to find a nice young lady there too. She turned back and put the tray on the table. Mr Roberts is courting busily, she said with a smile, his young lady comes in sometimes in the evening. It's against the rules of course, she said, but Miss Pritchard is such a nice quiet sensible girl.

Michael, who politely closed the door after her, returned to the fireplace and placed his elbows on the mantleshelf. He noticed three fire bricks in the grate, and smiled at himself in the mirror. Studying himself in the mirror, he thought of Watkins and his brother, of Coke, of all the students and the College. Quietly he decided that he would be President of the College before leaving. He thought of his career at college, imagined it. He took stock of his assets, his pleasant manner, his ability to get round people. He could speak quite well in public too, he thought. He should take care now to improve this art. He should take up a game, win his colours. He thought of tennis and badminton. But why should he want to be President, Why, he wondered? Not for love of position, of power, of influence alone, but in order that such power, such position, such influence should serve to advance the cause which he had made his own, the resurrection of Welsh freedom and honour. The more important his position, he argued with himself, the greater his service. Knowing what he intended to do, the certainty of purpose which this knowledge implied gave him a warm happiness and comfort.

He went upstairs to unpack, pulling a wry face at the small wardrobe, ugly washing-stand, and brass knob bed which confronted him. In dozens of rooms such as this his fellow-students slept, and went perhaps in summer, to study in quietness before examinations. Among such as these he had to make himself known and liked.

He had not been upstairs long when he heard a loud knock at the front door, hurried footsteps, then the commingling of two voices; one deep and fruity, the other ululating soprano, in a duet of introduction and welcome.

Michael finished unpacking. When he went down he found Watkins seated at the table, eating, with a large book open in front of him. Watkins got up to shake hands, pushing a ball of half-masticated food into his left cheek to free his tongue for talking. His body was thick and fat, and his tight shining blue serge suit looked as though it had been bandaged on him. His face was a glistening full moon, studded with pimples and blackheads. His hair, which was copper-coloured, stood up from his head in a manner reminiscent of coloured illustrations of the earth cooling.

While Michael arranged his books on the shelf, Watkins continued with his cold chicken. He smacked his lips frequently, sucking his fingers or the tea with which he washed down mouthfuls of bread and butter and chicken. Then he took the wrappings off a new bottle of marmalade and spread the stuff thickly on his bread and butter. Michael watched him, fascinated.

There was something excessively lordly in his manner in spite of his appearance. He seemed so self-assured, and his food and books showed that he was well-provided for.

When he had finally finished, Watkins came to the opposite armchair, and having made himself comfortable, opened a conversation like a lawyer cross-examining a witness, picking his teeth intermittently.

"History. I took a distinction in History in the State Scholarship. I have an unusual memory, you know. Very useful. When did the last black king of Naiti die? You don't know. 1825. Now you ask me a question. I doubt if you could catch me out in any of the last six centuries. History and Law, I think, are essential studies for anyone contemplating public life. My cousin says the law is the royal road to Westminster. They say at home that I am the best in the family for impromptu speeches — That's a game we play at home on winter evenings — I see you are a Welsh Nationalist, Edwards. I'm a Conservative myself. It's a good sound party which will live as long as the Empire lives. Mind you, I have ideals. I believe the British Empire has an essential part to play in the world and that it should be strong and healthy to play the part. Honestly, I have very little patience with narrow nationalism. Political suicide, as my cousin says. I should like to have a debate with you some evening . . . ."

Watkins rumbled on until he was interrupted by a rap on the door and the entry of Roberts and Jones. "Hello Freshers!" they said, and introduced themselves. Watkins showed resentment at their interruption and familiarity by sitting up and crossing his legs and answering them with prim, cold monosyllables. At an early opportunity he attempted to resume his diatribe on the principles of Conservatism. Roberts and Jones having listened curiously for a few minutes, they turned to Michael and screwed an index finger on their temples. Michael burst out laughing.

Watkins, enraged at their levity, jumped up and stalked out of the room. "Let's follow him up," said Roberts. All three dashed upstairs after him, and caught him just as he was about to close his bedroom door.

They rolled him up in his bed-clothes and Jones sat on his head. Roberts took away his mattress and then began to make a superstructure with his books. On top of these he placed a bedroom utensil and draped it with an old Union Jack.

When they finally left Watkins, they tottered downstairs weak with laughter, while their victim, robbed of his trousers, his braces knotted about his neck, harangued them from the top of the stairs . . . .

It was dark outside when Michael, Roberts and Jones, went out to buy fish and chips for supper. They took him for a stroll along the Promenade, introduce him to parties of acquaintances, and he became one of a long line that marched arm-in-arm along the promenade, 'kicked the bar' simultaneously, and then turned to serenade the women's hostel with lusty voices.

Chapter III

In a letter to the College Magazine the new President of Debates had deplored the behaviour at Debates in recent years. He reminded his readers that after the last war, when many of the members of the Union were army veterans, Debates Union attained its high water mark of brilliance. Things said, quips, mots, epigrams, still lived in the memory of the college, had become common coin in college conversations, giving it its own special distinction.

To what abysmal depths had they now sunk, he asked. Only the loudest voices were heard, only the most inane statements applauded. He appealed to speakers not to play up to the basest instincts of the house, the house not to encourage over-ribald and unseemly orange-box rhetoric. He cited the Freshers Debate of last year, which had coincided, unfortunately as it turned out, with Guy Fawkes night. Irresponsible elements had brought fireworks into the Hall, fused the lights and indulged in the grossest horse-play. Then two years ago, the lights had been fused, the President and Secretary carried off in the darkness, and left to spend the night locked in Professor Vaughan's room. Most humiliating of all for the College's reputation had not last year's Hon. President, a venerable world-famous elder statesman, been kidnapped at the station, having come to deliver his inaugural lecture? Such things the new President believed, should stop. He was no spoil-sport, but there was a limit to irresponsibility. He appealed for new and higher standards of decorum, as a foundation for new and higher debate sessions in the future . . . .

On the night of the Freshers Debate, Michael, George Kail, Betty Davies, Olwen Meynor and the secretary of Debates waited in the ante-room for the President. Michael stood by the window. It was a rough night and out in the darkness the waves, driven by the rising wind, dashed noisily towards the rocky shore. The wind threw gusts of rain like pebbles against the window.

"What time is high tide?" asked George.

Everyone guessed, none knew exactly. They were all pre-occupied. Betty smoked, plucked her gown, and blew the short gulps of smoke out through her nostrils. Olwen was reading through her speech, her lips moving silently. She lifted her head, laughed shortly, and then continued her silent reading.

Michael looked away from his companions seated about the small room lit by a bare powerful electric bulb. Outside he could barely see the white tops of advancing waves which seemed to sway like ghosts. He had learnt his speech carefully, then jotted down the headings on the postcard in his pocket. As far as he could, he had planned his every word and movement for the next hour or so. He had studied his audience with care.

At the Freshers Concert, when he first came up, he had been shocked at the noise. The Gods, who seemed to sway at the back

177

of the Hall with the effort of making noise, bawled, shouted and sang with frightening vigour. There were many groups among the crowd who every now and then crouched in an awkward circle to shush loudly, and having won silence, they recited together.

"Who thinks he's Romeo?" (*f*)

He thinks he's Romeo! (*ff*)

GERALD BLACK THINKS HE'S ROMEO!! (*fff*)

Up! Up! everyone roared. After a sharp scuffle the victim was caught and held up, high above everyone's head. The hall rocked with laughter.

Alexander Bowen, the oldest fresher as they called him, began to recite anecdotes about his experiences in America. He began confidently, putting his foot on a chair and bending intimately towards his audience. They preserved a unique silence, during and at the end of each story, until Alexander, red, desperate and unhappy retired, and then they laughed . . . .

> "When we leave this bloody college
> Oh! How happy we shall be.
> No more sausages for breakfast
> No more marmalade for tea."

was well sung to a famous hymn-tune. No one conducted. Every tune began and ended like a crude internal combustion engine, beginning in spurts and petering out.

Debates Union was not so riotous. There was no singing or horseplay, apart from very exceptional occasions.

Watkins attempted to speak at the first debate of the term. He was seated in the front of the house, so that when he got up he could not fail to catch the President's eye. He struck an oratorical posture and everyone watched him with interest. For a few minutes he was heard in silence. He paused.

"I cannot conceive," he began and paused again.

"Shame!," shouted a voice, "Why not?," shouted another. Everyone rocked with laughter.

Poor Watkins, thought Michael. They did not approve the budding orator. Nor for that matter the over-witty speaker. Their taste, he thought, could only be met by a careful balance, to be achieved like an intelligent recipe, by the sparing use of certain ingredients. A modicum of fact and substance; a modicum of moral; equal parts of humour, wit and sarcasm, to be served in an assured yet deferent manner, untainted by gestures or purple patches.

The President arrived at last, fingering his white tie nervously.

"All ready," he said hurriedly. He went up to the Secretary saying, "I think it will be alright. I've had a word with Bill, Arthur, Jac Bowen and Slap Lewis." He turned to the freshers, "Ready? Now don't be nervous — and don't be too cocky, whatever you do. I don't want riots. All ready? Off we go."

They entered the Exam. Hall and walked solemnly up the floor of the house. The President ascended to his chair. The speakers arranged themselves on either side of the Secretary's table. Someone had whistled 'The March of the Cuckoos' as they walked up, but it must have been an old joke for no one laughed.

The house appeared to be in a serious mood. On the left the women knitted, smoked or chewed sweets with cold indifference, on the right the men stared like blasé spectators at a second-rate bull-fight. For one nervous moment Michael considered mobs, Roman thumbs, Christian martyrs, peasants' revolts, scythes, hammers, guillotines and bulls. His heart thumped against his side.

But having settled in his chair, he was able to examine his audience individually. He picked out familiar faces, one by one. There in the top amid the Gods were Roberts and Jones, quietly chewing. Watkins as usual, had placed himself in line with the President's eye. He sat with legs apart, his hands and chin on the handle of his wet umbrella, about the ferrule of which grew a patch of wetness. Detail, Michael said to himself with relief, always is reassuring.

The President was talking, with growing confidence. The Secretary had got through the Minutes with only two fairly harmless interruptions.

"The subject matter before the house this evening is a debate: 'That Internationalism is the only remedy for the present world crisis.' Before calling upon Mr George Kail to open the debate for the affirmative side, I should like to remind the house that the Union Committee have this year deliberately chosen a subject of serious nature for Freshers' Debate. I need not elaborate on the reasons for this choice. All I intend to ask you, is to appeal to you to give the subject under discussion your serious consideration, and whatever you may think of freshers or of politics, please give the speakers a fair hearing."

Kail was a vigorous speaker. His deep harsh voice was emphatic, although his body seldom moved.

"How sincere he is," Michael thought, as he watched Kail, who gazed earnestly in front of him as he spoke, his wide lips moulding the shape of his words. Phrases such as 'The Russian Experiment', 'The Conflict now raging in Spain', 'The impotence of the League' and 'A World Order' occurred often. His audience was solemnly quiet, obviously sympathetic. He has struck the common cord, thought Michael; even I myself sympathise with him, although I know he is wrong, and wildly impractical. Ideals slipped from his lips like rabbits out of a conjuror's hat, sleek and transient.

When Kail sat down and the audience applauded, Michael grasped the postcard in his breast-pocket nervously. He felt the magnitude of his task — to find a common ground with this audience, and then attempt to disprove some of its most cherished ideas. As he rose, he felt the hiatus in the silence which would be broken when he opened his mouth. Silent, standing before them, he was a stranger, an object of curiosity, but when he began to speak, they would begin to know him, forming their opinions and impressions as his speech continued.

" . . . I too have enjoyed the speech of my opponent and, for an unguarded moment, revelled in the dream world which he outlined. But in the harsh light of reason I was forced to see in his blue-prints for a new world a striking resemblance to the story of the imprudent pig, who built his house of straw. For like the imprudent pig, our friend has omitted to take into account the big bad wolf . . . ." "Who's afraid of the big bad wolf," a voice called out. "We all are," said Michael as quickly as he could, "for in this instance the big bad wolf is reality, which we all appear to fear, for we do our best to avoid facing it . . .

" . . . Let us split up this word international into its

component parts. I hope I am not being too obvious when I say that it means 'between nations'. Yet we do tend to forget this simple fact. For good or for evil — for good I believe — the people of this world are grouped into nations, and surely such a fact cannot be ignored, as my opponent has ignored it, when considering any international system. However attractive the idea of a world state may seem to some of you, you must agree it would be sheer madness to ignore the present grouping, the grouping of history and geography, of time, place and space, God's grouping, if you like, of the peoples of the world. If you must build, build with the bricks and mortar of reality and not with the straws of the imagination which vanish before the wind . . . .

" . . . .This is the University of Wales, the University of one of the nations of the earth, one of the units if you like of any international order. This institution was fought for and established by men who believed in Welsh nationhood, who believed that the sons and daughters of Wales should have the privileges of Welsh citizenship and the opportunity to serve their country . . . . My opponent wishes us to become citizens of the world. But the world is not another city or another nation, it is a conglomeration of nations and we can only belong to one. If we are to serve humanity then let us begin in our own country, for service, like charity, begins at home. A man's first social obligation is to the community of which he is a member. A Welshman's first duty therefore is to Wales . . . and our birth-right is not only a duty, it is also a privilege. There is no need for me to catalogue the material and spiritual evils that are rife in our country, and must be faced and fought . . . . Our language, and culture, our Welsh way of life is in mortal danger. The storm which threatens to destroy Welsh nationhood is the storm which threatens European civilisation as a whole. Remember the story of the drowned land that lies in this bay — the youth of a country are its watchers in the tower, today we sleep while the waters that threaten our land are rising hour by hour. Our duty to humanity as a whole is to guard our section of the wall, for if Wales is annihilated, civilisation in our part of the world will be annihilated too . . . ."

As he spoke Michael became possessed with the importance of

181

his message. He felt compelled to drive his message home, it must reach the brain behind every one of the faces that now looked at him. It must penetrate every ear, into every brain, — into every separate consciousness in this room. The debate was not important, what mattered was the opportunity of driving the message home; he wished he could see it actually sinking in, like a nail into a bed of hard wood.

When he finally sat down he was exhausted. He felt isolated, foreign to the large warm hall and the students in it, and for a moment he felt an impulse to get out into the anonymity of the stormy darkness outside.

The Debate continued. Betty Davies was speaking, with rapid vehemance. "Narrow nationalism is the chief cause of war" she said, and the syllables of the phrase 'Narrow Nationalism' seemed to swirl from her throat, to her nostrils and then burst out of her mouth. Her speech and voice and manner appealed to her audience. She was small and pretty.

She was natural and unspoilt, they thought, unspoilt and plain spoken. She said what she meant, they thought, without a hair on her tongue. She was petite but lovably pugnacious. "Good old Betty," someone called out.

We shall lose this debate Michael said to himself in despair. But what is far worse is that my message has not reached them. Their feathers were impenetrable, my words rolled off like drops of water. Their minds are closed like vacant houses, there are shutters over their eyes.

Olwen did not like speaking in public and yet she tried her best to second Michael. She spoke with nervous quietness, but there was a tenacity of purpose in her voice, that made Michael regard her with sympathy and affection. When she looked from her notes there was a stubborn look on her gentle oval face.

When the debate had ended, the 'ayes' and the 'noes' filed out on either side of the statue before the Hall door into the quad. The President stood on the pedestal to announce the result of the voting.

"For the motion," he said with deliberation, "125; against 58."

Michael leant against the wall, watching the students talking to each other in groups or preparing to leave. Already, he

182

thought, they have forgotten the debate. They are thinking now of the best way home through the wind and the rain, of waves spreading fanwise over the promenade, wet silk stockings hanging in bedrooms to dry, socks on the fender in digs; of the joke at supper, the hateful sausage on the hostel plate, the unwanted visitor in one's room, the absence of friends expected, enemies sitting on one's bed, using endearments; of the unfinished essay, of the fixed cloud of fear in the back of minds, the fear of failure; of the arrangements for tomorrow afternoon, changing in dressing rooms, cold wind on bare knees, the steaming communal bath, the white bodies glistening with soapy water, the sobering cold shower, back in the digs making buttered crumpets for tea, or perhaps a quiet walk with a bosom friend in the dead winter lanes.

A familiar figure was approaching him; it was Idris whom he had met at the summer school, bringing with him a tall thin man whose spectacles had thick lenses, which, since he held his head high, often caught the light. At least, Michael thought, as Idris greeted him, you are a Nationalist. And he admitted to himself that he was glad to see him.

"This is Mr David Morgan, Edwards. He has just arrived back from the Sorbonne, to become assistant lecturer in French here. He's been impressed by your eloquence, I think, and wanted to meet you."

David Morgan spoke rapidly in a high pitched positive manner, making everything he said perfectly clear. Michael thought he had never heard anyone talk prose in so undiluted a fashion before. But his manner attracted Michael in a while. He was glad of the sympathy and understanding that Morgan showed. Before leaving he asked Michael to tea the following Sunday.

Michael went to the ante-room to get his mackintosh. Kail and Betty had left. Olwen was there alone putting on her overcoat.

"I'm sorry we lost," she said, tugging at her coat belt, "and I'm sorry that I spoke so badly."

With alarm Michael thought he saw a tear forming on her eyelid; he did not want to see it fall, and her face, usually so gentle and composed, crease up in sorrow.

"Nonsense," said Michael, "you spoke better than I did. In

183

any case, it's not our fault that the college is a hotbed for Philistines. We must educate them. Look, it's raining hard outside, you should have brought a mac. You have this and we'll call at my digs on the way."

Olwen refused the mackintosh with thanks. Michael looked around. "We'll borrow Prof. Williams' second best umbrella."

He looked at her as he buttoned up his mac. "Never mind Olwen. We'll convert them all yet. I've got one or two ideas now — for instance why can't we start a fortnightly News Sheet of some sort, something with a direct appeal to the college."

Walking through corridors to the Main Exit, Michael's voice echoed between the cold bare walls as he elaborated his idea. The wind swung the great door open out of his hand, and arm in arm they struggled against the turbulent weather, down the side streets towards Michael's digs.

"Come along in," Michael shouted against the wind.

Olwen screwed up her eyes when Michael switched on the light.

"Thank God," said Michael, "Watkins is out."

He glanced at Olwen. She stood by the door, strands of her hair stuck by the wind on her wet face. How fragile she looks now, he thought, but still dignified in her quiet way. Odd, he said to himself as he went to get a mackintosh from the hall-stand, I've never thought of kissing her before.

As he held the mackintosh and she put her arms in the sleeves his hands slid up to her shoulders and he turned her round to face him. He smiled at her wet shy face and then kissed her on the mouth. Her lips were soft and moist and to his surprise he felt her hands about his neck. Through half-opened eyelids he saw her eyes were closed, and her long black eyelashes sleek with rain. Involuntarily he tightened his grasp about her waist. Her body seemed small and tender pressed against his.

"Michael," she said, smoothing the back of his head with her hand, "I shouldn't let you kiss me; you don't love me. But you can see now how I feel. You know I love you, don't you? It makes me feel glad and sorry, proud and ashamed, all churned up together. I'm glad I kissed you because I love you, but I'm ashamed, humiliated too. Everyone wants to be proud in their love, I suppose. Oh, I don't honestly know how I feel, guilty or not guilty."

Michael thought, you are right. I didn't love you when I kissed you a moment ago. But you've made me love you in the space of a minute. Even now I am beginning to plan a complete story for us, you and I together, working. He said, "Olwen, I don't think I realised it before, but I do realise I love you now. Please believe me."

She smiled, "You don't have to ask me to believe you Michael. I think at the moment I could live on wishful thinking."

"I must go," she said drawing away from him, "or I'll be locked out."

They could not talk in the wind, Michael squeezed her arm and she smiled at him, so that her happiness infected him. On his way back, the wind helped him along, and he ran for short distances whistling and singing like a small boy.

Olwen ran up the broad staircase, excited with happiness. She passed the huge Rossetti woman leaning on a garden urn on the first floor landing without as much as a glance. (When she first came to college she had often stopped to stare at the drapery over the enormous hips level with her eyes.) She made straight for Room 51, eager for privacy. The fire she had built up before going out was still latently burning, and when she gave it a poke it responded immediately. As she took off her wet stockings she decided not to go to Mary's room for hot milk, she wanted to be alone to enjoy thinking about the evening. The edges of her skirt and sleeves were wet and she took off her clothes and rubbed her legs and arms with a towel. Opening the wardrobe to reach her dressing gown she surveyed herself in the mirror. She let the door swing open and studied the reflection of her body. My breasts are too small, she thought, my waist is not narrow enough. I like my legs. She bent her knee and lifted her heel. Above her shoulder she saw her father's photograph in his clerical collar on the mantleshelf, and hurriedly she took her dressing gown and closed the wardrobe door.

Returning to the fire, she took her father's photograph in her hands and gazed at his immobile unsmiling face . . . .

He had come across her diary once, open in the study. "My dear," he had said at tea, "Don't leave your confessions and impressions about in the study please." And she had blushed, and Mrs Thomas, the housekeeper, had wondered what they were talking about.

Poor father, she thought, I'm sure he misses me. My visits to the study before going up to bed. When he was in the mood for talking she would sit on the footstool, leaning against his knee. He always talked to her as though he were soliloquising, or talking to a companion of his own age and experience. Even when a child she had an idea of his theological and political views. He would tell her stories of how before she was born, her mother and he had allowed the bailiff to sell pieces of their furniture before paying the tithe; of how he had fought for a non-denominational school; of skirmishes with vicars and squires over Disestablishment, Temperence and other movements; of rousing public meetings of past elections and how he came to join the new Nationalist movement at its inception.

She wondered what he would think of Michael. They were so different, she thought. Michael made jokes about Methodists and mixed deliberately with the men who went drinking. Michael seemed such a stranger to the world which she knew, the Chapel, the Band of Hope and Missionary Societies, the life of the village which revolved about the Chapel. He was so obviously a vicar's son, belonging to the sort of people to whom the Chapel was naturally antagonistic. He was cold and distant, she knew, under his superficial charm, and naturally formal. At the branch meeting last week Idwal made a humorous remark and slapped Michael familiarly on the back. She had watched him over the rim of her cup and had seen the cold distaste in his eyes, in spite of his smile.

Getting into bed, she wondered whether Michael was capable of loving anyone. Had he inhumanly dedicated himself to a cause? How much did he need love and sympathy and companionship, shelter and comfort?

Having switched out the light she sat up for a while in bed. The embers of the sinking fire showed the room in a pleasant reddish twilight. In a light like this, she thought, on a stormy night like this, I should like to be with Michael before the fire, and hold his head in my lap or be in his arms. More happiness she could not think of than to be close to him, releasing the love that welled up in her heart.

186

A wave rose up thirty feet and the wind whipped its crest against her window. Startled, she put up the white shutters. She had not lain down for more than a minute when there was a short knock on her door and Mary hurried in. Short and stout in pyjamas and dressing gown too big for her she began talking before closing the door.

"Oh! Olwen, my love," she said, "are you asleep? Do you mind if I sleep here tonight? I'm terrified. I hate storms. Perhaps you are nervous too. Are you? Oh! I am. Sure you don't mind?"

She scrambled into bed alongside Olwen, and having hollowed out her place and settled down, talked on, her low tones rising and falling out of the pillow, the bedclothes shaking when she giggled.

All along the curving western shore of Wales the sea advanced in an abnormal tide. The waves rose and toppled over land usually untouched by water and all the shores were buried in the liquid fury of the sea. The wind too, abnormally violent, swept inland, bending the thick trunks of trees compelling them to creak and their branches to wail like human voices. Cattle and horses wintering out, stood in the shelter of the tallest hedges, and all the sheep on the mountains lay behind rocks or walls. Children who could not sleep, sat up in bed and asked what was the wind, who sent it, where was it going? In towns and villages policemen on night duty stood in the shelter of porticoes longing for the morning, apprehensive of falling slates. Tramps lying in hay barns, pulled hay or straw over themselves, scratched, smiled, and turning on their side, went to sleep. Some said "I like the wind, it makes me feel cosy in bed and sends me to sleep." Some sat up by the fire, made tea for themselves, and tried to read a book. In fishing villages everyone listened to the noisy treacherous passionate sounds of the sea. Wives whose husbands lay in bed beside them displayed unusual lovingness and affection; wives whose husbands were at sea sat at windows alone, cried alone in their bed and held their bodies tense and stiff, or went to sit up with neighbours, according to their natures. At the village of B — Mr Bright the rector, went about from cottage to cottage carrying advice, consolation and a friendly word. "Remember this is the age of steam, the machine age. We haven't so much to worry about as our grandparents had." As he walked down the village street the wind pulled his scarf and coat-tails about and strained at his shooting cap. Then grasping a loosened slate, aimed at his defenceless head and killed him instantaneously.

Olwen slept uneasily. Mary was restless in her sleep and her breath rumbled through the dried film in her nostrils. Sometimes Olwen dreamt of her father and Michael arguing in the study until she who watched them was hot with misery; then she dreamt of the story of the buried city in the bay, of the revelry on the night of the disaster, of Seithennyn drunk and helpless on watch at the floodgates. As in the cinema she saw the waters advance through the gate, the first low wave lapping at the banquet table and tickling the bare feet of the riotous ladies making them jump on the table in their alarm shouting "Mice! Mice!" Lovers on improvised beds sat up as they felt the touch of liquid and waking their partners, asked for an explanation. The king, a cousin of Canute, a man of undisputed valour, when aware of the situation marched forward through the water giving commands until the water entered his open mouth and swept the crown off his head. Citizens with two storey houses felt a glow of satisfaction as they watched their neighbours cling to the chimney pots of bungalows. But the two and three storey houses were also gradually submerged, until only the Cathedral belfry stood out of the water and there collected a handful of surviving clergy and thousands of rats and mice. Mary grunted heavily and pushed her elbow into Olwen's side. At three o'clock in the morning the storm was at its height. The promenade before the hostel was comparatively narrow, and built — it was said afterwards — on a very poor foundation. Tired of the ceaseless pounding of the waves at three o'clock it cracked. The sea rose and trampled remorselessly on the broken pavements and concrete blocks.

In the hostel the fire alarm was rung and out of different rooms two hundred women students, twenty maids, two cooks, a bursar, secretary and head warden and solitary male porter emerged and performed their fire-drill in orderly fashion. No one was absolutely certain what had happened. The warden ordered the drill to continue, realising that the responsibility was hers she kept her head. She 'phoned the Principal, then the Vice-

Principal, issued orders to responsible persons, ordered lorries, ordered the opening of the college refectory, the making of thirty gallons of hot milk.

The following afternoon in spite of the interruption in the normal tenor of college life, Michael and Olwen met as arranged at the south gable of the college building.

During the morning the collapse of the promenade caused a great hubbub and commotion in the town; at the Hostel the front of the building was declared unsafe and evacuated. All first year students at the hostel were ordered home for a week, while accommodation was sought for them elsewhere. Olwen had been busy packing, and 'phoning and sending cards and letters. She arranged to stay with an aunt who lived in a village ten miles away. Staying with her aunt in the meantime would save her the long journey home.

Workmen and volunteers from among students had been busy all morning sand-bagging the foundations, carrying furniture, boarding up windows, and the students enjoyed themselves immensely ("Wel, am hwyl," said Wil to his co-digger John when he came back home to dinner.) Nervous maiden ladies staying at hotels and apartment-houses near the hostel bought boxes of chocolates and sweets for the undergraduates and treated them like war heroes. Retired clergy-men discussed the theological significance of 'Tempests and Acts of God' and walked from the lounge fireplace to the window to see how the work was getting on.

Almost everyone in town came out onto the promenade during the morning to survey the damage. Reporters, including news-reel photographers, hovered about. An aeroplane flew over the site taking pictures. The Town Council had an emergency meeting, and the Town Surveyor sighed with relief when he noted that two dead predecessors were between him and the author of the promenade extension . . . .

Critically Michael observed Olwen walking towards him. He liked her straightforward walk (it gave him an image of the leather tongues of brogue shoes flapping up and down). But why, he wondered, did she hold her head down. It spoilt her appearance. He felt a strong desire to correct her, and then reproached himself for finding fault.

Olwen was not unconscious of his critical stare, and a feeling of resentful embarrassment overcame the buoyant joy that had made every yard of her journey a step nearer to happiness. All morning, during her many activities, she had looked forward to their meeting. Now she knew instinctively that she did not meet with his uncritical approval, and she rebuked herself for wondering what was out of place, for making rapid guesses at the fault in her body, face, manner, dress. If he loved her. she thought, he would not search for imperfections, and at least he would carefully conceal the fact that he was critical.

They walked out of town over the bridge along the main road south. She made no attempt to keep up a conversation and repressed her longing to talk freely, as she believed the most intimate friends should.

The afternoon was cold and calm, the winter sun lit up the stencilled trees, their wet bare branches, and in the meadows and on the slopes it made the white winterburnt grass gleam. They turned off the main road onto a path through the wood, and when they were out of sight Michael stopped and turned to kiss Olwen, but she insisted on their walking on. Why, Michael wondered, is she unwilling for me to kiss her now, and he stole puzzled glances at his companion as they walked along.

Side by side, and yet both conscious of an invisible intangible barrier between them, their conversation was spasmodic and almost formal. What is the matter they wondered? And both desired to pull the barrier down, but they did not know how or where to begin.

Now the path turned westward and they walked along a cob that led between marshy open fields to the sea. On the stony foreshore the sea had left a line of sea-weed that stretched thick and unbroken following the contour of the shore. Alongside the foreshore the path broadened into a rough road, and turning in the direction of the town, they saw in the distance the remnant of a cottage. The roof had fallen in and the jagged ends of joists and purlins stood out against the sky.

"That must be it!" Michael exclaimed. "The landlady said this morning that an old woman and a girl living in a cottage on the shore had been killed in the storm last night. The old woman had been crushed in the doorway."

Olwen shuddered and grasped Michael's arm tightly. Close up, the ruined building reminded her of a film of the Spanish war she had seen. The same tattered roof and cracked joists, the same heap of rubble vomited through a window and through a doorway. Sickened, she remembered a dazzling white hand sticking out of the rubble. Was it in such a position they found the old woman here a few hours ago? I must stop imagining about it she said to herself. I must stop thinking about it.

Through the window, part of the kitchen looked life-like in spite of the dust, a brass saucepan on the high mantelshelf still gleamed with the polish of a dead hand. The bedroom buried in stones, wallpaper torn revealing old wallpapers beneath, looked old and uninhabited.

"In Spain a bomb, in Wales a storm" . . . This phrase repeated itself stupidly thought Olwen. Do not think that this might have happened to me last night; do not think how easily a human life may be extinguished, nor how, in what manner: the motor accident, the finger on a trigger, a foot slipping. I am in the train that moves towards an accident, the ship that will be sunk. Death lies about us from our infancy. Fate hangs over us threatening the whole future, the next minute and next year. Only Now, the instant, was valid. Confused, her thoughts sharpened into fear, and turning to face Michael she buried her face in his jacket. Now, was Michael; his arm about her, the smell of his tweed coat, his voice, his breath.

Somewhere in the world someone dies every minute, thought Michael, and every minute a heart stops beating. Now there were wars, famine, diseases, earthquakes, in various areas of the world accelerating the natural processes of death, and here now a storm leaves two casualties, an old woman replete with memories, and a young girl living no doubt minute by minute.

Holding Olwen in his arms he thought — now for a moment we two have our heads above the waves. When we go back to our places in society we sink again, powerless in the cross-currents of time, place and circumstance. I am not Michael Edwards in whom the world revolves, to the dialectic of history — only an ant in the ant heap and like the ant powerless to escape or resist the hobnailed boot of Fate. I too, he thought, as he sensed of Olwen's fear, am afraid before the guns of chance . . . .

191

"Ahem!" Behind them someone coughed; startled, they turned to see a policeman regarding them with a curious mixture of benevolence and suspicion. He was middle-aged with a womanish face and a large stomach which interrupted the perpendicular procession of silver buttons on his blue coat.

"You don't," he said, "happen to have the right time on you? My watch has stopped. I've been here since mid-day and the relief is supposed to come at four. Quarter past three, thank you. Humph, another three quarters of an hour."

"Got to keep an eye on it." He jerked his head towards the building. "Not that there's anything worth much in it. 'Pears the old woman has a step-brother in Cardiff. Got to keep an eye on them. There are some people we know of about here would pinch their own grandmother's false teeth. Talk about a sense of decency. For that matter you'd be surprised what respectable people I've caught messing about when they thought no one was looking. I often say to my missus, 'My job makes you lose your faith in human nature'."

The policeman sat down on the window sill and folding his arms prepared to shorten his three-quarters of an hour by conversation. He was obviously disappointed when Olwen said she must go or she would be late for tea. He watched them with interest as they hurried away; what were their names and where did they come from? He wondered for a moment, and then looked at his watch.

Chapter IV

On a hot July morning in the year 1938, Michael sat at his father's desk in the study at home before the open french window, writing a letter to Olwen. He felt cool and comfortable in the study whose darkness was a pleasant contrast to the brilliant sunshine outside. Newly bathed and shaved and wearing a thin white shirt, Michael felt fresh and alert, out of the lethargic influence of the sun. Having come to the end of a paragraph he was for the moment at a loss for subject-matter, and he leaned back in his chair, and looked about him. I've described this study to her before he thought with a smile.

He got up to study a photograph on the wall. He admired its neatness; on the top, the college crest, then in a neat rectangular enlargement, the group and underneath in neat black lettering their names, and at the bottom in clear capitals 'The Taliesin Society' Oxford 1910. There were his father and his Uncle, young men with soft youthful faces. He knew the names of some of the others too, having heard his father talk of them when an old college acquaintance came to tea or supper or to spend the week end. Michael thought of the pleasant nostalgia they enjoyed leaning back in their armchairs, having said with a secretive smile, "those were the best years of my life." They recollected then, faces that had lain forgotten perhaps for decades in the unopened drawers of memory; old phrases, friends, old tutors, old affairs, old jokes, return like ghosts to the consciousness that first beheld or listened to them. They think, — and voice their intense desire to know what happened to old Jack? Where did he go and what did he do? They linger with eternal wonder and amazement, over fragments of the story of astonishing failure or unexpected success ("Remember Jason who took a double first? Poor fellow, he married an awful woman. She drove him to drink. When did you last hear of him?" or "Remember Julius, always so quiet and so reserved, 'Mouse' we called him. He's a General now you know.") But mostly, Michael thought, the outward facts of their lives were monotonously similar; from school to college, from college to profession, up the steps of promotion to retirement, and from retirement to death. So simple and so insignificant, Michael thought. What mattered he supposed as he turned away from the picture, was the indefinable and unchronological history of their minds and souls. Days and years in colleges and professions are reliably similar. A term was an exact dimension of time and a day was divided neatly into a table of time. Perhaps that was the special charm of college to old students; when they returned everything except faces remained exactly as before, so that they could enjoy sighing about old faces and at the same time feel "I am back in my youth again."

A foot ground the gravel of the drive outside; Michael looked up and saw an old man in shirt sleeves, carrying a light hoe. His thick stiff flannel shirt and corduroy trousers seemed like armour over his frail body and limbs, but his face was weathered, — toughened and birdlike.

Michael leaned across the desk and tapped the open window with his pen.

"Rodger Jones," he called out, "how are you today?" "I can't complain," said Rodger, "not on a fine day like this. And how are you, Michael Edwards?. You have done very well I hear, passed very high. Well done Michael Edwards, well done. And have you made up your mind what you are going to be? People of the village very often ask me, 'What is the Rector's son going to be?' and all I can say is the truth, that I don't know."

Michael laughed.

"I think I've made up my mind at last, Rodger Jones, I'm going to be a teacher."

"Well, that is a nice clean job I should think, and good long holidays too. I can't think what they do with themselves during holiday time, I remember when I was on Insurance for three months, — the time I broke my leg and hit my head, — I just didn't know what to do with myself. If I sat in the kitchen the old clock a-ticking seemed to be knocking against my skull. I remember how I hated a rainy day. And my poor wife poor thing, how she did nag. The time from dinner to tea and tea and supper never seemed so long. I reckon that is why I don't retire. Wouldn't know what to do with myself, having so much time on my hands."

Old Rodger continued his slow walk to the garden, muttering something about "those damn'd weeds" and Michael sat thinking about his career. Towards the end of his second year, when he went to share rooms with David Morgan, David had asked him about his career one evening after supper, and the question, coming from David, assumed a new importance. David so rarely asked personal questions, and when he did Michael felt compelled to face them.

Privately he considered his relationship with David as the first genuine friendship in his life, because he enjoyed it so much, and because it suited them both so well. A solid formal friendship, Michael thought, without any undue intimacy or friction.

David was a scholar and his books were his very breath of life.

Michael smiled remembering the pleasant confusion of David's untidy library, and his trunks in the attic full to overflowing with books, Welsh, French, Italian, English and Irish books were mingled without any attempt at order or index: Pascal with Rabelais, Kierkegaard with Malthus, Llywarch Hen with Lewis Carroll. David who talked of Thomas Aquinas and Maritain at breakfast and recited Baudelaire at tea. With the Tuesday morning post the 'Nouvelle Litteraire' would arrive, and David who had no lecture to deliver until eleven, lingered over his breakfast reading, laughing with his mouth full of toast and if Michael were there reading out snatches, usually too quickly for Michael to follow.

David loved long walks and spoke of them in miles: "I went for a *four* mile walk this afternoon." David was an excellent walking companion, Michael thought. He kept silent at the right moments, and yet vivified the countryside with his great knowledge of history and literature, with his critical appreciation and comparisons. Above all he was so entertaining. Michael saw him again climbing over a stile on the path over the cliffs, and with a leg on either side of the stile, saying, "Now if women went to war, war would be even more horrible, because women biologically have less sensibility than men, in order to bear children. The Arab women torture the wounded when the battle is over, and in the early Middle Ages Welsh women mutilated the dead on the battlefields . . . ." Or he saw him again seated on a bridge and dangling his long legs over a stream, saying, "In *Lear* the important drama is the psychological drama that goes on in the old man's mind; the actual dramatic events are so unreal and sensational as to become trivial . . . ."

But David wasn't entirely a walking encyclopaedia. He was nervous, almost highly strung. Michael recalled him at a public meeting. Someone had told him that a number of roughs had been paid to break up the meeting, and David, biting his nails, was on the look-out for them every minute, marching up and down the aisle, looking over people's heads. As he stood at the entrance to the hall a rough looking man had pushed him accidentally; then David hit out at once, striking him on the shoulder, and as it turned out afterwards, spraining his wrist.

Except when in a nervous pitch, David had an exuberant sense of humour and a merciless armoury of jokes. One joke recalled another and he went on and on, until everyone moaned with painful laughter, Was it last year or the year before, Michael tried to remember, that David spoke at the Celtic Society Dinner? Anyhow, there was tact in his humour, he suited his jokes to the company of the moment, although his own humour was almost universal.

Yes, David was tactful, thought Michael, remembering David's stay at the Rectory last summer. In this study they had sat talking, and David gave the Rector every opportunity to display his wide archaeological knowledge and his own erudition and eloquence helped to create conversations which delighted Mr Edwards so much that he could not conceal his annoyance when Mrs Edwards came in to say that supper was ready. They visited old houses, Cambro-Roman sites, old wells and market crosses in the vicinity, and Mr Edwards elaborated. Mrs Edwards was charmed by David's studious politeness and his detailed knowledge of Paris, where, she told him, she had spent a memorable holiday several years ago.

One evening when Mrs Edwards, David and Michael were out walking, she had paused, leaning on her walking stick, and said:

"Mr Morgan, don't you think it's time Michael made up his mind definitely about his career? I'm afraid he is so absorbed in these Nationalist dreams of his that he has become *quite* impervious to reality."

His mother, Michael thought with a smile, had always been inclined to his entering the Church. His father, he remembered, a few years ago had suggested the bar. He had a cousin who had done well and had chambers of his own now in the Temple. Once when he had gone to London he had written home:

"I called to see my cousin Lewis Vernon at his chambers. He made me very welcome. We had lunch together and he inquired about Michael, and he was very pleased to hear that he was doing well at Aber. He asked me what career Michael thought of following, and whether he had ever considered the Bar. Should he do so, he would of course do everything to help him . . . . While I was there Viscount S — son of the President of the Board of Trade, Mr E., the publisher, and the Bishop of N. called to see Lewis and I was introduced to

them. It seems to me that a career such as this would give Michael
every chance to get on, and, should he desire it, make a name for
himself."

Twisting his pen between his fingers, Michael confessed to
himself that at the time his father's suggestion had been a
considerable temptation to him. While working in the silence of
the college library he caught himself making academic plans for
himself in patterns on waste paper. He excused himself at the
time by arguing that power and position in England would
enable him to do more for Wales, although he knew the
hollowness of the excuse. It was David who unwittingly, finally
broke the spell of this particular temptation. One evening when
Michael was preparing an essay on Tudor policy, he and David
were discussing the psychological reasons for the popular Welsh
belief at the time of Henry VII's coronation and throughout his
reign, that Henry was the True Owain (the prophesied saviour of
Welsh freedom) and that Bosworth Field was a victory for Wales
and that Henry's coronation was the restoration of Welsh rule in
the island of Britain. The bards rejoiced at the thought that their
language was made safe and supreme for ever, and lost their
heads in adulation of the Tudors.

"The Scots made the same mistake afterwards," said David,
"Thinking that they ruled England and Scotland. The latter-
day manifestation of this hallucination in Wales has been the
idea of getting on in England in order to help the dear old folks at
home, or even worse, the using of nationalistic bluster at home to
step themselves up on the dear old folks' backs. Every time there
is a prospect of a Welsh Prime Minister in England, I groan for
my country."

Michael rose, and paced about the study. I must be quite clear
about this, he said to himself; I've had just about all the plums,
all the honours and all the praise, I can expect in my life. I am
President elect of a University college; I have a first class
honours degree in History, and I must expect no more, because I
am convinced that the well-being and very existence of this
nation depends upon the unstinted service of those who have
seen the danger and who are honest and bold enough to face up
to it. And because my nation is small and weak and corrupted,
and because the whole force of this inhuman, over-industrial-

ised, imperialistic age militates against its existence, for this single reason alone among many, I cannot expect in the course of my life from now onwards anything but humiliation, scorn, unpopularity, disappointment, poverty, persecution and imprisonment. I haven't a martyr-complex; perhaps it would be as well for me if I had. I am honestly afraid of the mad world which I know now I shall have to face; afraid even of its imagined threats, tortures, and cruelties.

He walked out of the house across the drive and on to the lawn, turning to look at the rectory. I could enjoy, he thought, a life like this. A quiet life in the country, married to Olwen, writing monographs of Welsh, English and Continental History. Perhaps even developing the inclination towards literary writing that was growing in him of late. What an interesting book I could make for example, he thought, out of the material in this village. A slightly humorous portrait of a Welsh village, featuring all the local characters; the postman who wrote poetry and had a secret weakness for backing horses with glamorous names; the family feuds that added spice to village life. They could have their friends down too to stay with them for as long as they liked.

He slumped down in a deck chair and took sunglasses out of his shirt-pocket. Professor Williams had given him an interview after the results. He had practically offered him a research scholarship; two years at Geneva. After some hesitation he had refused the offer. There was no time, he repeated to himself, no time. There was so much to be done and so little time. He could not afford to spend two more years on himself, remembering the threat of world war and the danger such a terrible event would involve for Wales. He wanted to get out of the unreal dream-like academic world as soon as he could. One more year of teacher's training and he could get out.

His mother, who had seen him come out, came towards where he sat in the deck chair. Michael could not help admiring her fresh and almost youthful appearance, and the tasteful summer dress she wore.

"Michael dear," she said as she approached him. "What's this I hear about an open air meeting you're arranging in the village. Your father tells me you intend asking Mr V, here to lunch. You know, darling, you are being inconvenient. People here are talking already. Mr V. has been in prison you know. And you might remember that I am the chairman of the Women's Unionist Association in this part of the country."

"I am sorry, Mother dear," said Michael as he rose, "but you know I'm an unrepentant fanatic. Really I hate to inconvenience you. I think I shall have to convert you without delay."

"Well dear, do something useful for me. Run down to the vestry to get your father's disgracefully grubby surplice, or he'll be wearing it again next Sunday."

Walking through the Churchyard, he put his warm hand on the cool slabs of a marble gravestone, and thought, how compromise and anti-climax were the natural features almost of human relations. When would the genuine climax climb out of the imagination and off the stage of dreams into the elements of external existence?

Inside the Church was dark and cool. Behind the marble font the single thick bell rope hung still and immobile. The pews were cold and empty, and somewhat self-consciously, even as though they were full, Michael walked down the aisle, and stood by the lectern, staring at the altar. "The House of God," he thought. Here in this island of grace, generations of villagers had been brought to be baptized and had come joyously to be married, and had been carried to be buried. "The still centre in a turning world," before battle here the knight had come, not to bless his arms but to commit his soul to God, and here the wounded defeated had returned out of the passionate shrieking of intense life and bathed in the prelude to peaceful death. In the midst of life, thought Michael, sinking to his knees at the altar, we are in death.

Then his cynical nature whispered, disturbing his settled knees, "In the midst of life we are in doubt." He shut his eyes as he had done once before when a small boy, and almost cried aloud, "Appear! Christ, appear! Now before the burning future advances to consume me, now in the unreal peace of a becalmed summer, now appear."

The Author

Emyr Humphreys was born at Prestatyn in 1919 and brought up in Trelawnyd. He read history at UCW Aberystwyth, where he became a nationalist. A conscientious objector, he worked on farms and as a relief worker in the Middle East and Italy. He has been a teacher, radio and drama producer for the BBC, and lectured in Drama at UCNW Bangor.

The author of eighteen novels, a collection of stories, four volumes of verse and a history of Wales, Emyr Humphreys is one of the country's most influential and important writers. He has won both the Hawthornden Prize (for *A Toy Epic*) and the Somerset Maugham Award.

The Editor

M. Wynn Thomas is a Senior Lecturer in the English Department of UCW Swansea. The author of a critical study of Walt Whitman, he is also the Chairman of the Welsh Arts Council's Literature Committee.